BLUE

D0882128

Visit us at www.boldstrokesbooks.com

BLUE

by

Russ Gregory

2011

BLUE

ISBN 10: 1-60282-571-8
ISBN 13: 978-1-60282-571-0

This Trade Paperback Original Is Published By
Bold Strokes Books, Inc.
P.O. Box 249
Valley Falls, NY 12185

First Edition: October 2011

CREDITS
EDITORS: GREG HERREN AND SHELLEY THRASHER
PRODUCTION DESIGN: SUSAN RAMUNDO
COVER DESIGN BY SHERI (GRAPHICARTIST2020@HOTMAIL.COM)

Acknowledgments

A blend of solitary and collaborative effort led to the creation of this book. I'd like to take a moment to express my gratitude to the people who contributed.

Over the course of the publication process I've had the pleasure of working with many talented and dedicated people. In particular I would like to thank Radclyffe and the team at Bold Strokes Books for their assistance, direction, and encouragement. Radclyffe's elegant leadership is truly something to behold. I'm constantly amazed by her ability to instill confidence, even in a very uncertain first-time author.

If the reader finds this story coherent, surely much of the credit goes to Greg Herren for his thoughtful editing. I don't know what other authors may think of the editing process, but my first experience was very positive. Greg's comments and corrections showed me the value of feedback from a knowledgeable and intelligent professional.

I would also like to thank my parents and siblings for the rich tapestry of love and support they have always provided. This story is fiction, but for some of my relatives, the shadow of family tales may be visible below the surface. I hope I don't offend anyone by acknowledging that much of *Blue* is rooted in whispered conversations overheard in childhood.

Finally, I would like to thank my dear friend Travis Hanes for his encouragement and assistance during the creation of this story. It is not overstatement to say that *Blue* would never have been written without him. Only my need to dedicate my first book to Tom keeps me from dedicating this work to Travis. (It was a pleasure writing this for you, Travis. Even though you supported my effort mainly as a path toward much needed self-therapy, I know that it was actually working with you that helped me let go.)

Dedication

In memory of Tom Barr.

CHAPTER ONE

RUTH

A pack of razor-thin dogs raised bloody faces from an unidentifiable carcass and turned their heads in unison as the cherry-red Mazda swept down the dusty road. Jerry Philips twisted his face into a wry smile as the car blew past a desolate feedlot. A vacant supply store sat facing an abandoned cinema house with its faded marquee announcing *Jaws* as the featured attraction. Through the car's fog-shrouded windshield, he could see the luminescent image of two corpulent couples in swimming suits reclined on chaise lounges. Above the chubby sunbathers, neon curlicue letters spelled out Clovis Heritage Manor and Assisted Living Facility—For the rest of your life.

Jerry pulled into the gravel lot and parked, waiting a few seconds before unfolding his lanky form through the car door in sections like an accordion. He was a tall man with a bad back. Driving for more than a few minutes always brought pain, so he stood, gingerly arching backward to stretch out the kinks. Tufts of fog trailed from his nostrils. When he inhaled, the smell of cow dung tempered the bitter cold. In the distance, the yapping snarl of fighting dogs intermingled with the sound of the gusting breeze. He looked around at the cloudless aquamarine sky that stretched from horizon to horizon. The sun blazed freakishly bright above the sandy plain. After the lush beauty of Austin, Texas, this dry landscape was stark and uninviting to his eyes, its glittering surfaces harsh, almost garish in their reflected brilliance. Squinting brought the unremitting hum of sinus pressure in Jerry's maxillary cavities to a full-blown buzz. He reached into his pocket for two little red pills, swallowed the Sudafed dry, and slid his sunglasses over his eyes before turning to scrutinize the building.

The nursing home was a stack of yellow bricks supporting a recently tarred asphalt-shingle roof. It sat at the edge of the parking lot just beyond two hedged patches of dormant lawn. Along one side, sagging awnings hung above carefully spaced aluminum-frame windows. A patina of dust coated each horizontal surface, and wind-blown ripples of fine silt sketched frothy wavelets on the roadway. Sand also piled up at the base of each west-facing wall. Yellow tufts of desert grass peppered the surrounding fields and sprouted from cracks in the walkway that curved from the lot.

Jerry could see indistinct shadowy movement behind a double set of glass doors.

It had taken just three phone calls to track Mrs. Brookes down. Starting with an address culled from a 1962 newspaper article, Jerry pulled the first number from an online crisscross directory. A gruff voice answered his call and denied any knowledge of Mrs. Brookes. The man reluctantly gave him the name of his old landlord, and Jerry found Cletus Thompson listed in the Clovis directory. A weary voice answering on the third ring rewarded his practiced persistence. Thompson told Jerry that he and his wife had been a neighbor of the Brookes back in the seventies. Ruth Brookes had sold them the ranch in 1976, two years after the death of her husband.

In a raspy Southern twang, Cletus explained they had been sorry to see the old woman go, but Mrs. Brookes seemed happy about moving to a place where she would have company and be taken care of in her old age. Jerry's hopes soared when Cletus mentioned he was sure Mrs. Brookes was still alive, "seeing as how my wife Evelyn received a letter from her just this morning." Cletus read the address over the phone, and Jerry thanked him for the help. The nursing home's phone number was listed online. His excitement building, Jerry dialed with sweaty palms. A perky receptionist/nurse patched him straight through to Mrs. Brookes's room, and Jerry fought to suppress his excitement when the hundred-and-three-year-old woman's crystal-clear greeting snapped back through the receiver.

The conversation had been pleasant and rewarding. Mrs. Brookes listened to Jerry's story without comment and answered his questions. He was relieved when she agreed to meet with him and eagerly booked a flight for the next day.

And so here he was—breathing the fusty air of Clovis, New Mexico with Mrs. Brookes's nursing home looming up the walkway.

Jerry reached back into the car for his camera bag. Ignoring the gurgling protest of his stomach, he scrunched across the gravel toward the entrance. As he approached, he glimpsed his ragged reflection in the glass doors. His crumpled appearance was scruffier than usual, his unruly hair mashed to the side and both eyes so bloodshot he looked almost demonic. Pausing to stuff his sunglasses into his shirt pocket and straighten his tie, he noticed a mimeographed flyer taped to the door, announcing the presence of pneumonia in the building. Great, he thought, and shuddered, imagining the microbes crawling over the door handle. He slipped a hand into his jacket pocket and opened the door, making contact through the coat liner.

A muggy, almost tropical atmosphere enveloped him as he stepped from the biting cold into an entrance alcove. He pushed through another set of glass doors and padded down a hallway. At the nurses' station, a woman in pastel scrubs directed him down a sunny corridor. Sweet grandmotherly smiles peered through crocheted shawls, and shrunken, wrinkled faces bobbed above aluminum walkers. He marched down the hallway keeping his distance, but nodding and smiling greetings to each haggard face.

Mrs. Brookes's room was the last one on the right. The door was propped open with a rubber doorstop and muffled sounds of activity emanated from within. Jerry knocked on the wall to broadcast his presence and peered inside.

It took a few seconds to register the scene, and then the bottom dropped out of his stomach. His knees nearly buckled and he steadied himself by leaning against the wall. Two orderlies stood on either side of a raised hospital bed clutching the ends of a large zippered bag. The smell of antiseptic permeated the air. One of the orderlies frowned a warning at Jerry, who dropped his eyes respectfully. The men counted down from three, then lifted the body bag and swung it gently onto a bedside gurney, pulling up the gurney's rails and unlocking its wheels. Jerry was just turning to leave when a vaguely familiar voice called from behind the door.

"Is that you, Mr. Philips?"

Peeking around a partition he could see the backside of a heavy woman as she struggled to lift a brittle, birdlike creature out of bed. A face as wrinkled as dried apricots floated above a powder-blue shoulder, and two claw-like hands clutched each other around the heavy woman's neck. A pair of coal-black eyes stared at him with laser-like intensity, and Mrs. Brookes spoke again.

"I apologize for the commotion, but I guess it really couldn't be helped. Death has its own time schedule, you know." Mrs. Brookes's lips smacked in a grimace. She had small ears and a sharp nose that drew the corners of her mouth outward like the bill of a duck. She closed her mouth and worked her teeth into position before speaking again. "We lost Neola this morning—God rest her soul. These boys are picking up the body. If you'll give me a minute, Sue will have me in my chair. Then we can chat in the hallway."

Jerry smiled politely and murmured agreement before escaping through the doorway. He pinned himself against the hallway wall and set his camera case down between his feet. The gurney slid by on whispering wheels. As it progressed down the hallway it drifted past onlookers like a procession of Purple Hearts in a Veterans Day parade; heads bowed in respect but furtive eyes darted upward to catch a glimpse of the prone figure.

He waited, rocking back and forth on his feet. In a few minutes, Mrs. Brookes's coal-black eyes appeared through the doorsill. The scowling, round-faced Sue ignored Jerry completely and positioned the chair next to the window.

"Thanks, Sue," Mrs. Brookes said. "This'll be fine."

"I'll be back in a few minutes to make the bed. Wave if you need anything." She tossed Jerry a threatening look before plodding down the hallway.

Jerry felt confused as he watched the nurse's ample backside lumber hippo-like toward the nurses' station. Mrs. Brookes said, "You'll have to excuse her. She's very protective of her old people."

"I guess I can understand that."

"She means well, but she can be a little rude."

The moist warmth in the building was starting to paint a patina of perspiration across Jerry's forehead as he turned his full attention to the twisted figure before him.

Mrs. Brookes's face was as folded and creased as crumpled parchment. Her cheeks and chin seemed to shift and slide in a rolling sea of wrinkles while an uncontrolled left hand trembled in her lap. Her head was a mass of tight steel-gray ringlets, each about the size and shape of a roll of dimes. Her shoulders hunched painfully forward and she struggled to lift her head, turning her face sideways to gaze upward at Jerry. She wore a hot-pink housecoat over a sea-foam-green flannel nightgown. Her legs were wrapped in layers of Highland plaid. Bunny slippers adorned her feet, but the tattered ears spoke more of comfort than whimsical fashion.

Jerry wiped perspiration from his brow with a handkerchief. "I hope this meeting isn't inconvenient for you, Mrs. Brookes. Perhaps we should reschedule."

The old woman ignored his offer. "I can see you're a little warm, Mr. Philips. Warm and upset...but you shouldn't be, upset, that is...warm is understandable since we keep the temperature at eighty. Most of these people," she gestured down the hallway, "complain about it being cold all the time. It's the thin blood and no exercise. It's enough to make me want to get up and go for a jog. But that's not really an option anymore." She smiled at Jerry. "It's a blessing, really, about Neola, I mean. Poor creature. It was well past her time."

Jerry smiled to himself. A hundred-and-three-year-old was referring to someone else as past her time. He realized he'd been unconsciously twisting the handle of his briefcase and set it down next to the camera case.

"Besides, Neola was my third roommate to pass." She waved a twisted hand dismissively. "The rules say now I get the room to myself. Live through three, private room for free." The phrase came out in the singsong cadence of a nursery rhyme. "Neola was good company, and I don't mean to speak ill of the dead, but she was a little…well…gassy, if you catch my drift."

Jerry snickered. "Yes, I think so." He squatted down in front of the wheelchair and added solemnly, "I'm sorry for your loss, Mrs. Brookes. God bless Neola."

"Yes, God probably does. Now, if I may ask, what kind of book are you writing? And take off that jacket, young man. You look like you're going to melt."

The coal-black eyes settled once more on his face. Jerry smiled and shrugged out of his tweed sports coat. He was finding her prickly ways endearing. He said, "It's about the persecution of…gays…in this country."

"Speak up, young man. I'm a very old woman." Again her words were derisive, but her smile beguiled him. Jerry repeated the words with a little more volume, then paused. He wasn't certain someone of her age group would understand "gay." She nodded, the corners of her mouth turned down in a little frown of irritation.

"I ran across your brother's criminal record during my research, and the documentation seems somewhat muddled. I was hoping you could clear up a few things for me."

"I see. And what is the point of this book, Mr. Philips?"

Jerry paused again. She was not at all what he expected. "It's a history," he answered. "I'm hoping to shed some light on these early stories to provide historical context for the current attitudes and prejudices."

"And you think my brother's story may be useful, do you?"

He nodded and loosened the knot of his tie. "Yes, I do."

She watched him closely. When she spoke again Jerry could hear the distrust in her voice.

"And which of my brother's many stories do you want to hear?"

"Excuse me?"

"Which deep, dark family secret do you want me to tell you, Mr. Philips?"

Jerry considered his options. Finally, he decided that anything less than the full truth would be a mistake with her. He said, "All of them...I guess."

"Speak up, young man. I have very old ears."

Jerry smiled and spoke louder. "All of them. I want to know all his secrets, the important ones, I mean, to put his life in perspective for the readers—to give them a chance to understand the context of his situation."

She nodded vigorously and stared off through the window. Jerry waited in silence, unwilling to rush her decision.

Finally, her glittering black eyes turned back onto him and she said, "In that case, Mr. Philips, you'd better push me back into my room and take a seat on the bed, because this story's going to take a while to tell."

Jerry smiled, tucking his jacket and camera case under one arm. With a nod of gratitude he grabbed the handles of the chair while her arthritic hands unlocked the wheels. He rolled her back into the now-vacant room and parked the chair next to the curtained window. He pulled out a small notepad and the video camera from the camera case. Holding both up, he looked at her questioningly. She stared a moment before smiling and nodding agreement.

"Well, if you're going to film me, at least you caught me after I've had my hair done." Her laugh was infectious.

Settling himself on the edge of the bed, just out of frame, Jerry nodded at his new star and hit the Record button on the camera. "Whenever you're ready, Mrs. Brookes."

"If I'm going to tell you this story, I'm going to tell it from the beginning."

Jerry nodded.

"Silas was born on Christmas day of 1898. Silas LeBlanc. LeBlanc is my maiden name, but then I guess you know that."

Jerry nodded again.

"Silas was born in an adobe farmhouse made of sod blocks cut from the sagebrush bluffs of eastern New Mexico. He was the third child Momma brought into the world in 1898, but the only one to survive the process. You see, back in January of that year,

Daddy had sprinkled lavender over the bodies of my twin sisters and wrapped them in French lace before laying the tiny bundles, side by side, into the same muddy grave on a grassy rise overlooking the bayou. I tell you that because that image, the image of delicate white lace against the rich black Louisiana soil, was forever seared into the minds and souls of my folks and in many ways was the backdrop of Silas's upbringing."

Mrs. Brookes paused, staring off through the window. Jerry waited, watching through the camera lens. Her words were almost lyrical, and her way of telling the story was even better than Jerry could have hoped.

"It was a very difficult time for Momma and Daddy. Oh, I know losing babies is hard for any young couple, but it wasn't just that. You see, the rural Louisiana community where they lived had shunned them long before the loss of their daughters. That's because Momma was an Okaloosa Indian and Daddy came from a Creole family. Their union shocked both groups, and their neighbors' reactions ranged from cold stares to jeering insults. Still, they clung to each other— even adding fuel to the fire by rejecting the religious convictions of their respective upbringings to become fervent Baptists.

"I really can't tell you how important their religion was to them, Mr. Philips. You see, I've thought about it a lot and it seems to me that a quiet strength of obstinate commitment grew out of that communal rejection, but with the loss of the baby girls, everything changed. The only thing they had left was their religion.

"Well, not long after the funeral, just two months, in fact, Daddy and Momma tied a few paltry possessions onto the yellow pine-board bed of a horse-drawn wagon and trundled westward through the pouring rain. It took eight weeks of slogging along boggy swampland, rattling over undulating hills, and rolling across Texas to reach a place so vast, so barren, and so inhospitable it was virtually uninhabited. Their search for solitude ended in New Mexico."

Again she looked out the window, pointing. "Not far down the road, in fact. There's not much left of Forest these days." Her eyes clouded, and Jerry waited for her to continue.

"Forest, New Mexico brought them relief from the gut-wrenching depression, sadness, and pain. Do you know the searing, bleak pain that rains down on the parents of dead children, Mr. Philips?"

Jerry shook his head.

"Well, they knew it. I hate to think what would have happened if they hadn't moved. Chances are good I wouldn't be here. But, with God's grace, they found escape among the sagebrush and cactus, escape from the agony of death and the scorn and ridicule that a mixed-race marriage spawned in insular Southern communities at the end of the nineteenth century.

"Daddy bought a small plot of land on a parched, windswept bluff a hundred miles east of the Rio Grande, and they settled among a sparse group of hardworking farmers and ranchers who were independent, forgiving, and—most important—kept to themselves. I still remember that old adobe farmhouse. It was dirty and lonely, and sat atop a bone-dry rise, overlooking a barren, snake-infested plain, but for Momma and Daddy it was a paradise. The property included enough farmable acreage to eke out a meager but sustainable existence. It had a deep well that brought up cool, clean water, even in the dead, dry heat of summer. And that was enough.

"Momma told me the first thing they did, as soon as their belongings had been stowed in the farmhouse, was pray. They sank to their knees on the hardboard surface of their new porch and gave thanks to God for bringing them to a place that was more accepting and less fearful of the societal changes they embodied; a place where they could start over, a place where they could heal and grow.

"And later that year, Christmas Day, in fact, Silas was born.

"Momma told me later that it had been a difficult labor. I know that when the worst of the struggle was over and baby Silas was sleeping soundly, Daddy prayed, once more—this time thanking God for the blessing of a son, on Christmas Day, a child to love and cherish, who would help with the back-breaking labor yet to be done on that rock-strewn patch of land. I'm sure Daddy also prayed for guidance, asking God to show him how to bring his boy up strong and true and worthy of His grace…because that's the way my daddy was, Mr. Philips."

Jerry nodded again and Mrs. Brookes smacked her lips and continued.

"And so, my big brother Silas was coddled and sheltered and loved, raised to shoulder the intense struggle, social void, and strict Baptist standards of his—well, *our* childhood. And despite the obvious hardships, he excelled in that world, Mr. Philips. Silas grew up to be a strapping, smart, attractive young man, well-liked by his neighbors, particularly the plain, sturdy girls that lived in the area. In fact, I know several of them harbored fantasies of settling down and building a family with him. They flirted, teased, and competed incessantly for his attention. But Silas ignored their advances. Of course, at the time I didn't know it, but obviously he had set his sights elsewhere.

"It seemed to me, as time passed, Silas gradually became aware that the fit between his inner self and the life on the farm was not comfortable. In his teens, he began to chafe at the role he was expected to play and began searching for something else. You see, another more-distant song tugged at his restless soul, and a desire began to awaken inside his mind, a growing yearning for a life of excitement and conquest. Does that make sense?"

Jerry nodded.

"It was like the childhood bedtime stories that Daddy told us, about our great-uncles' adventures. Uncle Wilton and Uncle Rufus had been Confederate soldiers, you see. I still remember the tales Daddy spun for the two of us, in the dwindling twilight hours. They were battle sagas full of heroism and near-death escape, stories of courage and nobility, and honor, just the thing to stir a teenage boy's imagination. I was just a girl, of course, and the stories were exciting and scary for me. But Silas, well, he replayed those stories over and over in his mind, and he dreamed…dreamed of escape from the farm to an exciting life elsewhere. Why, when war finally broke out across Europe, Silas could hardly contain himself. World events had produced an opportunity for adventure and an acceptable excuse for his departure.

"Silas was seventeen years old in 1916 when he bid a tearful good-bye to us before stepping onto the platform at the Abilene train station, the boarding point for his journey eastward. And I'm sure his anticipation never wavered as the train traced a torturous three-day route through sleepy Southern stations, gathering other anxious recruits, on its way toward the newly completed army training camp on the East Coast.

"A few short weeks later, he disembarked with his troop in an English seaport and was quickly shipped across the Channel. Silas's unit set up not far from the front lines and he found himself in a different world, Mr. Philips. Silas's letters home hardly mentioned the fighting, but long after our parents died Silas told me what Europe was like for him.

"It was a world filled with the drum roll of advancing artillery and the screams of horses cut down by shrapnel from exploding ordnance; a world where the acrid smell of sulfur mixed with the pungent scent of trench foot, and young men, faced with the transience of life, gave flight to their desires before marching out along the murky battle lines to bury their fears in foxholes and their fallen friends in shallow graves. It was a dark world, overflowing with pain and hardship and death, but it lit up like a beacon shining above the rocks for him. Because, finally, a half a world away from his family's expectations, in the wanton abandon of Europe's bustling streets and battlefields, Silas discovered an outlet for yearnings he hadn't even realized he possessed. In the drunken alleyways and shambled, shoddy houses near the war zone, Silas unleashed the shackled expectations of his childhood and became himself. Thousands of miles from his stifling Baptist upbringing, Silas found men."

Mrs. Brookes paused and the tremor in her hand was the only movement in the room. Jerry sat frozen, afraid to breathe lest he break the spell. After a moment, she seemed to recall herself.

"Of course I didn't know that Silas was gay back then. In truth, I didn't know that such a thing existed. The entire concept of homosexuality was alien, beyond comprehension. I just knew that Silas was my heroic big brother fighting for his country against the Kaiser, in the War to End All Wars.

"My upbringing hadn't been as challenging as Silas's—I'm two years younger. The jolting experience of our parents' early married days had settled somewhat by the time I joined the family, and the haunting presence of our dead sisters was never the hidden guiding force in my childhood that it had been for Silas.

"As for me, when Silas was off fighting the war in Europe, Floyd and I got married straight out of childhood. Floyd was my long-time sweetheart and you never met such a handsome, hardworking man. Together we settled into the dirt-poor life of subsistence farming, like all the families in this area. Despite Floyd's physical ailments—he was asthmatic, you see—our little farm succeeded and our family grew quickly. Silas had a young niece before he returned from Europe.

"The thing was, none of us understood the monumental changes Silas had gone through. We just expected his return to make everything like it was before the war. But the change in Silas was too big. He just was never happy back with us. I guess Silas, home from the war, found his old way of life unsatisfying and restrictive.

"So, when a job offer came from an army friend whose father owned a leather shop in New York City, well, I have to tell you I wasn't surprised that Silas hitched a ride to Albuquerque where he boarded another eastbound vehicle, this time a bus.

"Lord, lord…the things I know now that I didn't know then."

The old lady fixed her steely gaze on the camera. Even through the lens, Jerry could sense the intensity of her emotions as she said, "It was a trip that took him toward his destiny and disgrace in the eyes of his family."

Later, after Jerry checked into the Ramada Inn that night, he stayed up late trying to recreate the next scene that Mrs. Brookes had detailed to him. He tried to imagine the subtext as he typed, her words still echoing in his ears.

CHAPTER TWO

BILL

Once again, Bill was awake in the pre-dawn hours remembering that day at Granny Ruth's house. There were other childhood dramas for sure, more shocking images, vignettes that had altered the path of his future and molded his worldview. But most of those memories were sublimated in the murky haze of an abused past, much too painful to retrieve.

This scene was different; here it wasn't physical pain or even intentional mental torture. Here he wasn't even an actor in the drama; he was the watcher, anonymous and safely hidden from view.

Papa Floyd's wracking cough subsided at the doorway. He stepped into the kitchen and kissed Granny Ruth on the cheek.

"I'll be heading into town now to get the mail. You need me to pick up anything at Callahan's?"

"I need some paraffin, for the canning."

"Anything else?"

"That's all, but make sure you're back by sundown. I don't want to hold up supper. Lula needs to get the little ones in bed."

Papa Floyd gave her a quick hug and trailed his hand across Lula's shoulder on his way out of the kitchen. The screen door slapped shut behind him. The kitchen fell silent for a few seconds until Nelly banged through and bolted across the floor, followed closely by a speeding Ronnie.

"Mama, Mama—make him stop." Nelly ducked behind the sturdy kitchen chair and hid her face in the billowing folds of Lula's skirt.

Billy leaned back in the rocking chair and took in the scene reflected off the glass of the framed New York Botanical Garden print hanging on the study wall. He watched his mother shoot a curious look at Granny Ruth before glaring down at little Ronnie.

Ronnie huffed. "She started it." His face flared red with anger and he shook in his tiny untied sneakers. "She keeps taking the ball. She keeps—"

"Hush," Lula said sharply, "I don't want to hear it." Ruth, trying to hide a smile, turned her back and slowly stirred the soup on the stove.

Ronnie stomped a foot in four-year-old frustration and lost a sneaker for his effort.

"Put your shoe on," Lula ordered him. Her voice softened. "And you, little missy," she gently guided the three-year-old Nelly out from behind her chair, "leave your brother's ball alone."

Nelly's lower lip quivered while Ronnie wrestled with his shoestrings.

"You two go on out and play. And I don't want any more fussing." Lula pointed at the door. "Run along now and be nice."

The tiny figures ducked their heads. Bumping and nudging each other, they waddled out to the back porch. The screen door banged shut behind them.

"Lord, what am I going to do with those two?" Lula asked, smiling. The smile slowly faded and Lula dropped her head into her hands.

"Two little angels, you've been blessed with two little angels," Granny Ruth answered.

Finally Lula vocalized what both of them were thinking. "Two little angels...and Billy."

Billy's stomach tightened and he snuggled deeper into the wing-back chair, wanting to hide from the world. From his clandestine seat in the study, he watched the reflection closely, looking for Granny Ruth's reaction.

But Granny Ruth did not respond. Instead, she bent over the stove to look at the burner, tweaking the knob a fraction. When she was satisfied with the flame she stood up slowly and shuffled over to the table. She sat down across from Lula with a sigh.

Billy studied the reflected image of the women. Something important was going on, something important that Lula and her mother didn't want others to know. He had always been able to read his mother's mood from her eyes. But now those eyes were blank, and her face was like a silhouette etched in stone. Here, hidden in the darkened study, he could hear every word and see clearly into the kitchen, and the women couldn't see him.

Lula toyed restlessly with the tablecloth for a few seconds before lifting her head defiantly. Her dark eyes flashed and the warmth of her anger ignited. "When did you hear?" she asked.

Granny Ruth mopped her forehead with the back of a wrist and tossed a worried look toward the screen door before answering. "A letter arrived Thursday."

"He sent you a letter?"

The old woman nodded. She clenched her jaw and pulled a white lace handkerchief from her sleeve. She gripped it so tight Billy could see the tendons dance in her forearm.

"What does he want, Momma?"

"He's sick. He's alone and sick and he nee..." But the words died on Ruth's lips when she saw resentment blazing in Lula's face.

"Don't tell me he wants you to take care of him. Not after all these years, not after what he did."

Granny Ruth just shook her head and sighed. "He sent this." She pulled a small black leather-bound book from her apron pocket and shoved it across the table.

Lula took the book, leafed through the first few pages, and said, "A cookbook? He sent you a cookbook?"

"Can't you see? It's his way of making amends. I think he's trying to reach out to us."

Lula closed the book and shoved it back across the table. "After what he did, what he is, he can't make amends."

Ruth picked up the book carefully and stuck it back into her pocket. "He's your uncle, Lula. He's my brother and we're all he has left."

"And why is that, Momma?"

"What do you mean?"

"Why is it that we're all he's got left?"

"I don't know and I don't care, Lula May. He's family, and I won't listen to you if you're going to badmouth family."

Lula cast a wary glance toward the door and leaned back, scanning the hallway. Billy stilled his motion to avoid detection, even though he was safely hidden in the shadows. When she spoke again, Lula's whispered words hissed with disgust.

"But he's a homosexual, Momma."

The room fell still again and Billy could hear the soft sizzle of bacon in the frying pan.

Granny Ruth broke the smothered hush with a voice quivering with emotion and warning. "There are worse things."

"I won't let him anywhere near my children. Why now? After what he did to that boy, I wished they'd locked him up forever."

"Lula!"

"I do, Momma. I can't help it, I do."

Ruth shook her head in defiance. "You're wrong, Lula May. I'm going to see him...and bring him home."

"You can't be serious."

"Silas needs me and he's family."

Billy could see unfallen tears glistening in the reflected image of Granny Ruth's dark-brown eyes. The defiance was there but a slight waver warmed her voice as she said, "He's my brother, Lula. I have to help." And then, almost as an afterthought, she added, "Maybe you should worry a little less about your uncle and a little more about what your husband is doing to that child."

Billy could see that it took effort for Lula to hold her tongue because the words had stung deeply. Tears glinted in her eyes and she turned away to stare out the window.

Then Billy shifted in his seat to get a better view of his own reflection in the glass. *Shadows hid the split lip and bruises, but the swollen lumps on the side of his cheek and neck made the outline of his face look grotesquely distorted. As he turned his head, the light from the kitchen caught his left eye and the cloudy pupil glimmered in the shadowy reflection.*

The first indication of sunlight was beginning to warm the eastern sky as Bill rose and made his way to the bathroom. Time for a quick shower and then to figure out what to wear; thankfully his closet was full of things suitable for Sean's funeral.

CHAPTER THREE

SEAN

Dark clouds swirled overhead as a misty sprinkle began to fall. Danny shrugged into his trench coat and squeezed his arms around his chest. He sat tenuously in a lawn chair just beyond the range of the tarp's coverage and eyed the sky as the minister droned on.

"Ashes to ashes, dust to dust; we consecrate the body of Sean Perry and give it back to the earth from whence it came."

Whence it came? Whence it came? Who in this century uses the word "whence," he asked himself.

"Secure in the knowledge that Sean's immortal soul now dwells in the house of the Lord."

Danny rolled his eyes and tuned out the incessant religious muck. He scanned the audience and found Marco, who shot back a small, knowing grin and shifted his eyes toward the edge of the crowd. Danny followed Marco's line of sight and saw Sean's mother, frail and faded, clinging to her new husband's arm. Behind her stood Sean's teenage brothers, one trying to look strong and the other crying like a baby. Danny was surprised to see Sean's home-care nurse, Stephanie, comforting the weeping one.

Stephanie was bulky and strange looking. Danny had always found her presence unsettling, but maybe that was just his discomfort with Sean's dependence. Stephanie had taken good care of him. In fact, she had been a steadying influence in Sean's life ever since Sean had come home from the hospital more than twenty years ago now. It didn't seem possible.

Standing just beyond the family, a sulking figure drew Danny's attention. Wally slouched against a tent pole and stared in his direction or, rather, Marco's direction. Danny glanced back at Marco, who was now leering at Wally with an inviting smile. Danny turned his attention back to the minister, trying to block out the image of Marco cruising for sex at a funeral.

The sky flashed with a tremendous lightning bolt, and the crashing thunder hit just as the first fat drops pummeled the tarp. Danny was soaked before he reached his car. Water dribbled down his forehead as he sat behind the wheel and squinted toward the cemetery's gate. A steady stream of mourners filed toward their cars. Danny tried to figure out how long he would have to wait for Marco when he spotted him ducking into Wally's truck in the parking lot.

Danny shook his head in disgust. How incredibly tasteless—particularly since Marco and Sean had once been involved. But, Danny reasoned, that was long ago and Marco has clearly moved on. He started the car and pulled away from the curb slowly, sloshing over the rain-soaked pavement.

Jerry Philips leaned over and positioned his umbrella above Stephanie's head as she searched her purse for the car keys. She looked at him with an awkward smile. Water dribbled down her face, streaking her mascara and making raccoon-like rings around her eyes. She squinted at Jerry. "Thank you."

"You must be Stephanie Sheldon," Jerry said.

She pulled the keys from her purse and nodded, opening the car door. "Uh-huh."

"My name's Jerry Philips, I work for the *American Statesman*. Do you have a minute for a few questions?"

She looked at him warily. "About what?"

"About Sean Perry." Jerry flashed his best "aw-shucks" smile. "Just background information. I'm doing a follow-up article on the shootings." For good measure he added, "I won't name you as a source if that bothers you." He doubted she would give him anything he would want to quote. He watched the emotions play across her face, and her breathing picked up markedly—a good sign. He was totally surprised when she turned her back to him and sat down in her car seat.

"No, Mr. Philips, I don't want to answer your questions." She closed the car door sharply and pulled away from the curb with a chirp of her tires, leaving Jerry shaking his head in confusion.

CHAPTER FOUR

MATT

The New Mexico landscape mimicked pictures of Mars sent back from NASA's Pathfinder mission. Red clay arroyos pockmarked with sandstone boulders and coarse gravel edged right up to the tailings of bluffs, whose sides seemed to glow an iridescent Martian red in the afternoon sun. The color climbed the sides of the cliffs all the way to shadowy capstones at the top of the mesas. The flora was sadly lacking, mostly gray sage and tufts of desert grass. Pinion trees, whose ebony needles seemed to drink in the sunshine, shaded dust-covered prickly pear cactus. Every few miles, tumbleweeds blew across the pavement. The whole vista was vivid and dry and entirely void of the color green, as if some unknown, insidious agent had leeched all of the chlorophyll from the vegetation.

Only the wide desert sky, a soothing powder blue freckled with cotton-swab clouds, tempered the effect.

The car's radio blasted homage to a recently departed pope. Images of my father reluctantly welcoming Muggy into his house danced through my mind. I had made the arduous trip from Austin mainly to chauffeur the rental car northward from the Albuquerque airport, taking Mom and her best friend back to our family home. Mom had convinced Muggy she needed support following the horror she had recently endured. Alone in the Toyota Celica on the return journey, I tried to concentrate on the radio and avoid letting my thoughts wander.

If given free rein, they would inevitably lead back to unwanted images of things best left in the past.

I rounded another sweeping curve. A cricket smashed against my windshield. The iridescent blue-black creature drew my mind back to thoughts of that hot August night, nearly eight months ago, when I first gazed at the ghostly vision and sensed the trouble it foretold.

I had walked a lot that year. I'd start out from the wraparound porch of my red-brick house just before sundown and head southeast toward the University of Texas. I'd tramp through the sixty-foot pecan trees and four-hundred-year-old live oaks of Austin's urban forest with my footsteps muffled in an ever-present sea of fallen leaves. I followed varied paths, one night looping around the Law School, the next hiking along Waller Creek or strolling down the sidewalk on Duval. No matter how I arrived on campus, my route never varied once I got there. I'd make my way to Speedway and head straight to the Capitol, passing the Texas Historical Museum and the canyon of state office buildings named for prominent Texans.

Just past the light at Enfield, I'd creep by the state troopers manning the security barricade and practically levitate, my feet barely touching the ground, drawn toward the mammoth granite structure.

Regardless of the weather, I walked to the Capitol and watched people. On the university grounds I'd focus on the students, couples strolling hand-in-hand or groups scurrying between evening classes. In the residential neighborhoods I'd peer through the windows and glimpse scenes of shared contentment. On the streets I'd see clusters of happy young people. Everyone seemed to be talking and laughing, expressions of joy painted on their faces like Norman Rockwell paintings. Some evenings UT would host a sporting event or a touring Broadway show, and the boisterous crowds would bubble over into a cacophony of enthusiasm, totally oblivious to the desolate presence in their midst.

I wondered about these people, about their lives—all of them with futures and pasts, finding each other, enjoying each other while I contemplated my life—so different, so solitary. I always walked alone, by choice. I did have friends—Marco and Danny anyway—so I wasn't totally isolated.

I just preferred my own company to others'…or thought I did.

If asked back then, I would have said I was happy. Now, I realize how truly unhappy I was, and very lonely. But like all things, it takes contrast to see the details and my life had simply always been that way. It was the way I was.

I was raised to loathe people like me. I hated myself and felt disgustingly unwanted, unworthy of anyone's affection. There's a downside to being the gay son in a Southern fundamentalist Christian family. My life was full of discomfort and dissonance as the only openly gay member of a line that extends several generations in both directions. In my black-and-white upbringing, I knew two possible outcomes. But since I didn't actually die from embarrassment when my father walked into my room and found me in a romantic embrace with a neighbor boy in the eighth grade, ostracism seemed preordained. I left the arctic cold of my family's exclusion as soon as I graduated from high school, and going back was not an option.

But try as I might, I could never really escape the trauma of my childhood. A castaway, bobbing along in the ocean, years later I was still searching for salvation along the sidewalks of central Austin in the shadow of the Texas Capitol.

Late that summer, I started to feel the tug of emptiness and longing for something else, something more.

The crickets were swarming that night in August, and a mournful apprehension rumbled through my stomach. Unwanted images flashed in my mind as I passed into the neon light surrounding the Capitol.

Trying to avoid the teeming insects, I abandoned the sidewalk for the surrounding blanket of St. Augustine grass. The lawn was so thick it felt like a gymnastics mat as I made my way down the slope from the pink-limestone edifice. Austin's skyline glowed before me and I stood there, trying to block out a growing sense of unease, when I noticed a bluejay feasting on the crickets. They seemed to dance together, the bluejay hopping and flapping its wings, lunging at the darting iridescent blue-black creatures as they jumped and flicked in the neon light. Watching the crickets try to flee, I longed for my own escape.

In the eerie twilight I felt the uneasiness in my stomach again and squeezed my eyes shut. When I opened them, an image welled up in front of me, rising from the grass like tissue paper caught in the swirling gusts of a whirlwind. A vision of wispy indigo mist, a shimmering blue figure hovered above the grass.

I knew instantly that nothing would ever be the same.

With the wave of a shimmering appendage, the visage showed me my own jumbled, disturbed memory of the attack. A blaze of light blinded me, and the electric shock of searing pain shot through me as the Bronco squealed up the street again; without thinking I bent over trying to shield myself.

As fast as it had come, the hallucination disappeared.

I stood shaking from the image, and a jittery sense of impending transition settled over me like the ominous notes of a Bach fugue. My mind was empty except for a profound sense of isolation.

At that moment, I knew I had to find a way out. My life was on the edge of transformation, like when the tide shifts and the water flowing out begins to flow back in.

❖

I first saw him from a distance—a lonely figure walking along the sidewalk, head down, watching his feet.

I was making my way up Duval on one of my nightly walks through the deserted, shadowy side streets. The wind, whispering through branches, merged with the constant buzz of traffic from the freeway and created a muted hush humming in the darkness.

It was the first night of the year that actually felt like autumn. A Canadian cold front had blasted its way through the Midwest over the previous week and unexpectedly dipped south all the way into

Austin. The temperature hovered in the fifties and mist filled the air, surrounding streetlamps with glowing bubbles and wetting surfaces that glistened and reflected their radiance.

Cocooned in the gentle near-silence, I felt utterly alone—and there he was.

He strolled toward me, with broad shoulders over a narrow waist and the stride of a swimmer kicking across the water's surface. When he passed beneath a streetlight, I watched his sandy hair dance in the breeze. He kept his face turned down.

I climbed the hill to the intersection at Thirty-second Street and crossed. Distant headlights pierced the murkiness just above the horizon, and I could feel more than see the shape of a car turning off Harris Park. It was a silver Mustang, its purring engine muffled in the mist.

I walked on, watching him glide toward me. Dressed in black jeans and a long-sleeved black shirt, he moved like a panther in the night. I angled to the side of the walkway, giving him room to pass undisturbed. He passed without acknowledgement. I took a few more steps and stopped, turning to watch him walk on.

The Mustang approached the corner with its engine suddenly roaring, the driver accelerating to make the light. He ignored the car with his head down, his steps constant and unhurried.

The hair stood on the back of my neck as the image played out in front of me. Didn't he see the car?

Couldn't he hear?

My heartbeat quickened. "Hey," I said, then yelled louder, "Hey, the car!"

The lights of the Mustang cut the darkness as it topped the hill. The driver hit his brakes and the tires slid on the slick pavement.

"HEY, look out!" I yelled, running toward him. Still he walked on. I caught his arm just before he stepped from the curb, jerking him back to safety. The Mustang careened around the corner and roared back onto Duval with its horn blaring and the driver hurling obscenities.

"Are you okay? Didn't you see him?" I asked.

No answer. He just pulled away from my grasp. When he looked up, his eyes caught me completely off guard. They were glistening dark pools of pain. He lowered his head and walked on.

I stood and watched him, a solitary figure fading into the mist.

❖

Disorienting lights swirled and flashed from the dance floor. I closed my eyes, rubbing my temples. My headache was full-blown now, pounding with the rhythm of the dance beat.

"Danny, let's go." I tried to sound bored, not needy. Bored would get us out of there—needy would be ignored.

He ignored me.

"So did you have sex?" he asked Marco.

"Well, that depends on what you mean by sex."

Danny raised one skeptical eyebrow.

"What does 'having sex' mean anyway?" Marco said. "Is kissing sex? Is groping sex? Is kissing while groping sex?"

Danny shook his head and wagged a finger. "Honey, it's much more basic than that. If you ejaculated and he was in the room, you had sex."

Marco shrugged. "In that case I've had sex with my junior-high gym coach and the entire congregation of the Hyde Park Baptist Church, but not Wally."

Danny and I simultaneously pivoted our heads toward the patio. Through the window we watched as Wally clicked glasses with a black guy across the bar. Wally's blond curls bobbed as he tilted his head back and downed a shot. Then he licked salt from his knuckle and sucked on a lime wedge.

"Besides, sex with a bartender is so old school." Sarcasm dripped from Marco's voice.

Fleetingly, I considered the possibility that Marco's opinion of "sex with a bartender" would not have been so harsh if *Marco* had actually had sex with a bartender.

The three of us were perched along the railing at the Can. A twirling and flailing mass of dancers slithered and humped in front of us. I pondered another night of hunting but not finding.

Danny turned his back to me and leaned on Marco. "Let's dance, honey." He slurred his words—too much to drink again.

"Look who just walked in," Marco said, motioning to the entrance with his chin. Danny and I turned to scrutinize the line of excessively primped and markedly pumped young men filing past the bouncer at the door.

I knew which one had stirred Marco's interest. He had broad shoulders, narrow hips, and flashed a quick, sweet smile before dipping his head shyly. Sandy hair fell into his eyes and caught the light reflected by the mirror ball above the dance floor. The air around him seemed to glow with divine luminosity.

"Hello," Danny said. "Who's that?" His eyebrows lifted.

Marco grinned. "Forget it, honey, he's a heartbreaker."

To Marco, anyone he hadn't been with was a heartbreaker. I turned my attention back to the divine creation. He moved through the crowd like Moses parting the sea. At the bar, he leaned forward and grinned. The bartender grinned back and opened a bottle of beer, sliding it across the counter with practiced precision. Danny and Marco lost interest quickly and directed their hazy focus back to the dance floor, but I found it impossible to pull my eyes away. Despite my repeated efforts to keep from staring, I followed the sandy-haired Adonis around the room.

Other eyes followed him too. His presence seemed to draw interest like a black hole attracts starlight. He leaned back against the wall in the corner, sipping his beer and trying to avoid the attention. I dropped my head, trying not to stare.

When Danny finally managed to drag Marco onto the dance floor, I stepped around the railing to put the dancers between the lone figure leaning against the wall and me. This allowed me to watch him without being too obvious.

He was beautiful. The light played with the golden tone of his skin, catching the rise of veins that ran up the center of each bicep and disappeared under the sleeves of his black T-shirt. Its stretchy fabric pulled tight across his chest. His dark eyes stared into the distance. The hurt I'd seen was still there but tonight it seemed muted. He looked almost happy in the festive crowd.

From my perch along the railing I fought my attraction to him. I wanted to approach him, to ask about the first night I had seen him, establish a connection. But something about the way he separated himself from everyone else, avoiding contact, choosing the solace of a darkened corner to the comfort and companionship of the crowded bar or the furious activity of the frenetic dance floor, made me realize this wasn't the time.

So I stood there, pretending to watch the dancers—focused on him. It felt like we were the only ones in the room.

He stayed for one drink, then silently slipped through the crowd to the door. Half the boisterous crowd seemed to follow his exit with their eyes. A collective soft sigh was just audible beneath the dance beat as he tugged the door open and disappeared into the night.

I decided to follow. Catching Danny's eye, I cupped my hand and waved good-bye. I set my empty beer bottle on the counter. It took several minutes to navigate my way out of the bar.

Once outside, I searched for the trim dark figure. Fourth Street was particularly bustling that night. The Warehouse District was crowded with late-night partiers, the street clogged with heavy traffic. It felt like South by Southwest, Wurstfest, and Mardi Gras all rolled into one. Patrons strolled by bars, jazz clubs, and coffee shops, laughing and talking and waving to the street as cars rolled gently westward. Couples and rowdy college kids shared the sidewalks with gays and punks and heavily tattooed skateboarders wearing baggy shorts and facial jewelry.

He was nowhere to be seen. I had to make a decision: either turn left and head toward the Rainbow Bar, or turn right and hike up Congress Avenue. My gut feeling said turn left, but the bright lights of Congress beckoned. As I walked up Fourth, I looked down side streets and scanned parked cars. No luck. No luck at the lot on Congress either. By the time I turned north onto the Avenue I'd given up.

With the Capitol looming in front of me, I brooded over the situation. He'd vanished. This man was like a spirit to me, a shimmering vision just out of reach. A dream. Each step I took brought me closer to an epiphany. It came as I entered the Capitol grounds—the words echoed through my head like ripples on a lake and I knew it was futile to try to find him. *He will have to find me.* I walked home alone.

❖

"Hi," he said. He pushed his shopping cart into the checkout line behind me at Central Market. I glanced quickly into his basket—snap green beans, yogurt, whole-wheat bread, and mozzarella.

"Hi," I said, surprised.

"I saw you the other day at the Can." He smiled the same shy smile that had lit up the bar. A careless hand brushed sandy hair from his eyes.

I felt my face flush and fought to hide my excitement. I couldn't believe he'd recognized me. I couldn't believe he had even *seen* me. I swallowed awkwardly and said, "I go there a lot…probably more than I should."

"You were with some friends." It might have been a question.

"Yeah…well, sort of." I smiled.

His grin widened. "Not sure if you were there, or not sure if they were friends?"

"You have to get to know them." I shrugged.

His laugh was quiet and appealing, like a soft summer breeze.

"Paper or plastic?" the cashier asked. I turned to look at her. Her mouth was red and swollen. A small, round, silver stud protruded from below her bottom lip.

"Paper," I said as she began scanning items. I turned my attention back to him. "I saw you too. So do you go out much?"

"Not really."

"Didn't think so—you don't look like a regular." I grinned clumsily.

He smiled back.

"Matt," I introduced myself, offering my hand.

"Thatcher," he said, taking it. His grip was firm, his hand warm. Unintentionally I held tight for too long. It caused an awkward moment, as he pulled free. He dropped his head and brushed the hair out of his eyes again. I sighed.

The cashier mumbled something. I said, "Huh?"

"That'll be $22.47, Romeo." She sneered. "You wanna pay, I got a line here."

"Oh, sorry." I extracted two twenties from my wallet. He waited as I handed her the money.

"So, when do you expect you'll go out again?" I asked.

"Don't know. Like I said, I don't go out to the bars much. It was a special occasion—an exception to the rule."

"What rule?"

"My rule," he answered, ducking his head.

"Need to change that rule," I said.

He just nodded, looking at his feet.

The cashier handed me my change. I grabbed my bags and stood there like an idiot. The cashier glared at me again and I stepped aside.

"If I do, I'll look for you," Thatcher said, unloading his basket.

"That would be nice." I smiled. "Maybe we…" I let it drop, unsure how to continue.

"Maybe."

"Okay. See you later, Thatcher."

He grinned at me again and my heart skipped a beat.

I made my way to my car feeling somewhat elated and somewhat deflated. It had been a long time since I felt that way— too long. The gusting breeze picked up a few yellow leaves and skipped them across the brick lot in front of me. I squinted in the sunshine reflected from my windshield and smiled to myself.

CHAPTER FIVE

THATCHER

So you've been working for home-health care for quite a while?"

"That's right. I've been assigned to a quadriplegic since the eighties, providing nursing and support service."

"That's an odd career path for a registered nurse, isn't it? Did you find it challenging?"

"It was exhausting."

"Very few RNs spend...what is it, fifteen...twenty years... working with one patient."

"Nineteen...and this patient was special."

"Someone you knew?"

"You could say that, yes."

"Do you mind if I ask why you want to come back to emergency room? We don't usually get RNs returning to the ER."

Stephanie smiled warmly. "Well, it was a long, hard pull, and Sean passed a few weeks ago. I need a change. You might say I miss the action."

"Action we got...in spades." The administrator grinned wryly across the table. "Okay, your resume looks very good and I'll need to look into your references, but, assuming everything checks out, when can you start?"

Stephanie tried to hide her excitement, but the relief lifted the corners of her mouth and lit a fire in her eyes. She didn't really doubt that she would get the position, especially since RNs were in such demand. Still she was grateful that the job search had been easy. And Brackenridge was the biggest and most active ER in Central Texas, just where she wanted to be.

She offered her hand across the table and said, "Whenever you need me, Mr. Wallingford."

Wallingford took her hand with an emphatic grip and assured her she would hear from him shortly.

❖

Thatcher leaned back against the stack of pillows and stared through the bedroom window. The sky was suffused with purple, late-morning sunshine that bounced off the bottom surfaces of distant clouds, turning the entire landscape into a Van Gogh painting. Ottmar Liebert lazily strummed his guitar on the sound system, and Thatcher thought about Adam.

Somehow Thatcher's thoughts always seemed to find their way back to Adam. Ten years since he drew his last breath, and still Thatcher thought about him.

The room was naked. Bare walls, bare surfaces, and bare windows. The only furniture was a double bed, angled toward the window, and a mass of wires and boxes comprising his sound system piled on the floor.

The vacant room matched his barren, aching heart.

Thatcher stared at the clouds and felt empty. Adam would have enjoyed this sunset, he thought.

Adam understood beauty, its esthetics and elegance. He appreciated beauty for what it was—not for its effect, but as a thing alone, worthy of appreciation. Adam could find beauty in the simplest things. He smiled as he remembered.

Thatcher leaned against the screen door. The air on this springtime evening was cool, and Adam's emaciated body was all sharp angles as he sat wrapped in a quilt in the porch swing. The faraway storm sparked and flashed in the night sky. Thatcher scrutinized Adam's head as it weaved slowly up and down in progressively larger motions, finally dropping forward, his chin resting on his chest. The motion stilled for a few seconds until, with a start, Adam's head lifted again, his hooded eyes staring out at the storm as he struggled to stay awake.

Thatcher observed the cycle play out again and again until he finally pushed through the screen door and said, "Come on, Adam, let's get you into bed." He laid his hand gently on Adam's shoulder, subtly guiding him to stand.

But Adam shook him off. "No, Thatcher, I have to watch this storm. It's so beautiful."

Thatcher looked down at Adam. His hair was thinning and the skin hung around his eyes. His face was covered in blisters, and lines streaked up his arm from the needle marks. Unfallen tears in Adam's eyes sparkled in the lightning and Thatcher fought with his emotions, reluctant to let Adam know how much it hurt to see him like this.

The magnificent storm flashed and lightning snaked across the sky. Thatcher stepped around the swing and sat down. The two of them watched the billowing clouds as the drenching rain pelted the garden. After a minute, Thatcher laid his arm across Adam's shoulders and they rocked together in the muffled silence of the rainfall. In time, Adam snuggled against Thatcher, leaning his head back onto Thatcher's shoulder. His sleep came softly, and Thatcher slowed the swaying movement until they sat motionless. As he held his fragile lover, Thatcher wanted the world to stop too. He wanted time to pause, for the two of them to stay like that forever, warm and dry with the pelting rain falling around them. But the storm flashed again and, for the first time, he heard the rumble of distant thunder.

Thatcher's smile faded slowly. For so long, Adam had been the center of his life, and so many years later, Thatcher still couldn't figure out how to get past the emptiness he'd felt since his death.

That's how he felt now—empty, like this room. He laid his head back onto the pillows, closed his eyes, and let fatigue wash over him in a wave of sorrow. The void in his life was like darkness made gloomier by the dousing of a light. And strangely enough, that's the way he wanted it.

Without Adam, Thatcher preferred to be alone.

His cell phone chimed; he buried his head under a pillow. It rang again and he sighed. Rolling over, he stared at the screen. Caller ID told him it was Johnny.

He didn't want to answer it.

Johnny couldn't grasp that Thatcher wasn't interested in him. How could anyone not be interested? Johnny was beautiful. But Johnny wasn't Adam, and Thatcher wasn't interested.

I've got to get out of here, he thought, slipping out of bed. He padded toward the bathroom in sock-clad feet.

❖

"Hello?"

"Billy?"

He knew who it was. Only one person in the world still called him that, and instantly he was Billy again.

"It's Nell." His sister was always abrupt on the telephone. He sighed so loud he knew she could hear his frustration.

"Look, I'm sorry to call again—but it's Momma."

He rolled his eyes to the ceiling. "Yeah, and?"

"She's sick, Billy."

He felt a tickle in the back of his throat and the room began to rock. "What's wrong?"

"It's serious. Cancer, liver cancer."

Just like great-uncle Silas, he thought. His stomach clenched and he stared vacantly into the distance. He caught himself, astonished at this subconscious reaction. He hadn't seen his mother in twenty-four years—not since she threw him out of the house. He said, "Nell, she won't want me there."

"You have to come." It was more a request than a command.

Silence played on the phone line for a full minute while he concentrated on the ticking of the clock on his mantel. Finally, he said, "She kicked me out, Nell, remember. Told me she never wanted to see me again. In my book that means I'm no longer her son."

Nell's voice wavered a bit when she said, "Do it for me. Besides, you have to come home, Billy. You know that."

And she hung up before he could argue.

❖

"What is love, anyway?"

Marco spit the word out like he'd bitten into a wormy apple. Danny shrugged, and I stared at him in confusion. The three of us sat on bar stools at the Can. The afternoon crowd was an unattractive mix of hopeless alcoholics, hustlers, and twinks looking to score some E.

Marco answered his own question. "I'll tell you what it is. It's a God-awful obsession followed by a kick in the mouth and months of therapy."

Danny shot back. "Honey, you need to get laid more."

Marco agreed. "We all need to get laid more. But like Tina said—what's love got to do with it?"

A mischievous grin played across Danny's face. He turned his eyes and hazy concentration in my direction. "I could marry that woman," he said.

Marco and I both pivoted on our stools to look directly at him.

Marco said, "She'd be horribly disappointed."

I chuckled. *Marco's a cynic but Marco's a realist.*

Danny sipped his Scotch sulkily and sprayed a reply. "I don't know about that. I could maybe do it with her. I mean she's a woman and all, but those legs."

"She has the best legs in show business," Marco added emphatically.

"Except for maybe Ricky Martin."

I rolled my eyes. This would probably go on for a while. I tuned them out as they began to explore their *Live the Music* fantasies.

Across the bar, Gene, the afternoon bartender, set a bottle of Drambuie beside the cash register, climbed onto the top of the counter, and tugged off his T-shirt. A couple of hard-looking biker types slapped bills down on the Formica surface and stood in front of him, looking up at his crotch. Gene's muscled chest was extremely tan. I could just make out a thin line of curly dark hair that ran below his navel into the top of his faded blue jeans. He dropped to his knees, picked up the bottle, and leaned back. The first biker stepped forward, opened his mouth, and licked the hair under Gene's navel. He left his tongue there, cupped just below Gene's belly button, and gazed up as the bartender uncorked the bottle and poured a stream of golden liquid into the shallow spot between his pectoral muscles. The liquor pooled for a split second before the first rivulet streamed erotically over Gene's stomach into his navel. I could see the glint of voyeuristic eyes flash from the smoky corners of the bar. I couldn't stop watching as the little pocket of flesh filled and overflowed into the biker's mouth.

Self-loathing stirred me to action. I wasn't up to body shots on a Sunday afternoon.

"Well, I'm out of here." I stood, opened my wallet, and tossed a couple of bills on the bar.

"Where're you going?" Danny asked.

"Home, tomorrow's a school day."

"Bummer," Marco mumbled. I left the two of them staring at their drinks in the gloomy bar, made my way to the exit, and weaved through the next wave of alcoholics pushing into the entrance.

The late-afternoon sunshine blinded me as I stepped out, and I squinted at Fourth Street, trying to see through the glare. I turned toward my car, parked on Congress Avenue.

A collision nearly knocked me down.

"Whoa there," he said.

"I'm sorry, my eyes aren't used..." As my sight adjusted a familiar face came into focus. The surprise took my breath away.

"Been inside?" he asked, tilting his head toward the Can.

I smiled, trying to inhale, and nodded.

"How's the crowd?"

"Scary."

Thatcher smiled back. "Go figure. So where are you headed?"

"Home, I guess. What about you?"

"Early dinner at Sullivan's. You hungry?"

I tried to hide my enthusiasm. *Was he really asking me to dinner?* "Uh, I guess I could eat."

"Join me then," he offered, and I nodded.

The two of us ambled up the street in comfortable silence. I fought an inclination to fill the void with mindless chatter and he seemed happy with the silence. We rounded the corner at Colorado Street. The conversational lull lasted all the way to the restaurant's entrance. An attendant at the valet stand opened the plate-glass door, and a tall, gorgeous African-American woman at the hostess stand greeted us.

"Hi, guys." Her smile was dazzling. "How many?"

"Just two of us," Thatcher replied.

"I don't suppose you have reservations?"

"No." We answered in unison and grinned at each other as she ran a bloodred fingernail down her clipboard.

"No problem—you're early. We can seat you right away." She tossed her soft, dark hair over an ebony shoulder and murmured numbers to a pudgy blond waitress with enormous hips. The waitress nodded and grabbed a couple of menus.

"Right this way, guys."

We followed her to a booth in the back not far from the kitchen where she placed oversized leather-bound menus in front of us and set the wine list in the middle of the table.

"Robbie will let you know about our specials." She smiled again and trudged away, deftly avoiding a busboy carrying a tray of dirty dishes.

"Wine?" Thatcher asked.

I nodded.

"Red or white?"

"Red."

He glanced down the list while I scanned my menu. A young Latino with slicked-back hair dropped off a basket of bread, filled our water glasses, and lit a votive candle in a small jar on the table.

Robbie arrived and described the special selections, using ridiculous adjectives that made the offerings sound like they were antediluvian or, at the very least, pre-Mayan. Thatcher ordered a bottle of Silver Oak cabernet. Robbie shot off in search of the bottle of wine while the two of us perused our menus.

Hmmm, good taste in wine, I thought, stealing a furtive glance at those amazing eyes. His attraction seemed to shoot out like a searchlight between us. His golden skin glistened and flickered in the candlelight. He had great bone structure, a straight nose, and a strong, pronounced chin. But those eyes took my breath away. I'd never seen anything like them—blue and green at the same time.

Thatcher was distant and mysterious. And shy. I wanted to know him, understand him, and protect him. My heart melted for him, and I didn't know why. I could feel more than see a depth to his character that made me wary of idle conversation. So I sat quietly until the waiter returned and we had ordered dinner.

"Why don't you go out more?" I finally asked.

"What?" He looked up with a lost expression.

"The other day, at Central Market, you said you don't go out much. Why not?"

He brushed the sandy hair from his eyes. "I don't really like it, I guess. Too confusing, bad memories," he said simply.

"Confusing?" He looked down, obviously lost in thought, but didn't answer. I prodded again. "Confusing, how?"

He sighed. "I was in the military…army…don't-ask-don't-tell. Evidently frequenting gay bars is tantamount to telling. Funny about the army—shipping teenagers off to fight and die in foreign countries, lowering recruitment standards, ranks full of closet cases and gung-ho redneck lifers. But gutsy gays, who have stared down homophobes and fought off small-minded bigots forever, aren't worthy to serve."

"Tell it to the Spartans at Thermopylae?"

"Exactly." He grinned, but said no more.

I let it drop and the conversation lagged again while I wondered about those bad memories. He said, "Do you believe in kindred souls?"

Bewilderment must have been evident on my face.

"You know—like swans. Do you believe there is one and only one true love out there for each of us?"

I murmured, "I don't know." With my heart in my throat, I added, "Maybe."

He sighed and sat back. Watching him as he looked away felt almost voyeuristic. He was obviously wrestling with some inner vision, some storyline from his past. Thoughts played across his face in a series of subtle movements, his eyes unfocused, his attention turned inward. Again we sat in silence until I could remain quiet no more.

"Why?" I asked timidly.

He turned the question away with a disheartened shrug, and I silently vowed to wait out the arctic-like expanse of this lull in conversation.

But the silence lasted through dinner. And aside from murmured refusals of proffered dessert options, not a word was spoken until we nodded our farewells and strolled off in opposite directions on the sidewalk outside the restaurant.

The bright-pink hues of the twilight October sky clashed with my darkening mood as I pulled away from the curb on Congress Avenue. I kept replaying scenes from dinner, and the mystery of Thatcher deepened with each replay. The answer to one important question floated well out of my reach.

Who is this guy?

The sight of Adam shocked Thatcher. He hadn't looked this healthy in a long time. Adam was bathed in the golden glow of sunrise. Thatcher watched him from behind and felt the familiar apprehension. Will he be okay? When Adam finally turned to Thatcher, his smile melted Thatcher's heart, and Thatcher's throat constricted.

"Is it over? Did we make it?" he asked.

Adam just smiled and opened his arms. Thatcher felt warm tears of relief roll down his cheeks and he pressed himself against

Adam's body. The warmth filled Thatcher with joy and he laid his head on Adam's shoulder, inhaling his sweet smell. He ran his fingers across the muscular contours of Adam's back and Adam lifted Thatcher's chin, slowly tipping his face upward. They kissed passionately, then parted. Adam smiled again, softly wiping the tears from Thatcher's face. Thatcher looked into Adam's crystal-blue eyes, pools of sapphire.

Slowly the image began to fade. Adam's blue eyes misted in the haze and Thatcher fought to hold on—to pull Adam back. Thatcher strained to see through the mist, but Adam's presence flickered and faded even as Thatcher fought.

Thatcher woke in the dark empty room holding nothing. A familiar pain flooded him like a surging river, and a tidal wave of loss swallowed him.

❖

I lay back on my black leather couch listening to Train sing "Drops of Jupiter" and thought about dinner with Thatcher. A bulb, flickering in the streetlamp outside my house, cast strobe-lit lines from the mini-blinds onto the hardwood floors of my living room. Bare tree limbs, wobbling in the wind, painted dancing figures over the gleaming surface of my naked body. I watched the wriggling figures and pictured Thatcher's face. As Train sang softly, I pondered questions I couldn't answer.

What had he meant when he asked about kindred souls? I let myself consider his intentions. Could he really feel for me what I obviously felt for him? Could I be his "one true love"? And then the big one again…who was this guy anyway?

What did I really know about him?

The answer echoed through my mind. Nothing really, trivia. He shops at Central Market and goes out to the bars very occasionally. He may have been in the service…or was that just a metaphor? How could I feel so strongly for him anyway? Without knowing him— really knowing him—how had I built this…what…this love? Could it be love? Did I love him? I realized my feelings were irrational, baseless. What was he to me anyway? An image…a handsome, dark…what? As I formed the question the answer was obvious.

To me, Thatcher was a creature of pain.

I knew he was hurting. Thatcher wore his anguish like a nose ring in the middle of his face. Hurt, yes, but how? How had he been hurt—by someone or something? And was this…emotion…that I felt for him really just about that pain?

Maybe that was it. Maybe I wanted to save him, or protect him, or even deliver him, rescue him.

Headlights from a turning car flashed across the room, briefly illuminating the Russell Pavlicek abstract hanging on the far wall. Pinks and greens flared briefly and lingered in my eyes, melting and shifting for a few seconds. As the darkness returned, uneasiness settled into the pit of my stomach, and the seed of an idea germinated in the depths of my consciousness. Slowly it spurred me to action. I stood up and strode to the shower. In twenty minutes, I was bathed and dressed.

Marco knew Thatcher, or knew about Thatcher. I stepped out onto my porch and turned the key, locking the door. I didn't understand Thatcher but was determined to find out what Marco knew about him.

❖

Bright spots floated in Bill's eyes as he sat down on the pew near the back of the church. The optic residue from the flashbulb slowly faded from view. Bill didn't think a funeral was an appropriate place for a photo opportunity, but Nell's hen-pecked husband was dutifully following orders. It had been seventeen years since Nell had seen Bill, and she was determined to document the event.

The light from the nave was uncomfortable and his left eye, now permanently dilated, closed without willful awareness. Those who noticed him probably thought he was strange-looking and turned away with revulsion. He appeared drunk, leaning forward in the pew and awkwardly tilting to the side.

The service had been everything Bill expected. His mother's body, an aged façade with wispy gray hair and tightly pursed lips, lay in the casket and seemed to glower at him from the sanctuary. Nell, still freakishly girlish, softly simpered in the front row while pudgy, balding Ron worked unsuccessfully to corral the six wriggling kids squeezed awkwardly into the pew between him and his fat wife Jackie. And the preacher, with his pompous pronouncement of everlasting life and the blessings of family, figuratively wagging his finger from the pulpit, made Bill smile. It was perfect. Everything she would have wanted, he thought, everything she deserved.

Nell had even arranged for one-hundred-and-three-year-old Granny Ruth to be rolled into the chapel in her wheelchair. Bill pivoted uncomfortably on the hard surface and looked in her direction. The old woman appeared fragile, almost brittle. She was wrapped in black taffeta, her coal-black eyes hidden behind wispy lace cascading from the wide brim of her hat. Garbo in a wheelchair, he thought. As Bill watched, she pulled back the lace and stared at him. The skin in her face was translucent like waxed paper, and her shoulders hunched forward so that her head stuck out uncomfortably, but steely determination glinted in her eyes when she spotted him. Then the wrinkles of her face deepened and widened into a warm smile. Bill smiled back and tears shimmered in her eyes. Just like the tears he remembered that day when he first heard of Uncle Silas.

The thought brought on an unexpected reaction, and a wave of nausea rolled through his stomach. He lowered his head, closed his eyes, and stifled the urge to throw up.

CHAPTER SIX

THATCHER

The late-autumn sun shone brightly on the water and the air was just beginning to warm when Jim Avery pulled his red Toyota Highlander SUV along the curb and parked under Loop 1. He opened the driver's-side door and Venus bolted from the passenger seat across his lap. She jerked to a stop only when the leash, clipped to her collar, pulled taut against the door handle.

"Whoa there, wait for Daddy." Jim tugged the leash free and kicked the door closed. The car beeped an acknowledgment when he pressed the Lock button. The straining black Lab muscled her way across the street and onto the hike-and-bike trail. Gathering himself, Jim inhaled the crisp morning air and scanned the trail as Venus paused to sniff the base of the water fountain.

Foliage formed a tunnel to the east as the trail dipped through a forested area. In the other direction, the path moved first west before doglegging south, mounting a bridge that crossed the river under Loop 1. Solitary joggers shared the trail with groups of walkers and bikers. The walkers, scattered along in twos and threes, steered carefully to the sides of the passageway, allowing the bikers room to pass and runners space to maneuver.

As Venus pulled forcefully toward the river, Jim spotted a familiar figure dressed in running shorts sprawled on the grass alongside the trail. The sunshine sparkled off his golden skin and lit highlights in his sandy hair as the figure bent forward to stretch his hamstring.

Jim said, "Hi there, stranger."

Thatcher looked up with a wary expression before a wide grin of recognition broke through.

"Jim." Thatcher scrambled to his feet, brushing dead grass from his legs. He offered a hand to shake but Jim pushed it away dismissively and pulled Thatcher into a bear hug. They grasped each other awkwardly at first, but the unease faded quickly. Thatcher was five or six inches taller, so Jim found his nose buried in Thatcher's chest. They remained together for several seconds, and each seemed to hesitate before pulling back.

"Long time," Jim said.

Thatcher smiled. "Yeah."

"You look good."

"Thanks—you too."

"A little less up here and a little more down here, I'm afraid." Jim tapped his head and stomach at the same time.

Thatcher's smile widened. "Time marches on."

"So, how long has it been...two years?"

"Yeah, two years and two months."

"Tough years," Jim said, and he gazed deep into Thatcher's haunted green eyes for acknowledgment before adding, "They get easier."

They both knew it was a platitude. Thatcher chose not to respond. Instead, he bent to pet the Labrador retriever. Venus ducked her head in a sign of submission and wagged her tail slowly. "Is this Venus?"

"Yeah."

"She's all grown up."

"That's right. The last time you saw her she was a pup."

"Just a handful of wriggling fur."

Their eyes locked, and an unspoken message flashed between them. Their smiles faded before Thatcher looked away.

"Going for a run?" Jim asked, trying to change the subject.

"Yeah, just heading out."

"Great day for it." He inhaled deeply before offering. "You know…if you ever need to talk…"

Thatcher glanced up the trail nervously and murmured half-hearted thanks, then dropped his head and softly said, "Not yet."

Jim watched the sandy hair fall into those startling eyes and found himself thinking, He really is a handsome man. Venus whimpered at his feet. She was ready to go but Jim wavered. He wanted to break through the awkwardness and say what was left unspoken. He tried several approaches in his mind, but they all sounded trite and contrived. Finally, he said, "I understand, but if you ever need me…I'm there for you."

"You always were." Thatcher flashed another shy smile and they said uncomfortable good-byes, then Thatcher bolted up the trail and jogged quickly over the bridge.

Jim watched him run until he turned the corner on the far side of the river and disappeared from view. He shook his head and let the grin on his face fade slowly. Without warning, an image of Adam's emaciated body flashed in his mind's eye and an icy finger of discomfort trailed up his spine like an electric shock. Venus, tugging at the leash, brought him back to the present. She muscled toward the riverbank and Jim tugged her back onto the sunny trail; slowly, the disquieting sense of sadness melted in the warmth of the sunshine.

❖

"Greg!"

I cringed at the name.

"Aren't you Greg Palmer?"

I turned to see a short, bald man in his mid-fifties, he wore a gray, tropical-weight wool suit and sunglasses. The sunshine, gleaming off the top of his head, caused me to squint. Unconsciously I rubbed the scar under my arm. "Do I know you?" I asked.

He gave me a dejected look. "Don't you remember? I guess not. You were pretty much out of it the whole time." His lips parted into a small smile. "Understandable. It's been a while." He offered his hand. "It's Martin. You know, from Brackenridge Hospital." When I didn't react he said, "Martin Hansen?"

I remembered him. My mind replayed the scene from Brackenridge's recovery room. I recalled the pain and anesthetized surrealism, Martin's face floating in a drug-induced haze. The memory made me uncomfortable, like a friendly reminder of a youthful indiscretion. Reluctantly I shook his hand.

Twenty years ago I had cut through the secluded passageway between two buildings trying to catch up with my friends; we had planned to walk home together from a late-night party in the warehouse district, something we often did because no one wanted to be a designated driver. But that night I was delayed leaving Oil Can Harry's because the line to the bathroom was long. Marco and Danny went on ahead and, in a hurry to catch up, I turned down the darkened passageway between the buildings.

It was a decision I lived to regret.

I was ten feet from the sidewalk when a lone assailant fired a shot from the driver's seat of a passing blue Ford Bronco. The bullet slammed just below my rib cage on the right side. The force spun me around and dropped me like a brick to the pavement. The shot had barely missed my elbow, shattered a rib, nicked my liver, and pierced the lower lobe of my lung before tearing a nasty hole through my back on its way out of my body. Police later found the bullet embedded in the limestone façade over the arched entryway to the alley. It had bounced off a dumpster to get there.

That act made me the sixth victim in a series of seemingly unconnected incidents with no apparent motive, another casualty in a string of unexplained violence in Austin that year. The police were just connecting the previous attacks, four murders and one survivor, when I was shot, and they insisted on hiding my identity while I convalesced in the hospital. Over the next seven months, the staff of Seton Hospital knew me as Greg Palmer.

I hadn't been called Greg since then.

The "shooter" murders started again four days after I left the hospital. Six more bullets killed five gay men and put my friend

Sean Perry in a wheelchair. The murderer was extremely efficient: one bullet, one body. And then, just as mysteriously, the shootings had stopped. Twelve attacks, without so much as an inkling of who was responsible. No arrest had ever been made; no suspect had ever been named. The crimes remained unsolved and I had worked hard to forget that I was ever called Greg.

"Sorry, you must have mistaken me for someone else," I said curtly. I pushed past him into UT's Communications building.

I hustled across the lobby, squeezing by groups of students. The crowd in the Com building was harried. I joined the rush and scuttled past rowdy underclassmen scurrying in all directions. I hurried because I knew Marco's class had finished and I didn't want to miss him. I made my way into a crowded hallway with banks of elevators on both sides. Both Up buttons were illuminated. I squeezed into the queue next to a couple of nervous-looking females wearing sweatpants, their hair pulled back in ponytails. The three of us watched the numbers descend.

"So, are you ready?" one of them asked the other.

"Not really, but I studied all day," the other answered.

"I hope it's multiple choice, I can fake multiple choice."

The bell dinged and the doors opened. The three of us entered and I pressed Four. One of the girls pressed Five.

"Communications is not my favorite subject. I only took this class because I thought newscasting might be a cool job."

"You would really blow on TV," the other replied.

"You think so?"

"Yeah, I mean with your hair and everything—you'd be perfect."

I rolled my eyes and prayed the elevator would pick up speed.

"I know what you mean about Communication though. Who knew it would be this hard? Jamey said Mallory was easy."

"That bitch told me that too, and I need at least a B to graduate. Maybe if I slept with him or something. I mean he's old and ugly and everything, but I really need a B."

"Um hmm, I hear you there. I say a girl's gotta do what a girl's gotta do. That's exactly why I slept with Gravely."

"You slept with Gravely? Girl, he's hot. I'd do him even if I didn't need a grade. I mean I know he's just an assistant prof but he's got great legs and stuff."

The bell dinged and I sighed with relief; their conversation left me feeling disgusted and in need of a shower. The doors opened and I swept down the corridor, leaving them to discuss the vagaries of a slut's academic options.

I arrived at Marco's classroom just as he was gathering his things to leave.

"Hi, need a hand?"

"Matt!" He raised his eyebrows. "Trolling for a date or do you need some money?"

I shrugged off the put-down with a smile and said, "I was in the area, thought I'd drop by."

He stacked a well-thumbed notebook on top of two hefty textbooks. "Umm hum. So what's the catch, what do you need? I mean other than the obvious...fashion advice."

"No catch, just wanted to see where you worked."

He waved his arm expansively toward the empty classroom, "Well, there it is in all its glory."

"It's probably more exciting before the students leave," I deadpanned.

"Obviously, you've never taken my class."

I grinned and grabbed the books. "Well, it's glorious. I mean, compared to prison, of course. Want to do dinner?"

"Okay," he answered warily, "but this nice-guy routine doesn't fool me."

I gave him my best hurt look.

"You can buy me dinner, but first you have to tell me what this is about."

"What? I can't take my best buddy out to dinner once in a while without an ulterior motive?" I asked.

He looked at me with tired eyes that spoke volumes. "You are so transparent you might as well be made of glass."

I shrugged and said, "Okay, so I have some questions, but they can wait until we're drinking wine."

He grinned, lifting a ratty book bag onto his desk. I handed him the books and he stuffed them inside.

"Okay, darlin'—but you're buying…and I'm ordering."

❖

Twenty minutes later we were staring through the big picture windows at Brick Oven Pizza on Red River Street. The pink granite of the Texas Capitol building glowed before us. From our seat at the window, the edifice seemed to levitate with the magnificence of ten thousand watts. An eighty-dollar bottle of Sterling Merlot sat on the table and each of us held a glass of wine.

Marco clicked his glass against mine and took a swallow. His eyes closed slowly and he eased back into his seat savoring the "velvety smooth essence with hints of wood-smoke and berries." At least that's how the waiter described it. For eighty dollars a bottle, I thought the wine should at least foster world peace or cure cancer.

"So?" he queried when he'd regained consciousness.

"So, I need some information."

He raised an incredulous eyebrow.

"You remember that beautiful guy at the Can last Saturday?"

"I remember every beautiful guy at the Can last Saturday." His grin was sardonic.

"You know who I'm talking about. You said his name is Thatcher, Danny asked about him."

Marco frowned and his face darkened, his brows pulling together in the middle. "Yeah, so—what's he to you?"

"You know him, right? I'm interested, that's all."

"Um hmmm…so what exactly do you want to know about Thatcher?" he asked coyly.

"Just the basics really."

"Oh, you mean favorite sexual position, top, bottom, versatile? Or are you looking for an in-depth report on his physical endowments and his circumcision status?"

"Let's start with who he is and how you know him."

"What's going on here?"

My curiosity obviously annoyed him. I stared at him for a few seconds. Finally, I said, "I ran into him a couple of times this week." I shrugged. "Just wondering who he is, that's all."

"Right." Marco's doubt was predictable and unwelcome. I wanted straight answers, but the conversation would follow our regular pattern: innocent inquiry, incredulous cynicism, persistent prodding, put-down after put-down, angry declarations, pleading, and finally, reluctant truthfulness. The game was on.

"Come on, Marco. What do you know about him?"

"He has herpes and a fetish for farm animals." He was mocking me. "Don't tell me you're interested in the guy?"

I hedged. "Maybe."

"He's trouble, and that's all you need to know." Marco sipped his wine and turned away.

"Marco, I just bought you an eighty-dollar bottle of wine. Answer my questions."

He gave me a playful hurt look and took another sip. "And it's wonderful too, honey."

I fought the urge to roll my eyes and asked, "Where do you know him from?"

"Let's see, was it prison or did I rent him as an escort?"

I didn't laugh at the joke. The cold stare I shot back spoke for itself.

"I saw him on *America's Most Wanted*—that happens when you kill your mother."

Finally I said, "Marco, be serious."

"Look, Matt, he's no good. Take my word for it. He will break your heart. I don't mean to be negative, but better men than you have tried and failed. Leave him alone." The warning was delivered with as much sincerity as Marco could muster.

"Just tell me what you know about him, okay?" I looked directly into his eyes. "Please, it's important."

We stared at each other for a few minutes until my persistence finally broke through. He sighed in resignation, drank some more wine, and said, "I know he's trouble."

The waiter arrived with our pizza; I waited until he was gone before I started again. "Why? Why is he trouble?"

Marco reached across the table to grab a slice and trailed cheese all the way to his plate. "He just is, really, Matt. Hell, I know from firsthand experience. That guy's gonna break your heart."

"Where did you meet him?"

Still glaring at me, he said, "ASA, okay? I met him at ASA."

AIDS Service of Austin is a local HIV support organization. Marco volunteered there occasionally, manning the information line, giving advice to callers about how the virus was transmitted and what constitutes safe sex. A lump built in my throat and I swallowed hard before I asked, "Is he a client?"

Marco waved off my concern. "He's a volunteer…or was. I have no idea if he's positive." He carefully blew on his pizza then tested the temperature with his finger before taking a bite. I waited while he chewed.

"And," I asked.

"And he's got troubles." I waited for him to go on, but he was still being coy.

Finally I snapped, "Marco, just tell me." My frustration level was rising again.

He sighed heavily and shook his head with unenthusiastic resignation. "Look, his name's Thatcher Keeney. He lost someone, someone he loved. He's hurt…and he likes to spread it around." He paused, glancing nervously out the window, and took a sip of his wine. He shrugged and finished his dissertation with a look of annoyance in his eyes. "That's really all I know."

"Thatcher Keeney?"

"If you want to know more, ask someone else." He took another bite and wiped cheese from his chin.

"Who?"

"I don't know." He waved off my question with growing aggravation and grabbed another slice of pizza. "Try Jim Avery. They used to be close."

We ate in silence, sipping from our glasses and avoiding eye contact. Before I knew it, the wine had taken the edge off our confrontation and the conversation started up again, morphing, as is usual with Marco, in the direction of boys and salient rumors of bed partners. The more I drank, the less I thought about the price of the wine, and after a while, I was fairly convinced that I could just about taste a hint of wood-smoke and berries.

The morning broke clear and clean like a shining new penny. The pecan trees shed their pale-yellow leaves, which drifted like snowflakes through the clear blue sky. Almost overnight the crepe myrtles in Thatcher's garden had flared bloodred. From his bedroom window, they framed the deep-green lawn of the municipal golf course like rubies surrounding an emerald. But Thatcher had barely noticed the stunning foliage.

The sunset splashed golden hues across the landscape and drew purple edges on the scattered clouds. Slowly the color leached from view, and Austin settled into shadowy tranquility. When Thatcher walked that night, the still, cool air amplified the rhythmic pounding on the pavement. He turned his vacant eyes to the ground and watched as the sidewalk slid smoothly beneath him like a conveyor belt. Overhead, streaks of muted gray and indigo filled the sky and the nearly full moon was a perfect egg glowing in a nest of wispy clouds and halo. A trick of the night air appeared to shoot beams from the radiant object in symmetrical patterns, drawing first Xs, then crosses, and finally, eight-legged spiders. The sky itself was suffused with a soft glow, and the moon competed with Hyde Park's century-old moon towers for luminary supremacy.

On this night Austin was a Van Gogh painting.

But Thatcher was mostly oblivious to the effect. His focus was within. Confusing images swirled in seemingly disconnected patterns across the field of his mind's eye. A spinning kaleidoscope of emotions roiled inside his head. From the jumbled distance the rhythmic pounding slowly morphed into a familiar tune and his heart floated as he lost himself in memory. Thatcher's subconscious had pulled up the sound of Paul Simon softly singing about old friends sitting on a park bench like bookends.

Then a memory bubbled to the surface of his cauldron of thoughts.

Adam's eyes twinkled when he smiled in the sunshine. The New York skyline ringed Central Park like a Cherokee war party, and Thatcher watched Adam sitting on the bench. The fall air was cooler than it looked, but the bright sunshine felt glorious on his face. In the distance horse-drawn carriages lined up in front of the Plaza, and on a patch of yellow lawn in front of Adam a pair of nannies herded preschoolers toward a soccer ball. The nannies' efforts were only marginally successful, their charges lurching on wobbly legs, bumping and nudging each other, largely unaware of the purpose of the game. Thatcher snuggled into his sweatshirt and glanced again at Adam, who closed his eyes and tilted his head back onto the top railing of the bench. Thatcher's soul filled with joyful warmth and he smiled at the sight of Adam napping. Finally he closed his own eyes and they slept together on the bench, bathed in the glorious sunshine.

In Thatcher's mind Paul Simon sang softly about a newspaper rustling through the grass and dropping on the shoes of two old friends.

CHAPTER SEVEN

JIM

Jim Avery regularly used the weight room at Gregory Gym on the University of Texas campus. An average-looking guy without a lot of attitude...or hair, Jim liked animals and served as a nursing volunteer for the local AIDS hospice. I caught up with him in the gym's free-weight area the morning after my dinner with Marco. The two of us had a nodding gay-boy acquaintance—we were familiar fixtures at the gym and our screen names occasionally adorned the same chat rooms in cyberspace. Back in the eighties, Jim had briefly dated my college roommate, and over the years I'd run into him at various fundraising events, while shopping at Central Market or Whole Foods, and walking his dog on the hike and bike trails.

He was seated at a padded bench near the mirrored surface of the far wall when I entered the weight room. Hand weights of various sizes lay scattered at his feet, and a plastic bottle containing an orange liquid was tucked under the bench. I wove my way through the maze of exercise equipment as he rose and tugged a set of forty-pound hand weights from the floor mat. The weights clanged as he dropped them on a white-painted metal rack and glanced into the mirror. Red eyes stared back at me for a second, then he squinted and inhaled to sneeze.

I rounded the bench and sat down, while he wiped his nose with the tail of his shirt. He wore knee-length gray shorts, a blue Old Navy T-shirt, and Nike cross trainers with no socks. Rings of sweat darkened the underarms of his T-shirt, and the muscles in his arms were sufficiently pumped to draw attention.

"Hi," I said.

"Hi." His eyes squeezed shut. He covered his mouth and sneezed again. He wiped his hand on his shorts and extended it in my direction to shake.

"I'll pass," I said, waving off his offer.

"What? Are you afraid of catching something?"

I shrugged.

"I didn't realize there was anything microbial left for you to fear. Haven't you developed immunity to just about everything by now?"

"I'm not really sure how to take that." I grinned at him, grateful for the playful attitude.

"Take it as a compliment."

"I'm afraid you have a much-exaggerated view of my love life."

"Well, at least you have a love life, lucky bastard. I have a love life too, I guess, but it's mostly a solitary thing."

I sniggered. "Another reason not to shake your hand. And my love life is nonexistent at the moment, my friend."

"I find that hard to believe." He smiled again. For some reason, I felt a flush of embarrassment.

"So are you here to work out?" he asked, skeptically eyeing my jeans and street shoes.

"Not today. Today I swim."

"Ah, yes, you're a swimmer. I forgot about that."

"You look like you're working hard."

"Not really, I feel like shit." He sniffed. "Sinuses...I'm just going through the motions." He sat next to me on the bench and picked up a small towel, carefully folding it in half.

We looked at our reflections in the mirror and I said, "I know what you mean. My problem's ragweed and mold."

"God, don't I know it. Seems like everyone in Austin's got problems with mold. Three straight weeks of rain—then it's beautiful yesterday and today. Now the mold spores are everywhere. I'm just glad it's starting to dry out around here."

"Finally."

"Now if my sinuses would just follow suit." He wiped his nose with the towel.

I'd thought of a way to subtly steer the conversation toward Thatcher as we chatted. I smiled and said, "I think you know a friend of mine—Marco Padilla?"

"Guilty." He rubbed a wristband across his forehead. "He's an old friend, and I do mean old. So where'd the two of you meet—jail?" He giggled at his own feeble joke.

"Our mothers are friends." Jim looked at me quizzically. "I know…I find it hard to believe that he has a mother too."

He laughed again. I liked his laugh—it was open and friendly. "I did duty with Marco at ASA," he said. "We manned the phone lines together. He's a little twisted."

"Um hmm, like a pretzel." He laughed again. "If you worked at ASA you probably know Thatcher Keeney."

His red eyes squinted and he sneezed into his towel.

"Bless you."

He peered at me over the top of his towel. He raised his eyebrows and blew his nose. "Thank you," he said, adding, "God, I hate this. It's like Drip City in my head."

I waited while he wiped his nose again. "So, you know Thatcher?"

"Yeah. In fact I just saw him yesterday, at Town Lake, on the trail." He scanned the area for unwanted eavesdroppers and lowered his voice in exaggerated subterfuge. "And I'll tell you one thing, that guy looks great in running shorts."

I gave him a lecherous smile and wiggled my eyebrows before misquoting Groucho Marx: "He got his looks from his mother. She was a plastic surgeon."

He laughed again. "I love Groucho, ever hear this one? Outside a dog, a book is a man's best friend. Inside a dog, it's too dark to read."

We both laughed and he wiped his nose again.

I said, "That one's my favorite. I also like this one. 'It isn't necessary to have relatives in Kansas City to be unhappy.'"

He laughed so hard this time, tears came to his eyes. Watching him raised my spirits. He had the free, unhindered joy of a child. I waited until he wiped his eyes and blew his nose again before asking, "Did you meet Thatcher at ASA?"

"Yeah."

"On the phone lines?" I raised my eyebrows; he shrugged.

"Nope."

"Damn! I was starting to think the phone lines were a good place to meet guys." It was a really lame joke. I was struggling to keep the conversation going.

His grin was generous. "Not really."

I pressed again. "So how did you meet Thatcher?"

"I was Adam's case manager."

"Adam?"

He stared at me, confusion written on his face. I fidgeted uncomfortably. If he noticed my discomfort, he ignored it. He said, "Yeah, Adam—his lover."

My heart sank.

Jim waited a beat before adding, "The one that died."

"Oh." Relief tugged on the corners of my mouth before images of lost love swam through my mind as I thought about Thatcher's sadness. When I looked up again, Jim was eyeing me warily. I said, "I didn't know him."

"I thought you were friends with Thatcher?"

"Right." I wavered.

He shrugged but seemed to accept my evasion as an explanation. "Well, it *was* a while ago…nasty death." He paused, bending to tie a loose shoelace. "AIDS usually is."

"Oh. But Thatcher is…?" I let the question hang, unasked, in the air.

Again he fidgeted. His red eyes looked straight into mine, and his voice grew serious, "Maybe you should ask *him*."

"Yeah," I said, lowering my head. "Right, I didn't mean…I just…" This conversation wasn't going the way I wanted it to, but Jim seemed to want to ease my discomfort.

"Look, I understand. I just assumed you knew Thatcher better."

"I do, I mean." I tried to put together a meaningful sentence, but the words wouldn't come to me. I decided to go with candor. I sighed deeply. "Okay, I lied…sort of. I mean I do know him, but not well. We just met a couple of days ago."

"I see." Jim looked at me skeptically.

"I don't want to…well, I didn't want to pry. I just…I uh…I just want to know, I guess, know more about him."

"Right."

"I didn't know about Adam," I admitted.

He shook his head slowly. "Like I said, it was a long time ago."

"But it makes sense," I added.

He raised his eyebrows in an unspoken question.

"I mean, it explains why Thatcher seems so sad."

"Yeah, probably, but I was hoping that was over for him. Thatcher's been through a lot. Adam was, well…special, I guess. Thatcher tried everything, to make it better, to save him."

"To save Adam, you mean?" He nodded. "But it was AIDS?"

"Yeah, it was AIDS and it was the eighties, and AIDS in the eighties was a death sentence." He dropped his head and blew his nose again.

"I remember…every day someone new."

"Yeah…every day." We sat together in silence for a few seconds, each lost to his own thoughts.

"Sorry to bring you down. But thanks for the information. I should let you get back to your workout."

He smiled.

"Maybe we could get together for coffee or something," I offered.

"I'd like that," he said.

❖

This time Jerry Philips's rental car was a midnight-blue Buick. He pulled into the parking lot at the Clovis Heritage nursing home and parked under the neon sign. The fetid Clovis air hit him like a slap in the face as soon as he opened the door. He grimaced as a sharp pain shot up his spine when he grabbed his video camera from the Buick's backseat and slid gingerly out of the driver's-side door.

The whole world glimmered uncomfortably bright. The morning sun reflected sharply from frost-covered surfaces. Jerry squinted at the convenience store across the street. A window banner read Cigarettes, Beer, Milk, Bread, and Perfume.

Perfume?

Jerry grinned at the image and tugged a pair of sunglasses out of his shirt pocket. He slid them on and crunched across the frosty pavement toward the manor's entrance.

This morning Mrs. Brookes sat in a sunny spot in the hallway. She wore a fluffy sea-foam-green bathrobe and a blue flannel nightgown, her head a mass of spongy pink rollers bobbing gently over her wrinkled face. Her head seemed to be nestled in the nightgown's lace collar, and her emaciated body, looking frail and brittle, was shoehorned into the wheelchair, pinned in place by a tray table fixed to the front of the chair. Her legs were wrapped in layers of material, and her sagging torso appeared to be propped up by sharp-angled elbows that pressed down onto the tray. Jerry saw her intelligent coal-black eyes sparkle in recognition as he approached. She reached out a twisted arthritic hand in greeting. He grasped it carefully; the papery skin was like cellophane over a mass of blue veins and white bone.

"It's nice to see you again, Mr. Philips." Her voice was full of genuine warmth.

Jerry placed the camera bag on the floor before letting go of her hand. "Thank you for allowing me to come back and bother you. I just have a few more things to ask about."

The weathered features of her face twisted into a smile. "It's not like I have lots of pressing engagements these days. So you want to know how it all ended, don't you? The rest of my family's deep, dark secrets?"

Jerry smiled again. "Yes, ma'am, I would. If it's all right, I'd like to film you again too."

"Please sit down, young man. I'm getting a crick in my neck staring up at you there." She waved her twisted hand toward a padded bench perched along the wall. Jerry turned her chair toward the bench and took a seat directly in front of her.

"It's just that it's not a very easy story to tell," she said, looking off through the window.

"No, ma'am, I suspect not." The hallway grew silent except for the soft hum of the heater's fan and the distant shuffling of other patients. Jerry watched her patiently.

After a few seconds, the old woman's spongy pink head bobbed up and down and her twisted fist began to shake with palsy. She fixed him with her disconcertingly bright eyes and said, "Well, I guess since I've started this, I may as well finish it. Lord knows it's time someone hears what really happened. She glanced at the camera bag on the floor before fixing her coal-black eyes on his and said, "If we're gonna finish before I die, or they serve lunch, we'd better get started. As slow as they are around this place there's no telling which will come first."

He stared at his reflection in the mirror and sneered. His demonic left eye was fully dilated—it cast an ominous darkness over his face. In his forehead and cheekbones he saw the shadow of his mother's features.

He couldn't believe what had just happened.

Was this his mother's idea of a joke?

Deep down inside, he knew better.

Two hours earlier, Nell had handed him the letter along with small box wrapped in brown paper. She explained that their mother had prepared packages for each of her children before her death, as Nell put it, "a sentimental memento—something of personal significance."

Bill's letter said simply, "To show you how much I care." It was the package that delivered the real message.

He stared down at his hands, small and tapered like his mother's. He could see them shake. He struggled to control his emotion and still the motion. It took three flicks before the lighter ignited. He picked up the photo album by the corner and dangled it over the toilet. A grim picture of his stepfather stared back at him in mocking provocation as the other pictures fluttered down. The flame flickered and danced around the edge of the page. Slowly, a small trail of smoke rose to the ceiling. He watched the paper scorch and then the plastic covering burst into flame.

Seconds later the smoke alarm screamed from the bedroom.

"Fuck!"

He dropped the book in the sink and vaulted onto the bed, jerking the cover from the alarm. He pushed the Reset button and instantly the screeching became muffled. Bill stared at the box in confusion until he realized he was hearing the buzz from the hallway; the alarm system for the entire hotel was connected.

"Fuck!"

❖

Thatcher stood mesmerized, looking through the bedroom window. In the gap between the crepe myrtles he could just make out two figures, a couple, walking along the ridge of the distant fairway. Swathed in white and illuminated by the waning sunlight, the figures glowed ghostlike against the dark-green grass: ephemeral in their radiance, a pair of apparitions floating along the horizon, drifting in the breeze. Thatcher's thoughts drifted too, but not in the breeze. His thoughts swirled like a vortex, pulled by a powerful undertow from the past, toward the memory of Adam.

Thatcher pictured Adam from behind as he looked out over the ridge. Thatcher remembered Adam's smile on that day, the day he had first seen the house. It was the perfect lot on the perfect hill, the right place for their home. And the view had tickled Adam's imagination. Before the renovation could begin, Thatcher had altered the design to accommodate the bay window.

It was a big bay window angled awkwardly out toward the cliff edge.

The same bay window with the view of the golf course that Adam had imagined—this view that Thatcher now looked out on... but barely saw.

They leaned back, together, against the wall of the old carriage house. Thatcher thought to himself that the scrub oaks that lined the hill would have to go. Just above the trees, he caught a glimpse across the stream to the golf course. On the far horizon two figures, lugging golf bags, ambled up the distant fairway.

"Crepe myrtles." Adam's warm voice wafted through the still air like a butterfly. "Right there." He pointed to the cluster of hardy scrub oaks. "We need crepe-myrtle trees, two of them, with enough space in the middle to frame the view."

Thatcher tried to picture crepe myrtles.

"The bedroom needs that view, the bedroom screams for that view."

Thatcher looked at Adam. "And how are we going to do that, since this is the corner of the building?"

"Simple, we need a bay window—set at an angle."

Everything was simple to Adam. But Thatcher was the practical one. "Won't it destroy the building's proportions?" he asked.

"No one will even see it from the street, it won't be noticeable. Besides, it'll enhance the unique design."

Thatcher grinned. "What unique design? It's a box."

Adam gazed out over the tree line. "Well, at least it will be a box with a bay window—and a view."

Thatcher considered pressing his point, hardening his resistance. After all, he was the one with architectural training. And he had been the one who found the property in the first place. But Adam had vision—vision and an innate sense of design. And that smile. Adam's smile warmed Thatcher's heart, and deep down he knew that he would do anything to see that smile again. Thatcher's resistance melted like snowflakes in the sunshine.

"Okay." He shrugged. "So we build a box with a view."

Adam flashed the smile and leaned over, slipping his fingers inside Thatcher's palm. They stepped away from the building and strolled, hand in hand, up to the ridge. The sunset slapped pink hues across the landscape like a careless painter, turning the distant green lawn fluorescent and casting lengthening shadows all the way to the golf course.

The memory gradually faded until it was gone altogether. Thatcher stood motionless staring through the window, across the ridgeline at the green lawn in the distance. He felt the emptiness again, and darkness echoed in his soul. A surge of exhaustion washed over him in a tidal wave of depression. He was tired—tired of feeling empty, and lost. And tired, for the first time, he realized, of missing Adam.

Why? Why did Adam have to die? Why Adam? Why?

But his questions went unanswered as always, and the approaching darkness enveloped him like a cold, wet rain. He could feel his stomach clench. He could hear his heart pound. He could taste his loneliness. Thatcher was sinking back into an old, familiar place—back into the blackness.

His life was slipping away: he could see it, feel it, and taste it. He pictured his existence and the true loss—lost happiness, lost friendship, lost time—and his anger grew. The unrealized potential, unachieved goals, unshared love burned like a fire. For the first time since Adam's death Thatcher struggled with his feelings, his depression…and his obsession.

"No!" he screamed, and the force of his anguish surprised him. The sound of his voice echoed through the empty room as wet, hot tears welled up in his eyes and spilled down his cheeks. Softly he said, "Please, don't." Then even softer, "I can't do this anymore. I love you, Adam, but I have to go on…I have to."

Once vocalized, the concept crystallized and the words took on the power of a personal vow, sacred and inviolate. Release came quickly like the opening of a door and another, deeper, wave of sadness rolled in as he realized this was the start of letting go.

Of really—finally—letting go.

For the first time since Adam's death, Thatcher recalled that day at St. David's Hospital.

Adam leaned back into the pile of pillows. The late-afternoon sunlight, streaming through the window, caught the highlights of his eyes and they sparkled like sapphires. Thatcher sat beside him in a chair.

"I'm going to ask Dr. Byrd to stop the medicine," Adam said.

The room was so quiet Thatcher could hear the scratching of pen on paper from the nurses' station down the hall.

"I know." Thatcher's voice caught in his throat.

"It's time, Thatcher."

Adam paused and Thatcher strained to hear the scratching sounds. The world seemed to spin slower, and the only thing that mattered for him was Adam's face floating in front of his eyes.

Finally, Adam broke the stillness. "It's time to go home."

Thatcher nodded. He meant it was time to go home to die. "I just want to be with you," Thatcher replied.

Adam's voice was steady when he said, "All that I ever wanted was to be with you."

Thatcher laid his head on the bed, turning his face to the window. He didn't want Adam to see the tears in his eyes. Adam gently ran his fingers through Thatcher's hair.

"I love you, Thatch."

"I love you too." Thatcher's voice wavered.

"When I'm gone..."

"Please," Thatcher struggled to steady himself, "Adam, please...let's not talk about that n..." His voice broke and he swallowed hard, unable to finish his words.

Adam spoke softly as he stroked Thatcher's hair. "I have to, baby. We have to."

Thatcher turned to look at Adam, the tears flowing now, forgotten as they streaked down his face and spilled onto the bed.

Adam smiled sadly. "When I'm gone I want you to find someone else. I don't want you to be alone."

Thatcher's strength dissolved. He turned his face away again and stared out the window.

"I want you to fall in love again." Adam touched Thatcher's shoulder, the contact gentle and intimate. "I want you to be happy. All that I ever wanted was for you to be happy. Remember that, Thatch."

Thatcher's throat tightened and his tears dribbled onto the bedspread. He inhaled and spoke. "I love you, Adam."

The stillness in the room enveloped them in intimacy. Thatcher whispered, "Always."

"I know," Adam said. The words seemed to hang in the air like spring fog.

Gradually, the haze lifted and a peaceful calm infused their souls as a blanket of silence descended.

For the first time Thatcher understood Adam's words—*really* understood them.

Adam wanted him to find a way to go on and live again. Standing there, looking out his bedroom window at the now-darkened landscape, Thatcher resolved to let go of Adam.

Letting go would be harder than anything he had ever done.

CHAPTER EIGHT

MATT

I squinted into the late-afternoon sunshine—driving west was difficult at this hour. Thankfully, there weren't many cars on Bee Caves Road. Still, the winding lane weaved its way through Westlake Hills, dipping and turning past unpredictable parking-lot exits, changing construction sites, and abrupt stoplights. My grip on the steering wheel tightened and I stretched my neck to keep my eyes in the shadow of the rearview mirror. The glare was giving me a headache. The clock on my dashboard read 6:52, but it was ten minutes fast. I had eighteen minutes before practice.

My little green Miata sped through the light at Loop 360 with twelve minutes to spare, and five minutes later I pulled into the parking lot at West Austin Athletic Club. The sun had just dropped below the far horizon, turning the sky powder-blue and painting the scattered clouds orange. The hills were slowly shifting from warm sand and olive to taupe and tar.

I exited the car and maneuvered into my swimsuit under a towel wrapped around my waist while standing in the parking lot. The pool lights switched on as I hiked down the hill and the water became a glowing turquoise jewel, peppered with a few tanned bodies and streaked with the carnival-colored lane lines.

I marched across the deck and sat down on a bench next to the coach's whiteboard before carefully wiping the film from inside my goggles with my towel. When I stood and tossed the towel onto the bench, Coach Chris frowned in my direction. The message was clear—if I didn't want to deal with his retribution I'd better get in the water fast. I stretched the elastic band around my head, working the goggles over my eyes carefully. They made a satisfying sucking sound as I pressed the eyepieces into my sockets. I dove headfirst into the warm water and whipped two quick dolphin kicks, surfacing on my back and churning my feet as hard as they would go. With my arms stretched out above my head I pressed one hand into the other and extended my reach, forcing my biceps against my ears. I felt my elongated body slice through the water, cutting a straight line down the lane. I streamlined across the surface of the pool under the backstroke flags.

The water felt silky smooth sliding past my body and I breathed the cool evening air in big heaving gasps. I watched Coach Chris write on the board as I pulled up and clung to the gutter at the edge of the pool. A couple of swimmers dove into the lane to my right and a few stragglers were still making their way down the hill in the distance when Chris asked, "So are you ready for a little breaststroke, Matt?" He sat down in a deck chair with a silver whistle drooping from the side of his mouth and a clipboard in his lap.

I frowned my response and he said, "Don't ever let your coach know you don't want to swim his favorite stroke. That'll cost you."

I shrugged, and he added, "I think maybe a little death by breaststroke is in order."

My groan was almost involuntary.

More swimmers were arriving on deck now. They chatted in twos and threes and surreptitiously slipped into the water as Chris scribbled the workout on the whiteboard. I could just make out his writing. Warm-up would be 400 yards freestyle.

I was just about to push off the wall when I spotted Thatcher in the parking lot and shook my head in disbelief. I took off my goggles and squinted, unsure if I was hallucinating. But he was really there, all right. I watched as he poked his head tentatively around the corner of the dressing room and seemed to waver slightly before slinking very slowly down the hill. He looked uncomfortable, obviously reluctant to join the team in the pool. The evening temperature had dropped with the sun, and I could see him shiver as he set his black backpack on a deck chair and slipped out of his sweatpants. Underneath he wore a black Speedo. He shrugged out of a black T-shirt and wrapped his shoulders in a dark-gray towel. He slung the backpack over a shoulder, tossed his sandy hair out of his eyes, and paced around the corner of the pool. I couldn't take my eyes off him as his long, rhythmic strides carried him confidently across the deck toward Chris.

It wasn't unexpected for new swimmers to join a Masters' swim team in midseason—in fact, guys seemed to come and go without a specific schedule. But this was Thatcher, and seeing him with the team seemed foreign, like finding a Damron Guide tucked in the hymnal of a Baptist church.

He certainly looked like a swimmer, lean and athletic—and something about the way he moved was…well, smooth, like a finely tuned motor. Still, swimming was my sport and I was pretty sure I'd met every serious swimmer in Austin. And there was absolutely no way I would have missed Thatcher. If he had been using the local pools, I would have seen him. But then again, Thatcher evidently had lived in Austin for years and we hadn't met. He had volunteered at ASA, occasionally dropped in at the gay bars, and apparently knew Marco well enough for Marco to be wary of his presence—and still we hadn't crossed paths.

Until recently.

The West Austin Athletic Masters' swim team consisted of thirty or forty gay men and two or three lesbians. Usually only ten or twelve swimmers showed up for any given practice. The team swam together three times a week and wasn't nearly as serious about swimming as they were about cruising each other.

Every eye in the pool turned to watch as Thatcher walked across the deck.

Coach spoke first. "Hi. Is this your first time here?"

Thatcher nodded.

"I'm Chris." He offered his hand, "Coach Chris, welcome."

"Thatcher." He dropped his backpack and towel on the bench, shook Chris's hand, and turned his eyes toward the pool. "So how does this work?"

"You look cold," Chris answered.

Thatcher crossed his arms and rubbed his shoulders. "Kind of."

"Well, get in. Just grab a lane. We swim counter-clockwise, stay to the right side. Warm-up is 400 yards free. Lanes are arranged by speed, faster swimmers in the middle of the pool. Just jump in wherever you feel comfortable. We'll start the main set after everyone finishes the warm-up."

Thatcher nodded.

"Hey, stranger," I called from the water.

He looked down at me and a smile broke across his face. He shivered again and worked his goggles over his head. "So, you swim?"

"Yeah, I swim. It's warmer in the water." I nodded, grinned again, and he accepted my invitation with a nod.

I watched as he dove in. His lean, muscular body arched through the twilight sky and split the plane of the water like a knife. He surfaced past the backstroke flags and swam to the other side of the pool. His arms had the slow turnover of an efficient stroke and he moved quickly through the water—signs of a good swimmer. His hips rode high on the surface and his reach was long, strong, and even. He seemed to glide over the water.

He flip-turned at the far wall and swam back, pulling up next to me. We leaned back against the side of the pool together.

"Nice stroke," I said.

"Thanks."

"You're a swimmer."

"How can you tell?"

"You're wet." I shrugged. "It figures."

He smiled. "How about you? You look like a backstroker."

I smiled back. "Distance free, mostly."

"So, what now?" he asked.

I nodded to the whiteboard and said, "The warm-up."

He squinted at the board. "Four hundred yards free stroke."

We pushed off the wall side by side. I found my rhythm quickly and settled into a long, strong pull. I hit the far wall with a flip-turn and caught sight of him as he headed into the wall, a flash of black nylon and tan skin. I could see his muscles lengthen and contract as he pulled through the water. I was used to being faster than the other swimmers on our team, but the two of us swam at about the same pace. We finished the warm-up in just under five minutes. He pulled up beside me, struggling to catch his breath.

"Where did that come from?" His voice was raspy as he panted. "You're fast."

I smiled.

"I didn't expect that, I'm a little out of shape."

I eyed his body incredulously. "Right."

"It's been a while since I was in the water," he explained. "Looks like you swim a bit."

"A bit," I answered, turning the conversation back to him with a question. "So where do you swim, and I'm not buying that bit about it being a long time, mister."

Again the grin. "A couple of weeks ago, honest. I swim mostly at the Y." That explained why I hadn't seen him before. I swam in the city pools and on campus, but not at the Y.

"I'm not sure I can keep up with you," he added. "Maybe I should change lanes."

"Are you kidding? You're more than fast enough. Anyway, most of the workout's gonna be short sets. I'm not much of a sprinter."

Now he looked at me unbelievingly. "Right."

Still, the implied challenge kept him from bolting to another lane. I positioned my feet on the wall, getting ready to send off.

Just then, Danny and Marco arrived, late as usual. Marco's eyes bounced quickly from me to Thatcher and back again before he raised an eyebrow in disbelief and turned to whisper in Danny's ear.

Death by breaststroke entails short bursts of sprinting followed by even shorter bouts of swimming comfortably, all breaststroke. We moved continuously, toggling between fast and slow whenever Chris blew the whistle, and he blew the whistle a lot.

It turns out that breaststroke was one of Thatcher's strengths, and I struggled to keep up. Occasionally I would catch sight of Thatcher's extended torso and flexible legs smoothly whipping through the water. I fought hard to avoid being lapped. Afterward, my inner thighs burned from the exertion, and I silently vowed to avoid saying anything about Coach Chris's favorite stroke in the future.

When Chris finally gave us the thumbs-up sign indicating the set was over, I clung to the side of the pool, gasping for air. Thatcher pulled up beside me, his eyes scanning my body. I smiled inwardly and turned away, still breathing hard.

I was caught totally off guard when he touched the scar under my arm.

"What happened here?" He ran his finger lightly around my side, under my rib cage all the way to the distinctive exit wound, shaped like the number eight. He traced his finger slowly around the figure eight and the physical connection was electrifying. A chill radiated out from the point of contact, standing my hair on end. My legs tingled all the way to my toes. Thatcher's touch lingered on the wound while I gathered myself to speak. "An old accident."

Lying had become an unconscious reaction to questions about the scar. My natural aversion to the subject rose out of the need to forget. I expected interest in the injury, had dealt with it many times in the past. Over the years, I'd developed tools for allaying the fears of those concerned about my health and deflecting the prurient inquiries of those bold enough to ask about the scar. For me, the entire incident, from the moment I was shot until the day I left the hospital, had become a part of the past—like a bad dream or a disgraceful family secret best forgotten or at least left unmentioned.

And that's how I wanted it to stay—in the past.

❖

Bill's mother was dead, now. He was surprised how much her death bothered him. The old familiar ache throbbed from his side and he tried to ignore the pain. He knew it was psychosomatic, brought on by memories long-suppressed but recently rekindled.

She gave me a photo album, he thought, and his stomach tightened.

His right hand idly pushed the mouse, steering the cursor across the screen, but he wasn't paying attention. Unconsciously his left hand lifted his T-shirt and a finger traced the scar, a lazy figure eight on his abdomen.

A vivid image of the storm cellar flashed before his eyes and he flinched, pulling back from the computer screen. His mouth filled with a sickening taste and he started to shake.

He knew he couldn't hold back forever. Someday soon his resistance would fail and the hunter would hunt again. Even the thought stirred him below. He knew he would because he tasted the sweetness. The sweet taste that had returned after seeing…no, he wouldn't think of that anymore. Thinking of it was like doing it; the thoughts would become the deeds. For now he must keep the thoughts in check, the hunter at bay. He turned back to the computer screen in front of him and began another search.

Thatcher tossed his backpack in the passenger seat and climbed into his black RAV4. He stuck the key in the ignition and paused, smiling to himself. *So Matt has secrets.* And he winced, realizing he was starting to like this guy. *He's cute,* Thatcher thought. A little hyper, but cute. The image of the eight flashed in his mind's eye and he shook his head in confusion. It was uncanny, really, so familiar, so similar. What a strange connection, he thought. He stopped himself, realizing he was subconsciously molding the coincidence into a sign.

No, Matt was a nice guy. A nice guy with potential, he'd leave it at that.

He had had a good time tonight. Swimming with the team had been the right choice.

A few days before—when he had finally decided that he needed to break out of his old patterns and try to connect with life again—he'd considered his options. There were the bars, of course, but Thatcher usually tried to avoid that scene. His experience at the Can a few weeks before had shown him that he wasn't up to the hustlers, druggies, alcoholics, and strippers. That world would be full of old tricks and bitter one-night stands. Guys like Johnny Price, who wanted a relationship, a roommate, or at least another date—guys that hoped for more when all Thatcher was interested in was physical release. He cringed at the thought of bitter confrontations from the multitude of guys he'd left behind.

No, the bars were definitely out.

Then he thought about volunteering again. Good people were doing good things out there, and gay-related support organizations might lead to meeting someone. But then his mind wandered back to his time with ASA and he flashed to the image of Mike Frank.

Not long after losing Adam, Thatcher began to feel unsettled and detached. The long slog nursing Adam through his illness, and eventual death, had caused him to lose connection with almost all his friends and neighbors. That trend had only continued after Adam's funeral, and Thatcher caught himself spending more and more time alone. At first, he reasoned that his grief caused it; the new world he inhabited was a dark place where he felt isolated and cut off from society. After all, who would understand the depth of his sorrow and be willing to put up with his depression? But soon he realized it was more than that. Thatcher missed Adam, but he also missed a sense of purpose. He had become so used to dealing with the disease, with intimately handling all the horror of Adam's day-to-day struggle, that a world without that fight felt foreign. Like a soldier suffering post-traumatic stress syndrome, Thatcher mourned both the loss of Adam and the loss of that fight. He longed for that sense of purpose that caring for Adam had instilled in him.

Also, Adam's death had filled Thatcher with rage, spawned by the sense of his utter helplessness and his inability to stop the unstoppable. Missing the battle, Thatcher felt a deep desire to continue the fight, to do whatever he could to relieve the helplessness, to stop the disease. More than just wanting to help, Thatcher needed to find a way to help those still suffering from AIDS. But he didn't know that as bad as it had been for Adam, others had had it worse.

Thatcher found several volunteer options available at ASA, but only two of the programs called for working directly with people living with AIDS. The first, the Buddy Program, provided emotional support, and the other, the Helper Program, offered physical support to ASA's clients. Thatcher realized he was not ready to be a buddy. It was too soon after his loss to provide emotional support to anyone, and his temperament would never allow him to build the emotional distance needed for that kind of job.

But being a helper was different. He thought he could run errands while keeping enough emotional distance to avoid being sucked back into the inevitable vulnerability of the situation. The helper program would give him a chance for hands-on contact with clients, allowing him to contribute in a meaningful way and find the purpose his life had lacked since Adam's death.

So two weeks after the funeral, Thatcher signed up to be a helper and was assigned a client. Determined to work as long as the client needed his services and do whatever was required, Thatcher resolved to push ahead. After all, the program literature talked about running errands—like picking up drugs and grocery shopping, occasionally helping with the cooking or cleaning, and he knew he could do that. And that was how it started, when Thatcher began to work with Mike Frank. However, it ended differently.

He looks like a lizard. That's what Thatcher thought the first time he saw Mike, a big scaly lizard. Mike's battle with AIDS had stripped bulk from his cheeks and sharpened the contours of his bony face, making his nose narrow into a thin ridge terminating in nostrils. His dark eyes retreated deeper into their sockets, giving his brow ridge prominence. The edges of his mouth pulled back, making him appear to grin wickedly.

More disturbing than the changes to his face was the ruin of his body. Mike's arms and legs were thin, with folds of blotched and scaly skin hanging from the bone, like clothes on a clothesline. His stomach was disproportionately large, swollen from parasites and fluid retention caused by the drugs he was taking.

He reminded Thatcher of an anaconda that had just eaten a feral piglet.

Mike was bedridden, too weak to stand. He was also angry. His surly attitude had chased away two buddies and a handful of helpers. But Thatcher liked Mike's feistiness and angry outbursts. He saw Mike's sarcasm as an expression of an inward need to fight against the disease and his circumstances—a fight Thatcher hoped would ultimately lengthen Mike's life and give him the will to go on. Soon, Thatcher was dropping by Mike's little house on Carolyn Avenue twice daily, in the morning to deliver drugs and in the afternoon to walk and feed Mike's West Highland terrier.

Straight off the bat Mike directed his anger at Thatcher, calling him names and questioning his intentions. With his laid-back attitude, Thatcher easily weathered the storms and Mike turned his attention elsewhere. One day, while Thatcher was cataloguing Mike's meds, he heard Mike call his housekeeper a "lazy, jiggling lump of rancid jalapeño jelly." The housekeeper, whose English was questionable, caught the nasty tone and shot back, "Me no, you lacy, jiggle up racy jalapeño Jell-0." She turned and stomped out of the room.

Mike looked at Thatcher and they both broke out laughing.

It turned out Mike was wickedly funny, irreverently attacking anything and everything. He particularly liked to joke about his disease, his body, and the loss of yet another vital body function. For his part, Thatcher enjoyed the laughter and grew close to Mike.

But it didn't last. Two-and-a-half months after his first visit, Thatcher received a call at two in the morning.

"Hello?" Thatcher fumbled for the bedside lamp switch.

"Thatcher?" The man's voice was unfamiliar.

"Yes."

"This is Mitchell Jordan. I'm the night-care nurse working with Mike Frank." There was some rustling of paper. "It says here that you're his helper."

"Yeah, what's happened?"

"I need a hand. Can you come in and help do some cleaning?"

"Now?"

"Well, yeah, if you can." He paused again, and Thatcher tried to clear the muddle of recent slumber from his mind. Mitchell's voice softened. "Look, I know it's late, but Mike's time is near. I'm at his house. He needs help and I need help keeping him comfortable."

"Well, I guess I can. I'll be there in tw—"

"Great." There was a click, then the dial tone.

Thatcher arrived at Mike's house on Carolyn Avenue twenty minutes later. The entire street was dark, except for the lights shining through the bedroom window.

The scene Thatcher viewed as he stepped through the porch door burned an image into his subconscious that occasionally blazed across his mind in nightmarish half-awake moments of sheer terror.

The air in the room was fetid and humid, and the overhead lights blazed like the sun. Mike lay naked and sweating, curled up in the fetal position on the poster bed. His swollen, blister-covered tongue lolled out of the side of his mouth, streaked green and white. It reminded Thatcher of the pickles sold at ball games. Congealing red liquid pooled on the mattress and floor, blood-soaked sheets lay in a heap piled against the dresser. Red splotches discolored the walls around the foot of the bed, streaking the oak floor. A pudgy, balding man dressed in hospital scrubs stood over him checking the IV bag hanging from the corner bedpost.

The balding man looked at Thatcher. "You must be Thatcher. Could you grab a mop?"

Mike's unconscious body heaved forward, spewing bloody vomit across the bed and onto the floor. It splashed on Thatcher's shoes and misted the front of his jeans. Thatcher stood staring at his feet for a few seconds, too stunned to move. But soon the shock disengaged him from his emotions and he strode off in search of a mop.

For the next four hours, Thatcher cleaned like a machine. Mike's struggle ended just before dawn. As the morning sun rose over the freeway, Thatcher and Mitchell, both covered in blood, sat exhausted on the porch banister. Two somber-looking gentlemen zipped Mike's freshly scrubbed corpse into a body bag and hoisted it onto a gurney. As the gurney was rolled out of the bedroom into the warm sunshine, Thatcher's world tilted and darkened.

Later, Thatcher called ASA and dropped out of the helper program. He crawled into bed and slept for much of the next week. Soon the psychic scars from that night fused with haunting memories of Adam's last days. In Thatcher's mind, each scene deepened and emphasized the other to the point where he couldn't escape. Depression enveloped him.

Even though that had been long ago, Thatcher knew he couldn't volunteer like that again. The inner strength he'd found for Adam had disappeared after Mike so ASA was not an option.

Thatcher needed something totally different. Swimming might be a good way to meet people so he decided to give it a try. On the drive to the pool, he was full of apprehension. When he first caught sight of the pool, everyone talking and laughing, he wanted to turn around and go home. But he had made it through the practice and now, sitting in the parking lot, Thatcher had to admit he had enjoyed it.

He clicked on his headlights and shifted the RAV4 into reverse. After backing out of the space carefully he pulled onto Bee Caves Road and drove instinctively, not really seeing the road ahead of him. The image of Adam appeared in his mind's eye as he reached Loop 360.

"See, that wasn't so bad," Adam said, and smiled.

Thatcher smiled too.

❖

"I can't believe you."
"What?"
"You invited Thatcher to join the team?"
"Wait a minute."
"You're playing with fire."
"I did not invite him to join the team."
"He's going to break your heart."
"He came on his own." I was struggling to control the self-righteous indignation bubbling like acid in my stomach. Marco's anger was as unexpected as it was unwelcome and unfounded.

We glared at each other across the gingham-clad hardwood table. We were sitting in comfortable chairs on the deck at County Line restaurant. The lazy water of Bull Creek glowed green in the halogen illumination and slid slowly under the hardwood planks as it moseyed toward the inky black of Lake Austin. In the distance, a quarter moon poured a silver-white stripe out of an indigo sky onto the water's surface. The faint aroma of chlorine wafted from our bodies, mixing with the heavenly smell of Texas barbeque.

Danny sat studiously mute, his sticky fingers wrapped around the greasy ends of a rib.

"Puuleeeze," Marco moaned. "And he just happens to swim in your lane?"

"So now I own the lane?"

"You were all over each other."

"We were not."

"It looked really cozy in lane three."

"We were swimming."

"Some of the time—"

"Marco, what's wrong with you?"

This wasn't like Marco. Granted, he was always the first to put someone down. That was his way, but it never lasted this long. Eventually he'd come around…or at least turn to a new target. He fumed in his seat, glaring at me in anger as untouched sauce-laden brisket cooled in front of him.

"What don't you like about the guy?" I asked, trying to soften my tone.

"He's just bad."

"Why?"

"He just is." Marco shoved his plate away with a heavy sigh and turned to look at the water.

I sighed too. "Look at me." I waited until his eyes met mine. "Marco, I like this guy…*really* like this guy. I want to get to know him."

Marco looked away again. The three of us sat in irritated silence for a few seconds until I continued gently. "Marco, you're my friend. And I trust you, but you have to do better than that. If you know something about Thatcher, something I should know, then tell me. If not..." Danny dropped a naked bone onto his plate and grabbed another rib without looking down.

I sighed and started again. "Lord knows it's been a long time for me. I've been alone all my life, really...Well, I've been alone long enough. You should be happy for me. You should encourage this. I—"

Marco stood up, shoving his chair backward, and bolted through the restaurant without another word. I watched, dumbfounded, as he slammed out the double doors. Frustrated, I turned to stare at Danny and shrugged. He sighed and set the half-eaten rib on his plate, grabbing a napkin. He wiped his mouth, carefully cleaned each finger, and tossed the napkin onto the table before turning his gray eyes my direction.

"You really don't get it, do you?"

"Get what?"

"Clueless, and blonde. You're acting very blonde."

"What?"

"Matt, honey, it's not about Thatcher." He paused for effect. "It's about Marco."

"What about Marco?"

Just then a blue heron dove into the water a few feet from the deck. It surfaced, shedding droplets from its oily back, carrying a wriggling fish in its beak. I watched as it flapped its wings and lumbered out of the halogen light, down the creek toward the lake. It became a silhouette in the moon's glare before disappearing into the shadows.

"Marco is in love with you."

I stared at him, stunned. "Marco? And me?"

"Bingo," he said, turning his attention back to the ribs. I shook my head in disbelief and sat in silence, but the pieces started falling into place.

❖

The message light on my answering machine was blinking as I tossed my keys on the counter. After dropping Danny at his apartment I drove home, my mind muddled. I just wanted to go to bed and sleep my way out of this funk. I debated waiting until morning to listen to the message, but I pressed the Play button.

"Hey, Matt, I enjoyed swimming with you tonight. Thanks. I was just calling to see if you like jazz? Hiroshima's here next Friday. Wanna go?"

Thatcher left his number.

I lay down on my bed, the events of the day playing through my mind like a video collage. The world seemed to be spinning faster than usual and sleep seemed less inviting. I grabbed the phone, propped my head up with a pillow, and dialed.

"Hello."

"Hi, I got your message, I love jazz." I lied. I couldn't tell jazz from hip-hop.

"Great, so Friday works for you?"

"Yeah."

"You know where One World Theatre is?"

"Sure, on the way to the pool."

"How about I pick you up, say six. We can do dinner first." He added, "You got to eat, you know."

"Yeah, you got to eat." Anticipation built inside me.

I gave him directions to my house before we hung up then sat on the side of my bed, my elbows propped on my knees, holding my head in my hands. After a moment, I switched on my stereo system. I'd just started searching for a jazz station when I noticed a package leaning against the lower panes of the French doors.

I lumbered across the room and picked it up.

It was from my mother. *Not now.*

It took me ten minutes to unwrap the box, since Mom's penchant for overdoing everything reached its pinnacle in her wrapping skills. Every square inch of the surface of the brown-paper package was triple-wrapped in clear packing tape. The box looked as if it had been shrink-wrapped in plastic, the address barely visible below the layers. It took the combined efforts of a pair of pliers, a straight razor, and a serrated bread knife to break through the binding.

I had to dig through three layers of bubble wrap and Styrofoam peanuts to get to the CDs. The label on the boxed set read "The Christian Cure," the side panel touted a "spiritual method of healing homosexuality—twenty-five easy steps toward finding Jesus."

I tossed the CDs back into the box and sat on the couch, then switched off the room lights. My living room seemed larger in the darkness. I watched the shadow patterns shift. I just wanted to empty my mind of everything. I thought back to my discussion with Danny and glanced at the box on the floor. *God, what a day.*

I grabbed the box, strode back to the bedroom, and tossed the CDs into the basket tucked behind my computer cabinet. As far as I was concerned, those CDs could lie there unopened until I found time to bury the whole mess in the backyard.

My spirits were rising as I twiddled the knob on the stereo. It took a few minutes to locate a jazz program.

I grinned and lay back to enjoy the music.

I sat on the stone ledge surrounding the East Mall fountain and gazed into the distance. The cold front that had blown through the night before had stripped most of the leaves from the trees. Now, the embankments of Waller Creek were cloaked in yellow and orange. Fall color lay heaped in gutters and scattered across neatly trimmed lawns in front of brown brick buildings. I traced the line of black pavement sweeping around the turnaround that became Twenty-third Street as it climbed the hill between the football stadium and the Performing Arts Center. At the apex of the hill, the pavement seemed to pour into the yellow lawns bordering the LBJ library. A shimmering silver tower of water shot straight up and cascaded into the circular, tiled fountain filling the crook of the grassy-sloped hill.

I shifted my gaze to the right. Above the tops of the trees lining Waller Creek and the terracotta tiled roof of the Alumni Center stood the immense mountain of gray concrete—Belmont Hall and Royal Memorial Stadium.

A flock of forty or fifty pigeons wheeled in unison back and forth across the front of the stadium, rising ever higher, until finally topping the corner of the uppermost seats. They peeled off around the first pillar, playing a game of catch-me-if-you-can as they slalomed through the other pillars. Back and forth they flew, mysteriously turning as if following the same unheard signal, until finally they landed on the concrete beam at the base of the lights.

Behind me, the chimes of the University Tower signaled it was five thirty. The warm hues of sunset were leaking into the pale-blue sky as the sun dropped below the western horizon. I pulled up the zipper of my fleece jacket and slung my backpack onto a shoulder. I climbed the stairs beside the fountain and began walking across the East Mall in the general direction of the Communications Building, trying to play through various scenarios in my mind.

It was Thursday afternoon and Marco's class would be over soon.

I had spent an anxious day at work. I was supposed to be designing a Java class encapsulating a test structure, but I spent the day wondering about Thatcher and strategizing my next move with Marco.

My gut feeling was that Marco's infatuation was a sort of a cry for attention. He was my best friend and I loved him, but he was notorious for his need for attention and the brevity of his romantic obsessions.

Danny had called me at work, telling me I just needed to weather the storm. Danny believed Marco would soon move on to another equally unattainable target. He was probably right, but inactivity had never been my coping mechanism. So I marched across campus, trying to come up with the appropriate words to not hurt him or, God forbid, lose his friendship.

I turned past Hogg Auditorium as the lights began kicking on across campus. A streetlamp cast an uneven, speckled shadow pattern through the rustling foliage of magnolia trees onto the lawn in front of the Littlefield Home. I stepped over a shifting mat of dead leaves that swept past me in the breeze. The leaves blew into the brick courtyard of the Littlefield Carriage House as I climbed the stairs to the Communication Building. The concrete courtyard in front of the building was packed with students jostling through the glass doors. Like a salmon swimming upstream, I made my way into the building, shoving past the youth of Texas as they elbowed and tugged with the current intent on escaping. In the building's foyer, I fought my way to the elevator, but the doors slid shut before I could reach them.

Fine, I'll take the stairs.

I pushed through the heavy metal door, letting it swing shut behind me, then started to climb. The solid concrete walls amplified the echo of my feet as they beat an awkward rhythm, skipping every third or fourth step. I paused to catch my breath at the fourth floor, grabbing the railing and glancing up just as Marco shoved through the stairwell door on the fifth floor. He bolted down the stairs, his head turned down, with a book bag slung over one shoulder and a briefcase in the opposite hand. He was obviously in a hurry.

"Hey," I said as he approached.

His eyes widened. "What are you doing here?"

"It's called stalking in forty-nine states. Fortunately, we live in the other one."

"Very funny." He wasn't smiling.

"We need to talk."

"Sorry, not now." He shook his head, waving me off with the flick of a wrist. "I'm late." He pushed past me and hurried down the stairs.

I followed in his wake. "When then? When can we talk?"

Without turning, he asked, "What is it you want?"

"Just…well, I…um—"

"Look, this isn't a good time," he said as we reached the third-floor landing. "Is it important?"

"I just…I mean I…well, I…"

He pushed through the doors to the third floor with annoyance. "Yeah?"

I trailed him down a tiled hallway past metal doors with important-sounding names like PHOTOGRAPHY LAB, SOUND STAGE, and CAMERA ROOM printed on signs above them. I grabbed his elbow to stop him just as we reached the Production Facility. "We need to talk about last night."

"What about last night?" He raised one eyebrow.

"Well, I…umm…" Again, I found what I wanted to say hard to get out.

He opened the door marked PRODUCTION FACILITY and paused, leaning against the jamb. A sign hung from a string hooked over a peg on the outside of the door. It read, TAPING IN PROGRESS—QUIET.

"Look, I'm really busy right now," he whispered. "Why don't you think about it and give me a call when you figure out what you want to say." He stepped inside and slid the door shut with a muffled click.

I stood staring at the QUIET sign swinging back and forth for a full twenty seconds before I walked back toward the stairwell. My mood didn't improve until the tower bells rang at six.

My date with Thatcher was just twenty-four hours away.

❖

Bill sat in the backseat of the black Ford Explorer, staring through its tinted windows, his heart rate beginning to climb. Not yet, he told himself, and leaned back. Restlessly, he scanned the car's interior. His feral mind noted a thousand details—the sharp shadows cast from the parking-lot lights, the soft glow of the leather seats, and the scent of his own anticipation. He reached over the seat and adjusted the rearview mirror, sneering at his reflection. He pulled the stocking cap down to his eyebrows and caught sight of his dark eyes sparkling in the shadows. The pupil of his right eye had widened to match his left and they looked balanced, almost normal. A sinister smile curled across his lips.

The dashboard clock's numbers glowed emerald green: 2:10. That explained the increasing street traffic. The bars were closing. He watched groups of drunks sway and stumble as they made their way, in twos and threes, through the parking lot.

A group of college-aged women dressed in short skirts and tight tops talked nonstop, high-pitched voices tumbling and falling over one another just like the way their lithesome bodies nudged and stumbled together. The sound of high heels clicked a staccato rhythm across the poorly lit pavement. He observed the women as they congregated around a red Volvo. A delicate-looking Asian girl shivered in the northerly breeze as a buxom redhead started searching through her purse. He fingered the trigger of his Bushmaster .223 and licked his chapped lips, watching as the redhead found her keys. The Volvo stalled as it pulled onto Fourth Street. He heard the grinding of the ignition before the car jumped to life, weaving westward into the traffic.

Typical, he thought. Women are so inferior.

He pictured himself regal, tumescent, and omnipotent as he fondled the stock of the Bushmaster. His sexual interest swelled as he stroked the cold steel. Shivers shot through him and his arousal came on like the wind stirring the trees outside. He glanced at his watch, 2:12. He turned his eyes back to the alleyway and slowed his breathing. He pictured himself as an animal, stalking his prey in the night.

Careful, he thought, not too soon. The best hunts built slowly. The escalating anticipation was half the fun. He diverted his attention by concentrating on his heartbeat, steadying his pulse while the parking lot gradually emptied.

Eventually the Explorer was one of only four vehicles left in the lot. Briefly, he considered moving to a new location. No, he thought, this is the only place with an accurate sight up the alley. He would stay. He glimpsed a police car driving slowly down Fourth Street. First it concerned him, but the concern turned to titillation. A challenge, a foolish challenge, he thought. So what if they spotted the Explorer? Who else would think to steal the car in Waco and change the plates in Killeen before using it to hunt in Austin? His resolve stiffened with the rising heat in his crotch. The police car crawled by at a snail's pace. The officer's attention was on a pair of winos huddled in the threshold of the bank entrance across the street. He watched the patrol car stop, the officer roll down his window and speak to the winos. The words weren't audible inside the Explorer, but soon the pair bundled together a cache of ratty blankets and cardboard boxes before stumbling off to find another nighttime shelter. The cop car followed them slowly down the street in the direction of Town Lake.

Moisture began accumulating on the inside of the Explorer's windows. It annoyed him. He reached over the seat, turned the key in the ignition, and pressed a button. The rear window rolled halfway down. He breathed in the still, cold air and leaned the barrel of the Bushmaster against his knee, poking its tip out of the window. He turned and stared down the alley.

At 2:47 the gate behind the Can swung open. A tall man stepped into the alley wearing a ball cap and a black leather jacket, a moneybag tucked under his arm.

Got to be his tips, Bill thought, and his heartbeat quickened again. He lifted the rifle butt from the floor and slipped a Styrofoam container over the barrel. He wrapped the trigger mechanism in the towel and pulled two cotton swabs from his pocket, twisted the cotton and carefully stuck one into each ear. He readjusted his stocking cap before resting the encased barrel on the edge of the windowsill, sighted down the barrel, and tasted sweetness.

He pulled the trigger.

The dull thud of the muffled gunshot echoed in the car. He knew it was dangerous, but he took a few seconds to watch through the sight as the bartender crumpled to the ground.

Bill's eyes rolled back into his head, and he imagined his tumescent penis pumping in his shorts. The intense energy of the moment was prolonged. When the throbbing stopped and the interior of the car shifted back into view, he wiped the sweat from his forehead and crawled over the seat.

Carefully, he guided the black Explorer out of the parking lot and headed north first before turning right onto Fifth Street. He stopped, waiting on the light at Colorado Street and again on Congress Avenue before the lights synchronized for him. He drove just under the speed limit all the way to the interstate, savoring the sweetness in his mouth.

CHAPTER NINE

JERRY

Jerry Philips's back was killing him. He stood up awkwardly and arched his spine, and a sharp, shooting pain cut through him. "Fuck!"

Carla Sandoval exhaled in frustration and pushed back from her computer, rolling her chair through the entrance of her cubicle. She hooked her head around the partition and glared over her reading glasses at Jerry. "You want to keep it down over there? Some of us are trying to work."

Philips smiled back at her. "I'm sorry if my intense pain is interrupting your flow of brilliance."

Her head disappeared around the partition and Jerry silently mouthed *bitch* as he eased back into his chair, picking up the next folder from the stack.

He flipped the cover and read the top page. Silas LeBlanc, WWI veteran, served with distinction in Europe, arrested in 1923 for "perverted sexual relations." Jerry noted the euphemism. In the vernacular of the era "perverted sexual relations" meant sex with another man. Jerry read on.

LeBlanc had served fourteen years in Ossining prison, formerly known as Sing Sing, just up the Hudson River from New York City. He had been released in 1938—no further incarceration was listed.

Philips flipped to the next page: a death certificate. LeBlanc had died of advanced liver cancer in 1966 at the age of 67. He thought back to Ruth Brookes's interview and smiled. What a story! If he could just put the pieces together…He needed to track down a few loose ends and it would be complete. This one would really be something.

He flipped back through the folder to the next document, the investigating officer's report. His phone rang as he scanned the details.

"Philips," he answered.

"Hey, Jer, could you come in here a minute?" It was his boss, Metro Editor Ron Billings.

"What's up?"

"Just come in here, will ya? We got something you need to see."

Philips heard a click as Billings disconnected. He shoved the police report back into the folder and tossed it on his desk. Gingerly, he stood and began shuffling down the hallway toward Billings's office.

❖

Slivers of morning sunlight sliced through the mini-blinds and painted stripes across Matt's back. Thatcher watched the gentle rise and fall as the slumbering naked man breathed. The stripes became a sea, with the fluid shadows sliding over the muscles like waves ebbing and flowing with the tide. Thatcher looked on, mesmerized by the sun as it lit tiny gleaming hairs along Matt's back, its rays twinkling and flickering across the golden surface of his shoulders.

Thatcher thought back to the previous evening and smiled. Things had started slowly. Dinner conversation was halting and uncomfortable. But finally the talk turned to swimming and music, and the more time they spent together the more comfortable it became. They had a lot in common, and by the time they ambled into One World Theatre for the concert, they were joking like old friends.

Thatcher sensed Matt had been surprised by the music. He'd tried to hide his ignorance, but Thatcher could tell this was his first experience with live jazz. It was sweet, though, the way he labored to sound knowledgeable. Matt was cute, but had been so obviously out of his element.

He replayed the trip home and the unspoken decision to sleep together. It had felt so right. And the fit was good, sexually—the sensual touch, the tender approach, the slow buildup before, finally, the heated rush. And the tender touch again as they lay together covered in sweat until they drifted off, their bodies pressed together so naturally each felt like an extension of the other.

Thatcher let his hand trail across Matt's body and looked up into the sunshine streaming through the bay window. He felt happy, truly happy. This was the first time he had felt this way since Adam. A thought flickered through his mind. *I feel full...of...what?* But he caught himself before forming the word.

Wow, he thought and closed his eyes, sighing. Adam's smiling face flashed before him.

"That wasn't so bad, was it?"
"No, it wasn't."
They both turned and looked at Matt. Adam said, "I like him."
Thatcher smiled, "Yeah, me too. I didn't expect to."
"I know you didn't."
A lump built in Thatcher's throat. "Adam, I don't..." But he couldn't finish the statement.
Adam took his hand. "It's okay," he said softly. "I know."
Tears filled Thatcher's eyes and he smiled weakly, laying his head on Adam's shoulder.
They turned to watch Matt sleep in comfortable silence. Gradually the sun lifted and the rippling waves slowly crept down Matt's back.
Finally Thatcher said, "I didn't expect this."
Adam just smiled, nodding.

Adam's image slowly melted in the morning sunshine until Thatcher was alone again, watching Matt sleep.

CHAPTER TEN

MATT

I dried my damp hair with a towel and hung it on the hook screwed to the back of the bathroom door before stepping into my underwear and strolling to the living room. I sat down on a club chair and grinned to myself. I was in Thatcher's house. I was very happy, yet a touch of uncertainty tempered my elation.

I wasn't quite sure if it was smart for this to happen so fast.

The night before had been wonderful. And the morning, especially the morning, when the tangle of bodies and contact had been so frantic, so full of emotion—and Thatcher seemed to want me as much as I wanted him.

Right now, I wanted nothing more than to spend the entire day with Thatcher, just be with him. But I was beginning to understand him, and soon Thatcher would need his space.

As I dressed, I ran through several monologues in my mind. I was getting ready to say good-bye, something expressive but not melodramatic. I wrestled with the subject for several minutes. I finally gave up, deciding to let the passions of the moment dictate the conversation, and sat back to take a look around his place.

The walls of his place were empty, painted pale-blue; the floors were hardwood, covered with light-beige wool rugs. The only furniture was the club chair I sat in and a cherrywood desk with a computer display and keyboard positioned behind a comfortable-looking office chair. I sat facing the east wall, which held three large wooden framed windows. The window trim, baseboards, ceilings, and mini-blinds were all white. Behind me a white cabinet with glass doors looked through to the kitchen. Stacks of sturdy white plates and a few wineglasses were displayed in the cabinet, which hung over a small countertop of contrasting blue-flecked Corian. To my right, a French door framed a small garden area, and to my left, two steps led up to a landing, lined in bookshelves, which bordered the bedroom entrance.

The bedroom was austere like the rest of the house. It had hardwood floors, wool rugs, and window treatments, while the walls were a slightly darker smoky-blue. The only furniture was a cherrywood sleigh bed and a Harman Kardon stereo system piled in the corner. A slatted white closet door and an oddly angled bay window provided the only relief from the otherwise stark interior.

I heard Thatcher humming in the bathroom. A photo hung near the door. Framed in silver, it was the only wall decoration. The picture itself was black and white. It showed a handsome shirtless man holding a tiny puppy out to the camera. The puppy fit neatly in the man's hands. *Was this Adam?*

And why is this place so Spartan?

The barren walls, uncluttered surfaces, and empty space gave the house a vacant feeling. The sound of my breathing echoed, almost like I was in a cave.

The morning paper sat on the floor next to the chair. I idly thumbed through the first section before turning back to the first page.

I caught my breath.

The article ran down the right column of the front page just below the fold. The headline read DOWNTOWN SHOOTING. My cell phone vibrated. I walked to the couch and grabbed my jacket, digging it out of a pocket.

"Hello."

"Did you hear about the bartender at the Can?" It was Danny.

"What about him?"

"Shot, early yesterday morning." He paused for effect. "They found him behind the bar."

"Is this the 'downtown shooting' thing in the paper?"

"Yep."

"Hold on, I'm reading."

I sat back down and scanned the article. There were no details other than the body was found just before sunrise on Thursday in the Fourth Street alley. The victim had been shot once and there was no sign of a struggle. His name was being withheld pending notification of the family.

"How do you know it's the bartender?" I asked.

"Marco and I were down there last night…at the Can." Another pause. "Where were you?"

"On a date." The shower shut off in the bathroom.

"With who?"

I paused for a moment. Danny, sensing my uncertainty, asked, "Wait a minute. Are you at home?"

"Nope."

"You're still with him, aren't you?"

"Um hmmm."

"It's Thatcher, isn't it? It's got to be Thatcher, I know it's Thatcher. I can't believe it. You're at Thatcher's house, right now! You spent the night there? This is gonna kill Marco. I can't believe it."

"I have to go," I said. "I'll call you later." I disconnected before he could respond and turned my phone off. I didn't want to discuss my date while sitting in Thatcher's living room waiting for him to get out of the shower.

A few minutes later, Thatcher came out of the bathroom with only a towel around his waist. He was unbelievably beautiful, his wet hair darker than normal. I fought the urge to grab him, instead saying, "I guess I should be going. Thanks. I had fun."

His look of disappointment was the best gift he could have given me. He said, "Okay, if you must. Hold on. I'll get dressed and drop you at your place."

"Don't hurry. I think I'll walk." I hoped he wouldn't catch the reluctance in my voice. "I really enjoyed it, Thatcher. Can we do this again soon?"

He smiled and my heart filled with joy.

"I'm game if you are," he said.

"Anytime."

We kissed and I made my exit quickly, before I talked myself into staying. It took twenty minutes to walk to my house on Texas Avenue.

I'm pretty sure I smiled the entire way.

❖

Detective Sergeant John Reed poked his head around the doorway of Lieutenant Sam Griggs's tiny office. Sergeant Reed waited for Griggs's slate-gray eyes to look up from the computer terminal before he spoke.

"Got the slug results from the Fourth Street stiff. You won't believe it."

Griggs scratched his head and sighed in exasperation. "What now?"

"A match." Reed stepped around the corner waving a manila folder.

Griggs's eyebrows were dark, showing the youthful color of his hair before it had turned gray. They lifted in expectation. "And?"

"It's Blue."

The lieutenant's jaw hardened. He pushed back from his desk. "Blue? Are they sure? Give me that." He pointed at the folder.

"They're sure." Reed stepped through the doorway, dropped the folder onto the oak desk, and sat on a ratty couch shoved against the far wall. Griggs reached for it and flipped through the pages, pausing occasionally as he surveyed the contents. Reed waited in silence.

When Lieutenant Griggs was promoted to head of Homicide for the Austin Police Department a few years earlier, his first official act had been to establish a team to review unsolved cases. The

APD's Cold Case Unit's mission was to review and follow up on dead-end cases, and since its inception, it had resolved more than a dozen murders and rapes.

One of the techniques the new group implemented was a color-coded system for classifying active cases. Most of the cases were either yellow for active or green for under review. Orange meant solved, pending trial. Gray cases were resolved. Three colors had been reserved for the highest profile outstanding murder cases that had yet to be solved.

The yogurt-shop quadruple homicide was Red. In the early nineties, four girls had been brutally murdered after hours at an I Can't Believe It's Yogurt store where two of the victims worked. After years of searching, the CCU scored its greatest success when four young men were arrested and charged with the crime. Red went gray.

White had been the murder of the notorious atheist leader, Madelyn Murray O'Hare, and her son, in the mid-nineties. This case had also been solved and an angry ex-con, briefly employed by O'Hare, was eventually indicted for murder. Evidence was presented to the effect that the body of "the most hated woman in the country" had been cut into pieces and either scattered or buried in a South Texas field. The White case had also turned gray.

But Blue was still blue. The Blue case involved the serial shootings of young gay men in downtown Austin between 1984 and 1986. Despite being the top-priority case left on their agenda, they had no leads, no suspects, and no reason to believe that would ever change—until now.

When Griggs finished scanning the folder's contents he peered over his reading glasses at Reed. "The ballistic reports are solid?"

"Looks like it. The slug showed consistent markings, matching the bullets retrieved from Sellers, Conway, and Fielding. Most of the other slugs were so badly damaged they couldn't be typed. But there were no contradictions." Reed sat forward on the sofa and glanced down at the open folder.

"So it's the same weapon. After all this time, you really think he's started again?"

"The evidence says so. Same gun, same MO, same victim profile." Reed shrugged.

Griggs pushed his chair back and sighed heavily. He clenched his teeth and felt his blood pressure begin to rise. He let his eyes drift to a set of framed photos on his desk.

Griggs had been in service long enough to know that every good cop eventually comes across a lifetime case—one that slides under his skin like a junkie's needle and keeps him up into the night with stomach-clenching uncertainty—a case that won't let go, no matter what.

Blue was Griggs's lifetime case.

He'd drawn the original assignment. He'd fixated over it long before he was promoted, its unfathomable sequence of violent murders constantly occupying his subconscious mind. Just thinking about the case could raise his stress level. Griggs knew he was obsessed. He had skipped vacations, avoided downtime, and spent every spare moment on the case long before creating the CCU.

But Blue had cost Griggs much more than headaches and lost sleep. He had sacrificed his marriage to it. The obsession had driven his wife and sons away.

And still Blue wouldn't crack.

It was a tough case—and now it was back. Griggs knew it would be, hoped it would be. He locked his eyes onto Reed and said, "Okay, I want the casebook in my office now. Blue has just gone hot, red-hot! Get Cooper in here, and Mattock. And call the Bureau."

"The FBI?" Reed shook his head in disbelief. "You sure you want to involve the feds?"

"No," Griggs admitted. "But they're already involved. This is a serial-murder case, remember? We need to talk to their talent. We need to figure out, if it's him—"

"It's him," Reed assured him.

But Griggs remained cautious. "*If* it's him, we need to know why he's started again. We need a profiler."

"Well, the feds have got the resources. It's just..." Reed shrugged.

"What?"

"They'll try to take the case, Lieutenant. You know that."

"This isn't a competition, Reed. Besides, we have the on-going investigation. We have the evidence. We made the match. There's plenty of glory to go around here—and work, plenty of work to do too."

Reed nodded.

"Okay, let's get started. Ask Mandy to pull the casebook and set up a conference room. Right now I've got some phone calls to make."

Reed nodded and bolted through the doorway. Lieutenant Griggs turned back to his computer and clicked a few keys. His personal case file for Blue opened on the screen. He searched through the contents until he found the page listing the victims, then grabbed his phone and punched in a few numbers.

"Hello."

"Adam Malloy, please."

Griggs waited for a response but the line was silent.

"Hello? Hello?"

"Who is this?"

He caught an unexpected note of rage through the phone and paused before answering, "This is Lieutenant Griggs of the Austin Police Department. I would like to speak with Adam Malloy. Is he available?"

"No, he isn't." The words were clipped and angry.

The hiss of the telephone connection filled the dead air until Griggs, keeping his voice as neutral as possible, asked, "When do you expect him back?"

"Adam is dead, Lieutenant."

The statement took Griggs by surprise and he paused, searching his memory for Adam's face. But it was too long ago. Finally, he said, "I'm sorry." He read quickly through the victim's profile while the hiss filled the void between them. "Who am I speaking with, please?"

"Thatcher Keeney." Thatcher's resentment was palpable. "What is this about, Lieutenant...Grigson, is it?"

"Griggs, Lieutenant Griggs." He ignored the first question. "I'm sorry to bother you, Mr. Keeney." He was about to hang up when an ugly thought crossed his mind. "Do you happen to know how Mr. Malloy died?"

He sighed heavily before saying, "Yes, I do."

Griggs waited, but Thatcher waited too. Griggs could tell he wouldn't give up the information without a direct request. After a moment Griggs said, "I'm not trying to bring up difficult memories, Mr. Keeney, but I need to know how Adam died."

The use of Adam's Christian name seemed to annoy Thatcher even more and he spat out the words, "It was AIDS. Adam Malloy died of AIDS, Lieutenant."

"I see," Griggs said. He thanked Thatcher and hung up.

Thatcher sat staring at the phone, emotion and confusion coursing through his mind in a stew of bewilderment. Lieutenant Griggs, he asked himself, where have I heard that name?

Almost before he formed the question the answer floated into view. He remembered that Griggs had led the sniper investigation. An image flashed through Thatcher's mind of the first of many very black days.

Thatcher leaned his head against Adam's bed and closed his eyes. The heart monitor beeped a steady rhythm, and the sound of the ventilator was vaguely reminiscent of Darth Vader's raspy breathing. A tube ran up Adam's nose and emptied into a large glass bottle on the ICU floor. The bottle was half full of a viscous bloody-brown liquid. A clear plastic bag containing mustard-colored sludge hung from the IV stand. Another tube ran from it into Adam's forearm. The mustard-colored liquid dripped steadily into a bubble-shaped chamber at the base of the bag.

Thatcher sat next to the bed and held Adam's warm hand on top of the blanket. For the past hour, he had tried to will Adam awake, to bring him back to consciousness with the sheer force of his determination, but it hadn't worked and his desperation was growing.

Thatcher was not religious; he wasn't even sure he believed in God. But in the bright room, listening to the steady beep of the monitor and the hiss of the ventilator, he closed his eyes and whispered a prayer. "If you're there, God, could you please send him back to me? I love him so much that I don't think I can live without him; and if he leaves me...I'll..."

Just then Adam squeezed his hand and Thatcher raised his head. He stared at Adam with tears streaming down his face. Adam's eyes flickered open and he felt the bottom fall out of his stomach.

"Adam..." Thatcher's voice was thick with emotion and the words caught in his throat. Adam's eyes searched the room in confusion. Thatcher inhaled and started again. "You were shot, baby. You're in the hospital."

Adam nodded and lay back down without speaking. Relief filled Thatcher's soul. It coursed through his body and poured from his eyes onto the bed. With conviction Thatcher said, "You're going to be okay." And he knew it. He knew the truth of it. This would not be Adam's day to die. They would have more time, more precious time, together.

More precious, Thatcher thought, than he even knew.

Three hours after the nurses had moved Adam from ICU into a room on the surgery ward of Brackenridge Hospital, Lieutenant Griggs appeared at the doorway. Thatcher tried to picture the man. What he remembered was a swath of dark hair atop the sturdy body of a drill sergeant, a bull neck, and a surprisingly respectful bearing. Griggs had gently questioned Adam about the shooting, right up until Adam's pain medication began to fail, and then he left without pushing. Thatcher remembered being relieved when he left, and thankful that Griggs appeared to respect Adam's condition.

Adam retained no memory of the actual shooting, so in a follow-up interview, Griggs asked about Adam's activities leading up to that afternoon. Thatcher recalled listening quietly as Adam detailed the activities of a normal day. Griggs took notes and left without any indication of the investigation's direction as the nurse arrived with more morphine.

Griggs showed up two more times during Adam's stay at the hospital. From the questions he asked, it seemed to Thatcher that Griggs was tracing seemingly unconnected details. It was pretty obvious that the investigator was shopping around for a new lead, that the investigation was directionless.

Thatcher took Adam home a couple of weeks later. That was the summer of 1985. Adam had been the fourth victim and the first to survive a serial-sniper attack. As Adam convalesced under Thatcher's nursing care, the sniper continued. Many men died as a result. And then, without explanation, it all stopped.

Thatcher had been there when the doctors assessed Adam's condition. The gunshot had missed Adam's heart and most of his internal organs, but it had nicked his liver. There had been a lot of bleeding in his abdomen. In the first of many ironies, Adam had given blood at Brackenridge Hospital's blood drive the morning of the attack.

In the emergency room, the hospital gave blood back to him.

When he thought about the irony of the situation, Thatcher's mood would blacken. The way he saw it, the whole situation was ironic.

It was ironic that Adam, the careful one—the one who double-checked door locks, shunned trips through bad neighborhoods, rarely traveled alone—was the one who was shot. It was ironic that Adam, who worked for a drug company, died a few months before the drug industry released protease inhibitors and doctors began prescribing the three-drug cocktail that moved AIDS from the list of always fatal to mostly manageable diseases. But the biggest irony, the irony that really roiled in Thatcher's gut, was the fact that the treatment that saved Adam in the ICU that dreadful day was the very thing that ended up costing him his life years later.

Blood products in the early eighties were not screened for HIV.

CHAPTER ELEVEN

MATT

If I had to describe Texas weather in a word, that word would be *erratic*.

As I walked home from Thatcher's house, Austin's beautiful morning sunshine gave way to gray skies as the wind shifted. By the time I'd arrived at my street, the temperature had dropped ten degrees and a syrupy mist floated down from the thickening sky, coating the seams of my jacket and the hairs on my head with translucent droplets.

Stepping through the front door, I saw the flashing number 3 on my answering machine. I shook the moisture from my coat in the entrance hall and hung it on a wall peg before dragging the soles of my shoes over the throw rug and marching across the living room to my desk. I pushed the Play button.

The first message was from Mom, the second from Danny, and the third from Marco. I listened to all three a second time, pressing Delete. I had no interest in talking with Danny or Marco. That could wait, so I picked up the handset and dialed my mother's number.

"Hello."

"Hi, Mom, how are you?"

"I'm fine, darling. You sound scratchy. Is your throat scratchy?"

"No, Mom, my throat's fine."

"Good. Honey, listen. I was just calling to make sure you got the package I sent and to tell you some good news."

"I got the package." I rolled my eyes. "What's the news?"

She cleared her throat. "Well, you remember Debbie Conway, don't you? That pretty dark-haired girl, lives over in Fruitland? Her mother goes to our church."

"Not really."

"Sure you do. You went to kindergarten with her before she was home-schooled. You rode bicycles together. She came to your sixth birthday party. You two were always so cute together."

"I don't remember her, Ma. What's Debbie got to do with me?"

"Well, she's going to be in Austin." I rolled my eyes again. "San Antonio, actually, but that's close enough. So I thought you could drive down there and take her out to dinner. She's such a pretty girl."

I sighed heavily. "What are you doing, Mother?"

"What? I'm not doing anything. I'm just thinking you would like to see an old friend, that's all."

"I don't know her, Ma. She's not a friend. At this point she's barely an acquaintance."

"Sure you know her. You remember, she rode that red bicycle, always had skinned knees. She came to your sixth birthday party."

"I don't remember her, Ma, and I don't remember the party either."

"Well, she remembers you. Her mother told me so. And she's grown into such a lovely woman."

"So?"

"So I mentioned that you live in Austin and her mother told me that Debbie was moving to San Antonio."

"Wait a minute. I thought you said she was just visiting."

"Well…yeah, she's just visiting this trip. But she's going there to hunt for a place to live. Her job is being transferred. She works for a computer…something company…doing computer…something. Like you. Anyway, I thought, wouldn't it be nice if my kind and considerate son would make her feel welcome in her new state." Her voice became warm and sticky.

I rolled my eyes again. "Why do you do this?"

"Do what?" She was trying to sound innocent but I wasn't buying it.

"You know I'm gay, Ma. Remember our little talk?"

"Gay-shmay, it's a phase."

I rolled my eyes again. "It's not a phase." I sighed in exasperation. "It's who I am and the sooner you accept—"

"It's a phase. Our minister tells me there are places that can help. Have you listened to the CDs yet?"

"The only thing I need help with is my laundry." I enunciated each word carefully. "You don't get it, do you? Let me try this again. There are just two things I have to do in this life and that's be gay and die. "

"It's a phase, I tell you."

"I'm thirty-nine years old, Ma." I was becoming despondent. "It's not a phase."

"You just need to meet the right girl."

"Well, sure…but the right girl for me has a penis, and they're so very hard to find." I sighed heavily into the receiver. "Why do you always do this, Mom? Why do you push so hard? I wish you would listen to me, just once really hear me. I don't need to meet a girl. I need for you to accept me the way I am."

"Well, think about it then. I'll call you soon."

I sighed again.

"I love you, Matt."

"I know," I said, and hung up. I collapsed onto the couch, my mood darkening. I replayed the conversation in my mind, totally awestruck at how an aging, ninety-pound, Southern woman could destroy the best day I'd had in months from fifteen hundred miles away.

When the phone rang again I answered on reflex.

"Hello."

"May I speak with Matt Bell, please?"

Though I couldn't place the voice exactly, it sounded familiar. "This is Matt," I said.

"Mr. Bell, I don't know if you remember me. My name is Lieutenant Griggs with the Austin Police Department." A connection stirred in the primal part of my mind and I shuddered. An image of a dark-haired, thick-necked man in a rumpled gray suit danced into view and I squeezed my eyes shut.

Lieutenant Sam Griggs was just an officer when we first met. I still remember his image weaving into view like a hazy apparition floating through the fog of drug-induced sleep. I was lying in a bed in the Brackenridge Hospital recovery room. I ignored his presence, trying to subdue the natural movement of the world with my mind. I pictured a rock, a smooth, hard river-bottom stone. I attempted to become as motionless as that stone, so stationary I could feel my body melt into the soft surface of the bed.

I remember seeing Griggs's liquid face float into view again.

He had rattled off incoherent phrases and disconnected words in a jumbled mix of sound. He blurted out his cacophony like a news flash. And without giving me time to process it, he launched right into another series of discordant noises, charging ahead heedless of my inability to respond. Even if I could have understood, I couldn't have answered.

Eventually Griggs gave up. Perhaps my silence or the tears in my eyes convinced him. Either way, the interrogation was pointless. His image melted like a Dali painting and the pudgy, balding recovery-room nurse shot me full of morphine. The edges of my consciousness blurred again, and soon Griggs's shape-shifting head drifted back into the ether.

I don't remember falling asleep. The next image my mind processed was a private hospital room bathed in the eerie dark-green-gray of nighttime. Sergeant Griggs sat, submerged in moonlight, on a folding chair at the foot of the bed.

That's when he calmly told me I had been shot.

"Yes, Lieutenant, I remember you." I answered slowly.

"I have something to tell you. Mr. Bell, is this a good time?"

Just like that. As if I had a choice and could decide to listen to what he had to say or could switch his words off, like a light or a radio.

"What is it?" I held my breath as I waited for the answer.

"He's back," was all he said.

I could still hear Griggs breathe, as the room began to spin. He didn't need to explain; we both knew to whom he was referring. Finally I asked, "Are you sure?"

"Yes." He paused and I could tell he was struggling to find the right words. "I wanted to let you know, to warn you to prepare. I'm not sure how long before the media finds out."

The room swirled around inside my head like a fighter plane in a death spiral. I clung to the receiver. Finally, I mumbled, "Thank you, Lieutenant." We said our good-byes and I hung up quickly.

I sat back on the couch and stared at the ceiling. After a moment, I stood up and strolled out to my front yard. I found my paper lying in a bed of pansies beside my porch. I brushed off the dead leaves and bits of mud as I walked back inside the house and sat down on my black leather sofa. I reread the entire DOWNTOWN SHOOTING article three times before I dropped the paper on the floor, lay back, and stared up at the ceiling.

❖

Thatcher never thought about God. But everyone who knew him understood if there was a God, He had bestowed on Thatcher many gifts.

In his youth, Thatcher saw these gifts as his birthright. They had simply always been there. He did realize that he was lucky—and to a certain extent he was thankful.

After Lieutenant Griggs's phone call, a black funk seemed to surround Thatcher again. That afternoon, he found himself aimlessly wandering the streets of Austin. Through the thickening winter mist he walked with his head turned down and a sea of feelings swirling through his mind. Thatcher was confused and enraged. One thought kept bubbling through the cauldron of his anger.

Thatcher climbed the hill from the golf course realizing he could not let go until he found and destroyed this monster. Only then would he be free. Thatcher knew it was ridiculous for him to assume that he could do this, of course. The police had failed. Still, his whole being cried out for resolution, and resolution meant finding the man who shot Adam.

Only then could he truly put Adam's memory to rest and begin to pull the pieces of his life back together. Nothing else mattered.

❖

The quickening breeze cleared the skies over the pool and wafted steam from the exposed skin of my shoulders. Still, I felt comfortably warm in the turquoise water under a canopy of stars that stretched from horizon to horizon. I finished the last set of intervals, pushing the pace and feeling a burning sensation deep in my chest as I gasped for air while I clung to the gutter at the end of the lane.

It had been a disappointing workout. I had come hoping to see Thatcher but he was a no-show. Though full of familiar faces, the crowd that did arrive lacked anyone close enough to talk to about recent events without having to explain ancient personal history. It didn't help that the team had a new swimmer today: Martin, from Brackenridge Hospital—the same pudgy, balding guy who knew me as Greg Palmer. He struggled to keep up with the swimmers in the slowest lane. It seemed doubly ill timed that he picked this day of all days to start swimming with the team. His face at poolside was not only an unwelcome reminder of Lieutenant Griggs's phone call, but a remnant of my painful past. Several times I caught him staring at my scar, and I feared being cornered in the locker room and pressed for an explanation. If he continued to be a part of the team, at some point I would need to deal with the whole situation.

It had been two full days since Lieutenant Griggs had called. It had also been two full days without hearing from Thatcher. I had dialed his number twice with no answer and hung up without leaving a message. What could I say anyway?

Mercifully, Marco and Danny were also absent from the pool. I'd managed to avoid that whole confusing situation. Soon enough I would need to approach Marco again, but I wasn't ready for that, not yet. Truthfully I only half-expected to see them at the pool. They skipped practice often, choosing instead to hoist beers at the local watering hole.

Overhead, the breeze ruffled the backstroke flags while I considered my options with Thatcher. Nothing looked good. I could call him again, be the one to make contact. That could set a dangerous precedent and possibly label me as needy. I could wait, running the risk of letting him drift out of my life much as he had drifted into it.

Or I could try something else. What that something else could possibly *be* was the stumbling block.

I was deep in thought when Coach Chris called down from his chair on deck, "Four-hundred cool-down and we're out of here."

I nodded, slipped my goggles over my eyes, and pushed off the wall slowly. As I swam, questions ran through my mind. What was the right road? How should I play this strange and wily hand I had been dealt? I was considering my options when Jim Avery's image popped into my head. Jim knew Thatcher. Jim would counsel, not preach.

I would call Jim.

❖

"Hello."

"Jim, hi! It's Matt."

"Matt?" The confusion on the phone was evident in his voice. "What's up?"

It was a sunny Saturday. Thatcher had not appeared in over a week, though I had managed to make contact with Marco at the bar on Thursday. We had talked, obtusely, about the situation. The two of us agreed, through nonverbal communication, to avoid unnecessary unpleasantness. I was more confident than ever that Danny's advice was right. In time Marco would redirect his attention elsewhere.

"Don't ask," I answered. "I was wondering if you have lunch plans?"

"Nope. You want to do lunch?"

"Sure, we can catch up."

"Sounds great, but first I need to take Venus for a walk. You want to join us?"

"Venus who?"

"She's my baby."

"You have a baby?"

"For sure, she's a black Lab."

"Oh, you had me going there. I thought maybe you'd made a big life change."

"What? Like fatherhood? Are you insane?" He chuckled.

"Good point. Walking your dog sounds like fun. Want to meet at Town Lake?"

"Great. Just so you know, she's a bit of a sled dog on the trail. Luckily, the leash has been tested for four hundred pounds of pull. But it'll be a workout."

"Well, I'll try to stay out of her way and let you do the heavy lifting."

We agreed to meet at eleven.

❖

Since Lieutenant Griggs's call, Thatcher had executed his plan. He needed action to keep from falling back into his funk, so he started trying to track down the shooter. He spent two days researching old *Statesman* articles. Articles written about the shooter were much too old to be archived online, so he patiently tracked them down on microfiche and photocopied every report available in the UT campus library system. He sat at his desk reading the articles, jotting down notes on a yellow legal pad.

The early stories were the most direct, carefully listing the facts of the investigation and providing locations and times of the shootings as well as details of the victims. The press had not connected the first three shootings. By the fourth attack, it was obvious both the reporters and the police had linked the crimes. The investigators must have become more careful with the details released to the press—the later articles were less detailed and heavier on speculation.

The first shooting occurred in October of 1984. John Carlton, a twenty-one-year-old student at St. Edwards University in south

Austin, was gunned down shortly after leaving the Private Cellar, a gay bar on Austin's notorious Sixth Street. Sixth Street was the heart of the bar scene in the 1980s, a noisy collection of discos, jazz clubs, and sports bars intermingled with a few high-dollar restaurants and the elegant Driskill Hotel.

Carlton had been shot in the upper abdomen as he arrived at his car, parked in the lot under Interstate 35. The crime occurred right in front of the Austin Police Department headquarters. He bled to death in transport to Brackenridge Hospital. There was one witness to the shooting, a Willy Philips. The witness sounded like a vagrant in the quotes printed in the paper. He was indignant when police picked him up for questioning the following morning. The *Statesman* article, written by Bob Jones, described Philips as "a drifter with a drinking problem."

Thatcher took note of both names and moved on to the next murder.

Sam Malden died four weeks later. A twenty-seven-year-old unemployed carpenter, Malden was gunned down outside a flophouse in a seedy section of South Congress Avenue in the early hours of a Saturday morning. Thatcher knew that hookers and drug dealers frequented South Congress in the early 1980s. No mention was made of motive, or family, or witnesses.

Thatcher thought about the two men, both in their twenties, and he pondered the similarities and differences. Both men were alone at the time they were attacked, and both were out late at night. Carlton was obviously gay, while the second article sounded as if the police suspected Malden was a hustler. Perhaps he was out picking up tricks, working the street, when he was killed.

The third murder occurred a month after Malden. A young man was gunned down on December 22, 1984. That was roughly a month before Adam was shot. John Wilson, a thirty-five-year-old father of two, was walking on Seventh Street not far from the police station, in the early hours of a Saturday morning. The details of the shooting were sketchy at best. The article, also written by Bob Jones, mentioned that the neighborhood was known for its illicit drug activity. The article seemed to indicate it was a drug deal gone sour, although two different co-workers of Mr. Wilson's were quoted expressing doubt regarding his involvement with drugs.

A couple of articles had been written about Adam's attack. After Adam was shot, the shootings stopped for six full months. Adam was in the hospital for much of that time. He had been transferred from the Emergency Room to ICU and into surgery. He recuperated in the surgery ward at Brackenridge until Thatcher brought him home after a nightmarish six months of procedures and physical therapy.

Thatcher scanned the rest of the articles. They told stories of gunshot victims very much like the others. Young men shot in the central city, late at night. Most were alone, but a few had been with friends. Witnesses were few and far between and their accounts were sketchy, only covering the barest details of the incidents.

No mention was made of anyone providing a description of the shooter.

It was an article written after the sixth shooting that knocked Thatcher for a loop. The victim, whose name was withheld, had survived. The shooting had occurred in the alleyway in the downtown area just as the young man was hurrying to catch up with his friends after an evening out. The shooter had driven a Ford Bronco and sped away from the scene just as the victim's friends arrived. One of the friends was quoted in the article.

He was lying in a pool of blood on the pavement; we didn't know where the shot came from until we saw the Bronco speeding up Fifth Street. By then it was too far to see who was driving; the windows were heavily tinted, too dark to see inside anyway.

The quote was attributed to Marco Padilla, Matt's best friend.

❖

I was leaning back against my car, enjoying the sunshine on my face, when Jim Avery's red Toyota Highlander pulled to the curb and parked under the Loop 1 Bridge. He opened the door, grinning as a large ball of wriggling black fur leapt across the seat. The creature was all tongue and tail and straining at the leash.

Venus.

"Hi," Jim said. "Are you sure you're up for this?"

I took the leash from him. "You bet." He climbed out of the driver's seat, and the three of us tramped off toward the bridge. Venus pulled up to relieve herself at the first grassy spot she came to and I turned to Jim.

"Beautiful day."

"Yeah, Venus and I love to do this when the sun's shining."

Venus finished her duties and jerked me in the direction of the trail.

"What'd I tell you, she's a sled dog." Jim smiled, and I handed him the leash.

We took the three-mile loop—south over the bridge, east along the park, and turning north again, climbing the stairs to the new pedestrian bridge. Several times along the way we stopped for Venus to sniff the foliage and relieve herself.

She seemed to need a lot of relief.

Venus was bedded down in the back of the Highlander, safely parked on West Sixth Street, and the two of us were seated in a booth at Hut's Hamburgers when I asked, "So do you like being a case worker?"

"Sometimes, but not often," Jim answered. "It's just that there are so many problems, so much to be done. And with funding the way it is, the system's overrun."

I nodded my response, which Jim took as an invitation to explain.

"The legislature's the problem. They set up the State School and State Hospital to house people in need of mental-health services and then hold back the funding. It's the damn Republicans, and it's everywhere—means fewer people are served, right? More people being taken care of by their families?"

He went on. "Well, that's the thought, but unfortunately it doesn't work that way. In the first place, a lot of these people don't have families. Or, more likely, they have families that don't want to be bothered with their problems. So they're shipped to Austin during a crisis, get funneled through the State Hospital and dumped on the street, long before they're ready."

"But that doesn't really happen all the time. I mean, most of the time people are taken care of," I said.

Jim sighed. "Truthfully, I think it's more common for them to end up lost and forgotten. Some of them want to be on the street. They'd rather be left alone—their psychosis is too extreme for them to interact normally. It's a lousy system."

"But where do they go? The streets aren't full of insane people."

"Yes, they are. Open your eyes, darling. Austin is full of psychotic people. Most of them aren't a threat to anyone but themselves." As if on cue, he nodded toward the entrance. "See that guy over there?" I followed his gaze to a thin man wearing forest-green corduroys, a button-down white shirt, and a tweed jacket. He was quietly sorting through a pile of newspapers. Nothing about the man was unusual, but something about him seemed familiar. He must have been in his early thirties, and the tweed jacket gave him the air of a college professor. His straight brown hair was unstylishly long, like he was a couple of weeks overdue for a haircut. His bangs hung over his eyes as he meticulously arranged the papers in a stack, taking care to align the edges.

I nodded, and Jim continued. "He's one of Austin's deinstitutionalized homeless."

I looked more closely at the man. He was attractive and obviously cared for, but was apparently not totally aware of his surroundings. As I watched, he turned his back on the noisy crowd surrounding him in the entrance of the restaurant and continued stacking the newspapers.

"His name's Stanley Church," Jim said. "His family lives here in Austin. Well, his sister anyway."

"And he was in the mental hospital?"

Jim's eyes squinted at the use of the term. "He was once a patient at the State Hospital, yes, but now he's homeless."

"But he doesn't look homeless."

Jim's smile was patrician, like a teacher gently guiding an errant student. "And what does a homeless person look like?"

"Dirtier, I guess."

Jim laughed. "There is that," he said. "But Stan is a bit of a neat freak. It's part of his obsessive compulsion."

We ate in silence. After a while, I decided to change the subject. "Have you heard from Thatcher lately?"

Jim stuffed a French fry in his mouth. "Nope, not in weeks. You?"

"Yeah, I saw him a few days ago."

"In general, he's a recluse—kind of like Stanley." He grinned at me.

I nodded. "We had a date."

Jim looked up at me with his mouth open. "A date with Stanley?"

"No, with Thatcher."

"You and Thatcher?"

"Yeah."

He cleared his mouth with a sip of iced tea. "A real date, like dinner and a movie?" He was clearly not convinced.

"Dinner and jazz," I answered.

A grin crept across his face. "Yep, jazz…that's Thatcher all right. And that is really good news."

I squinted at him in confusion.

"Good news, for Thatcher, I mean—and you too, I guess. Maybe he's finally moving on."

I nodded. "You mean from Adam."

"I mean from Adam's death." His smile widened. "So how was it?"

"It was great."

My smile must have faded because he looked at me and said, "But…"

"But now he's seems to have disappeared."

"Disappeared?"

"I haven't heard from him in a week."

"Umm, like I said…a recluse." He nodded to himself and took a bite of his burger.

"So what do I do?" I tried not to sound desperate.

"Do? What…with Thatcher?"

"Yeah."

"I guess you find him." He shrugged. "Shouldn't be too hard."

"You think that's the way to play it?"

He grinned. "He's really got you worried."

"Yeah. I guess. It's just that things seemed so good then… nothing."

"Why don't you give him a call?"

"I've tried but—"

"Don't tell me." He stuffed another ketchup-laden French fry in his mouth. "No answer."

I nodded.

"Hmmm, so that's what this is about. Lunch, I mean?"

I looked sheepishly into his eyes. "Sort of, but I wanted to see you too, of course."

He smiled an acknowledgement. "Right, well. I don't know what you want from me exactly."

I took another bite of my burger and stared out the window. Clouds were building in the western sky, but overhead the sun was shining brightly. As I scanned the horizon, dead leaves skittered across Sixth Street from the north and I could tell the weather was about to change. I cleared my mouth, wiped my chin with a napkin, and looked directly at him. "Tell me about Adam."

He swallowed roughly and sat back, staring at me for a few seconds. Finally, he said, "What do you want to know?"

"Just tell me about him. You know…just stuff."

Jim raised an eyebrow. "Not much to tell really. He was a sweet guy with some health problems. Always a little sickly, even before the AIDS. He was an artist, a painter or sculptor, I think."

I thought about the lack of paintings on Thatcher's walls and sat trying to remember the man in the picture. Jim went on. "They were together for several years. I didn't really get to know them until near the end. I was Adam's case manager at ASA."

I nodded.

"He was my client for the last two years of his life. Thatcher took care of him, the primary caregiver. No other family. They were together, but they were alone. Together alone, if you get my drift."

He sat back and took another swig of iced tea. I stared through the window; the clouds were moving in now, much closer than before.

"Was it a bad death?" I asked.

He set his glass down and looked at me coldly. "It was AIDS."

I let my eyes drop to my hands folded together on the top of the table. Our waiter appeared, cleared the table, and left the check.

"How did Thatcher take Adam's death?"

He looked at me. "How do you think he took it? He was devastated."

I nodded. "You said Adam was sick before the AIDS. Do you know what he had?"

"I don't think he had anything. It was an injury, I believe. Like I said, I didn't know either of them well back then."

We sat together in silence while the waiter charged the bill to my credit card. When he returned, I signed the receipt and looked up into Jim's eyes. "The thing is, I want to see Thatcher again. But he's hard to understand."

Jim nodded.

"How would you play it?"

"You mean if I were in your shoes?"

"Yeah."

"I guess I'd call him." He smiled at me again. "Look, Matt, it's not rocket science. He's a different kind of guy, but he's still a guy. I imagine he's hoping you'll call too. Better yet, drop by. Go see him."

I grinned. The idea sent joy rippling through my body.

"And another thing…"

I watched him closely.

"I don't say this often, but I think he's worth it."

As we exited Hut's, I took note of the neat stack of newspapers on the counter. Stanley Church had vanished without a trace. I walked Jim to his car with the first heavy drops of rain falling from the sky and we said our good-byes quickly. I barely noticed the gathering gloom. My world was surprisingly sunny.

Chapter Twelve

Dorothy

Dorothy Bowles was a child of the sixties. In the most tumultuous of decades, she'd weathered Woodstock, protested Vietnam, and chained herself to a redwood trying to prevent its removal. Now in her mid-fifties, Dorothy had graying hair cut fashionably short, and Armani suits and reasonable pumps had replaced peasant dresses and Birkenstock sandals in her wardrobe.

And the one-time protestor of government control now worked for the FBI.

Dorothy knocked once on the conference room door before pushing it open. She tossed her shoulder bag onto the conference table and sat down, shooting a smile toward the front of the room. Lieutenant Griggs gave a quick nod in her direction and turned back to the blackboard. Every other eye in the room remained on her. Dorothy noted all the men sitting around the table wore cheap, rumpled suits, except Lieutenant Griggs. He looked fresh and crisp, despite the fact his jacket was off and his tie loosened around his neck. Several heads pivoted and furtive smiles flew toward her from all around the table. Dorothy was used to attention from men. Even in her fifties, she had a powerful sexual allure. Experience had taught her to use her appeal to her advantage.

Griggs drew the group's attention back to the front of the room with a question. "Time frame?"

John Reed leaned back in his chair. "Got that nailed, Lieutenant. It's pretty tight, between 2:40 and 3:45 on Friday morning, probably closer to 2:40." Reed didn't need to consult his notes; he'd committed the details of the murder to memory. He said, "The bar owner, a Thomas Lilly, usually closes the bar around 2:40, but he was out of town on Friday, so O'Conner closed. The cleaning crew arrived at 3:55. They discovered his body. 911 records show a Mr. Padilla called at 3:57."

Griggs wrote on the board, which was covered with phrases detailing a rough chronological listing of the case facts: times and names and seemingly disconnected tips assembled in a jumble of potential evidence.

There wasn't much.

He said, "Padilla found the body?"

"Yeah, Rubin Padilla, he works for the cleaning company. Lilly told us the bar has contracted cleaning duties from Padilla's company, Three Guys' Industrial Services, since 1998." Reed grinned, adding, "The three guys are Padilla and his two nieces... must be strong women."

There was a murmur of suppressed laughter and furtive glances toward Dorothy, the only female in the room. Griggs quelled the twitter with a cold look.

"Okay, Agent Bowles is here, we can finish this later. Are you ready, Ms. Bowles?"

Dorothy nodded. Once more, heads swiveled in her direction. Lieutenant Griggs cleared his throat before offering a small introduction. "I'm sure most of you know Agent Bowles is with the FBI's criminology division. I've asked her in today to give us any insight she can offer into the Blue investigation. Dorothy."

Dorothy stood up, heaving her computer bag onto a shoulder. She smiled and strode to the head of the conference table. Most of the men's eyes followed the gentle sway of her hips. She carefully placed her computer bag on the ground and unzipped the pouch. She pulled out an IBM ThinkPad and set it on the table, plugging her power supply into the wall mount before she sat down. She flipped on the power, reached back into the computer bag, and extracted a small projector, which she hooked to the back of the computer.

"Could someone get the lights?"

There was a short scramble before the lights dimmed and Dorothy logged on. After a few minutes, an out-of-focus view of her computer screen's image appeared on the wall above her shoulder. She pressed a button on the projector and a map of Austin's downtown section came into focus. "What I've got here is a map that shows the relative locations and times of all of the Blue shootings. Xs mark the locations where the victims' bodies were found. They are color coded, moving from gray to pink to red. The more red, the earlier the attack."

She moved the cursor across the screen, landing on an X.

"This gray X here indicates last week's shooting. You can see that all the attacks occurred within a forty-block radius of the downtown section, nine of them within the downtown corridor. All of the locations in the midst of the city, yet all of them isolated from traffic and view."

She clicked on a different X. A crime-scene photo appeared on the screen. "I assume your guys are familiar with the MO and the facts of the investigation?" Dorothy looked at Griggs, who nodded. "Good. I've been asked to analyze the mental state of the perpetrator, to try to point out some of the things that make him tick. Perhaps illuminate what makes him different from everyone else."

"What makes him different from everyone else is that he murders people." Sergeant Stephen Connors scowled at Dorothy from his seat at the conference table.

Dorothy looked at Connors, unfazed. "That's pretty obvious."

"So if it's obvious, why are you wasting our time with your guesses?"

The entire crowd shifted uncomfortably in their seats. Griggs opened his mouth to speak, but Dorothy stilled him with a gesture.

"I'm sorry you feel that way…officer…"

"Sergeant." He corrected her. "Sergeant Connors."

"Sergeant Connors, if you all feel that way then perhaps I'm wasting my time." Dorothy scanned the faces at the table. When no one responded, she moved to close the display of her computer.

Reed said, "Let her speak."

There was a buzz of communal acquiescence before Lieutenant Griggs stood up. "No, we don't feel that way, Agent Bowles." He scowled at Connors. "We need your help. In fact, we need all the help we can get."

The rest of the room shot darting glances between Griggs and Connors.

A young pudgy officer in uniform said, "Well, I, for one, appreciate the cooperation. It could be the key to figuring this thing out, right?" He fixed Connors with a determined stare and added, "Don't you think so, Stephen?"

Connors shrugged and sat back in his chair. Griggs leaned against the wall and said, "Please continue, Agent Bowles."

"If I may go on then." Dorothy smiled at the pudgy officer and glanced quickly at Connors, who sulked in his seat. She forced her attention back to the computer screen and moved the mouse.

"Yes, our killer kills, as the sergeant pointed out." She smiled at Connors. "Serial killers murder as a reflection of their inner state. You might say they murder in response to their inner state. Take this victim, for example." She clicked a dark-pink X, and the image of a body lying next to a Dumpster in a pool of blood appeared on the wall.

Dorothy said, "Sam Malden, the second victim, a twenty-seven-year-old single man, moved to Austin just three months before his body was found on South Congress Avenue. That was on…" She clicked a document icon under the picture and a small window opened. Dorothy read, "November 22, 1984. Just over twenty-nine days after the first body was found." She pulled her head up and glanced over the audience. Every eye in the room was on her. "Twenty-nine days has great significance. For one thing it's approximately the period of the phases of the moon. In fact, if you trace the lunar calendar with respect to the first six attacks you will see they all occur within twenty-four hours of a new moon. Is this fact significant?"

Dorothy knew she had their attention now. She left the question hanging in the air and shifted her tack.

"Sam Malden was a gay man, like many, perhaps all, of the other victims."

"We know this, they all were queer," Connors snapped. "Lieutenant, what is this garbage...lunar calendars? Next she's gonna bring out her Tarot cards?"

Griggs sat back in his chair, crossing his arms over his chest. "Agent Bowles?"

She gave him a small smile of recognition. She knew she needed to establish her position before her advice would be taken seriously. She said, "I know you know the obvious stuff, Sergeant, that the killer is probably a white man in his late twenties to mid-forties; that he is an intelligent loner, most likely thought of as odd or completely ignored by the people who he comes in contact with. That he might keep trophies of his victims and that the root of his psychosis is most likely childhood trauma or abuse.

"But did you know this particular shooter is impotent or sexually frustrated? Did you know that the shooter has significant medical knowledge and is most likely trying to wound, not kill, his victims? That he is either right-handed, with the left eye stronger than the right, or left-handed, with the right eye stronger than the left? That his victims most likely represent an important figure from his childhood, a family member or close friend, that he is fastidious in behavior, introverted, and awkward socially? Has suppressed or confused homosexual tendencies and a strong, probably religious, family background of homophobia...probably not unlike your own bigotry, Sergeant?"

Connors fidgeted uncomfortably in his seat. The rest of the room watched in stunned silence, clearly impressed. Dorothy had expected this reaction. It was always like this, every time she helped with a local investigation. She had learned to hit them quick and hard with the facts. She had to prove her value early because, until she did, their interaction would be adversarial—or, worse, her advice would be ignored.

Now was the time to follow up with the justification. "I realize that many of you may wonder about these assertions. And as good investigators, you should question them. I know you may find some of these things far-fetched," she tossed another small smile toward Connors, "but hear me out."

Connors looked at Lieutenant Griggs, who raised an eyebrow.

Dorothy Bowles built her explanation carefully, first piecing together the case for each claim before explaining its relevance. She based her allegation that the shooter was impotent and sexually frustrated on trend analysis and historical research of previous serial murderers. Evidence indicated that the Blue murderer killed from a distance, never approached his victim. The shooter also chose a rifle as a murder weapon. Both of these characteristics were highly statistically correlated with other serial killers who were either impotent or had serious emotional or physical problems that interfered with their sexual function. Distance from the shooter also indicated a fastidious nature, perhaps stemming from a reluctance to get close or touch the gore associated with violent death. Dorothy explained using charts and tables to emphasize the logic behind the science. She knew that psychology would not fly with these men. She relied instead on cold, hard numbers: a sophisticated statistical analysis of past patterns and an objective consideration of the facts, carefully avoiding references to soft science or anecdotal evidence.

She explained that the basis for her assertion that the shooter had significant medical knowledge and was not trying to murder his victims resulted from a careful study of the shootings. Most of the victims had been shot on the right side of the abdomen below the rib cage. She explained that the bureau had questioned a panel of trauma experts who generally agreed that this particular target was the perfect location to place a bullet intended to wound or maim a victim, serious enough to force hospitalization but, in general, not kill.

John Reed raised his hand.

"Yes?"

"If he was not trying to kill them, how can you explain the fact so many of the victims died, Agent Bowles?"

"Good question." She glanced at his nametag. "Sergeant Reed." Reed smiled shyly. "Detective Reed."

"*Detective* Reed." She smiled back at him and Reed's pale complexion flared red. "I'm glad you're paying attention. That can be attributed to two factors. The ammunition used, which was overpowered for the intended purpose, and the isolated nature of the crime scenes. Most of the victims died from blood loss. In fact, statistical analysis of the time differences between the three survivors and the victims that died shows a strong correlation between the length of time it took to find the victim and the resulting mortality. In fact, statistically, survival can be almost totally attributed to this latency between attack and discovery. The three survivors..." Agent Bowles clicked on an icon that opened an Explorer window and searched for a document. It took just a few seconds to find it. She dragged it into her word-processor window and its contents filled the screen.

"Yes, here it is. Matt Bell and Sean Perry were out with friends when they were shot. Their companions found them minutes after they were shot. Adam Malloy managed to drag himself out of the alleyway and was discovered bleeding in the street ten minutes later." Dorothy ran the cursor down a column on the screen. "As you can see, none of the others, those that died, were found within the first thirty minutes of the time of attack."

Dorothy went on to explain her assertion of the shooter's hand and eye preferences based on the pattern of missed shots. It was founded on an assumption of the shooter's target. When she assumed the shooter was trying to hit near where most of the victims were shot—the right abdomen area—the missed shots showed a regular pattern consistent with overcompensation that comes about when a rifle is held in a manner consistent with adjusting for a weak eye. To prove her point, she again referred to research conducted by the Bureau. "When Bureau sharpshooters were forced to wear glasses that selectively reduced the sight in one eye, scatter patterns began to emerge that were coherent across a wide variety of attempts. In general, the pattern that resulted from the testing was the same for a right-handed shooter with a weak left eye as for a left-handed shooter with a weak right eye."

Dorothy presented pictures that displayed the expected scatter pattern found in the Bureau's research. "When I overlay this pattern with a composite of our shooter's scatter pattern..." She clicked on another document and dragged it over the displayed image. The two patterns matched up so closely Dorothy could hear a gasp escape from the back of the room.

She watched her audience. Before wrapping up her presentation she had one more surprise. She fought to keep the smirk off her face. She had saved the best for last.

"One more thing." She turned back to her computer and opened another file that showed a timeline of the attacks graphically. The irregular period of attacks was interrupted occasionally at seemingly random patterns.

"When you compare the attack timeline with the survival data," she dragged the timeline image into another window, "you can see that the period between deaths is clearly discernable. The shooter attacks in regular intervals until he has a survivor. There are three lulls in his activity, each following an attack survivor. Significantly, the length of time that the shooter lays off from his pattern seems to match the length of time it takes the survivor to recover from his wounds. And the last survivor, Sean Perry, never fully recovered and was cared for until he passed away eighteen days ago."

Dorothy looked up from her computer. Her audience sat in rapt silence. She said, "That was two weeks before the last murder, which means this murder occurred on the first new moon following Perry's death. We don't know the importance of that yet, but we do know one thing." She closed her computer and paused, letting the tension build. Finally, she said, "Your shooter will shoot another gay man in downtown Austin in the late evening or early morning hours of December eleventh or twelfth. That gives you just two weeks to find this killer, or another dead body will be lying in the morgue."

❖

Bill lay back onto the cold tin and shuddered, gazing into the night sky. Clouds skittered past the effervescent moon. It was full again, and his thoughts trailed back to the alleyway. Briefly, he tasted the sweetness as he visualized the shot—the boy, framed in the scope spinning from the force of the bullet, the muffled bang ringing in his ears, the boy dropping like a marionette with cut strings. He imagined the pulsating stiffening rise from below. It had been a good shot, it was always a good shot, he thought, and corrected himself. No, mustn't be too confident...curiosity didn't kill the cat...overconfidence did. He inhaled deeply and could smell the sulfur. His mind's eye flashed to an image of the others—glistening, smooth, strong—and he tasted the sweetness again. Clouds chased over the moon but in his mind he could still see it. It was an eyehole, the light through the eyehole, and soon the eyehole would be covered. And when the eyehole was covered...He shivered again, but this time it wasn't from the cold.

CHAPTER THIRTEEN

MATT

The rain ended at dusk. The air was crystal clear and felt fresh and clean. The wind rolled around to the west just after sundown, and the mercury began to drop. By morning, the temperature hovered below freezing and the puddles in the gutter were slushy with ice forming at the edges.

Thatcher sat at his desk, under the glare of his desk lamp, flipping through the police report of Adam's shooting. He had managed to secure a copy from an acquaintance that worked at the police station. In exchange for a date, the young man had given him the report just fourteen months after Adam's death. Thatcher reread the ballistics section for what seemed like the thousandth time, wading through the familiar stilted technical jargon that explained the probable path trajectories and markings left on the bullet and perusing the analysis of the weapon.

The shooter had used a Bushmaster .223. Thatcher read the name again and looked at the disassembled weapon at his feet—a Bushmaster .223. He had purchased the gun to help him understand the report. He wanted to recognize the difference between the casing and the cartridge, the barrel and the stock. But now that he had it— held it in his hands, felt its smooth black-steel surface, and sighted down its barrel—Thatcher realized he really wanted knowledge of the shooter, not of the weapon. Thatcher had bought the gun because of what it told him about the killer. And as he looked down at the disassembled pieces, he realized the story the gun told was muddled.

The Bushmaster was a hunter's rifle, a sniper's weapon. It was not what the shooter would use if he wanted to experience the victim's pain up close. It was a cold, impersonal weapon, accurate from far away, which was evidently how the killer wanted it. This murderer did not want to sully his hands with the gore of his victims. He wanted to control the situation, he wanted death served up, sanitized.

The thought infuriated Thatcher and he sat at the desk, stewing in anger. The doorbell brought him back from his dark meditation. Quickly he gathered the pieces of the Bushmaster and carried them to the closet.

As he hurried back from the bedroom, he called out, "Be right there."

❖

I stared at my finger on the doorbell and prayed following Jim's advice would not be a mistake. I heard Thatcher call out and inhaled deeply, trying to still my pounding heart. When he opened the door, my uncertainty was not alleviated. Through the screen, he glared at me in ambiguous antagonism—or at least distracted annoyance. I feared that showing up unannounced was a bad idea and considered making some lame excuse and beating a hasty retreat. A smile broke across his lips and a surge of relief coursed through me.

I smiled back.

"Hi," he said, nudging the screen door open.

"Hi, I was just in the neighborhood and thought I'd drop by. If you're busy I can come back."

He smiled again and shivered in the unexpected cool. "Come in."

He brushed the straw-colored hair out of his eyes and held the door. As I stepped into his barren living room, it was apparent he had been working at his desk. His PC was off, but I could see a notebook beside the keyboard, a pen wedged in the binding. The pages were covered with neatly printed paragraphs with hastily scribbled notations crammed into the margins. A tidy stack of photocopies was tucked next to the overhanging paper tray of an ink-jet printer. What looked like an instruction manual was serving as a paperweight. It lay facedown and open on top of the stack.

I nodded toward the desk. "Really, if you're busy..."

"No, just doing a little research." He stepped over to the desk and grabbed the manual, shoved the photocopies inside it, and picked up the notebook. He slid the whole lot into a drawer and turned back to me with another smile. "It's time for a break anyway. I'm glad to see you."

"Me too." I shrugged. "I missed you at practice this week. I was expecting...well...hoping anyway—"

"Yeah," he snapped. "I've been busy." A quick grin lessened the sting. His grin faded as he leaned back on the desk, sliding the desk drawer shut with his hip.

I nodded a response, fighting my curiosity. He waved me to the club chair and turned his desk chair around to face me.

We both sat down and I studied him silently. Thatcher looked disheveled. I could tell it had been a couple of days since he'd shaved, and his hair was spiked and tussled like he'd just rolled out of bed. Still, he looked wonderful with the sunshine streaming through the window on his golden skin. Again, I said, "Is this a bad time?"

He shot a furtive glance toward the closet before answering. "Will you relax? It can wait." He leaned back and the light twinkled in his eyes. "It's really good to see you. I've missed you."

It was exactly what I wanted to hear and my spirits soared. "I've missed you too."

He stretched a leg out and gently kicked the sole of my boot with his bare foot. We both looked down. He nudged me again before offering his apology. "I should have called. I'm sorry."

"Me too." I paused, still watching his foot. "I mean...I did. Call...Well, sort of."

He looked at me with his eyebrows raised.

"I didn't leave a message."

I thought I saw a note of sadness flash across his brow. He nodded and said, "Tell you what, I'm hungry. Are you?"

"A little, I guess." I had just eaten.

"Can you give me a minute to get ready?" He rubbed his head and grinned sheepishly. "You caught me before my shower."

"Sure, take your time. I'm in no hurry."

"Great! Figure out where you want to go. I won't be long." He stood and squeezed my shoulder as he strolled to the bathroom. I sat back, looking at the sunshine streaming through the blinds, and felt like singing. In a few seconds, I heard the shower kick on.

Thatcher called out, "Turn on some music."

"Okay." I plodded toward his stereo system in the bedroom.

Clean laundry was folded in neat piles on top of his unmade bed: T-shirts and underwear and socks. I walked around the bed and found his CD collection stacked in columns leaning against the wall. The stereo tuner and tape player were arranged on the floor next to his CD player. I knelt and sorted through the CDs. They were all jazz recordings. I was just about to close my eyes and grab one when I spotted a Hiroshima disc, their *Black and White* CD.

As the first Asian notes of the koto wafted through the room, I let my eyes wander. They trailed across the bay window and landed on the closet door. I flashed back to Thatcher's furtive glance in that direction and, without considering my motives, opened the door. On the floor, wedged in the gap between two pairs of shoes, was the cold, black-steel tube of a rifle barrel. The disassembled stock and trigger mechanism were scattered on the floor. I bent down to look at the pieces. The weapon was an XM15, E2S Patrolman's A3 Carbine .223. It had a sixteen-inch barrel, an M4 step cut, and a one-in-nine-inch twist with a removable carry handle. I could see the A2 rear sight on the barrel, with a forward assist and brass deflector. The gun was a Bushmaster .223. The music drowned the sound of my gasp.

I knew a lot about this type of gun because I had been shot by one once. My stomach clenched as I closed the closet door quickly and returned to the living room.

I paced back and forth across the small space, unable to focus. A jumble of possibilities percolated up from my subconscious. Finally, the rest of the world seemed to fade away and my eyes were drawn to the desk.

The sound of the shower running in the bathroom was just audible under the ethereal notes of Hiroshima's *Dreams*. My hand trembled as I reached for the drawer handle. I tugged it open, shoved aside the notepad, and pulled out the stack of photocopies. It was obvious that the Xeroxed copies were made from microfiche; they showed the telltale signs of folds and inconsistent graying patterns. I scanned the top one and my pulse began to quicken. I frantically flipped through the others. They were stories of the sniper shootings, arranged in chronological order.

The last in the stack was cut from Friday's paper.

I was wondering what it all meant when my mind stitched together an unexpected connection—an image of Thatcher's face when he saw my scar in the pool—and I began to hear the distant drumbeat of a coming revelation. It rattled me. I shook my head, trying to dispel the vision. In my mind a question floated into foggy view.

Could Thatcher be the shooter?

It explained Thatcher's unexpected attention. It explained his strange behavior, dropping in and out of contact. I tried to think back to the time of the last murder and realized it had been the night before we slept together. An unsettling vision of the first time I saw him floated into view. The shadowy figure emerging through the fog, his head turned downward, lost in his own thoughts, almost animalistic. *Like a panther. He walked like a panther.* I remembered the ambivalence when he almost stepped in front of the car. Was he distracted or suicidal? And the far-away hurt look I had seen in his eyes—was it a sign of his loss, or some deeper inner conflict?

A wave of nausea radiated through me and my knees felt weak. I shut my eyes tight and leaned back on the desk to keep from falling down. My brain churned with thoughts of the gun on the floor of the closet, the articles—the incriminating evidence—spread on the desk in front of me.

Slowly, unwanted thoughts receded to the back of my mind and another feeling came forward, accompanied by an impression of Thatcher the first time I saw him. He was like a hurt child, oblivious to his surroundings. And the sound of Thatcher's voice floated through my thoughts, asking, "Do you believe in one true love?"

I had to know more. Before I took action I had to know for sure. I turned my attention back to the notepad but heard the water go off in the shower. Hurriedly, I gathered the articles, stacking them in order and shoving them back into the manual. I slid them into the drawer and tossed the notepad in on top. I stepped away from the desk and shot a quick glance into the bedroom before breathing a sigh of relief. *Thank God I remembered to close the closet door.*

Thatcher came out of the bathroom wearing a towel around his waist. He finger-combed his damp hair and tossed another furtive glance toward the bedroom before moving in my direction. He kissed me gently, brushed past, and sat down on the chair.

"Nice choice," he said.

"Hmmm."

I sat on the club chair and watched him.

"Hiroshima." He smiled.

I nodded. I tried to reason with myself, to still my pounding heart and deal with the headache beginning to assert itself at the base of my skull.

Thatcher grinned at me and stood up. "I'll just be a minute," he said, and ambled into the bedroom. I watched as he opened the closet door, reached inside quickly, and grabbed a pair of jeans. It might have been my imagination, but I thought I saw him glance down at the gun before closing the door.

He tugged the jeans on, under his towel, before he spoke. "So, where are we going?"

"What?"

He dropped the towel on the floor, pulled a T-shirt off the bed, and worked it over his head. "I asked where you want to go eat. Man, where are you?" He smiled. "You're a million miles away."

"Oh, sorry," I said, trying to focus. "I don't know. Wherever you want."

My growing headache was working its way down to my stomach. I had no appetite. Thatcher looked at me as he bent to tie his shoes. He raised an eyebrow quizzically before shrugging. "Okay, how about Hyde Park Bar and Grill?"

"Sure," I said.

God, I wish he wasn't so beautiful. My mind was racing. On the one hand, I knew I was falling in love with Thatcher. Already had, in fact. But on the other hand, the gun and the articles, what did they mean? I shuddered.

Thatcher said, "It's such a beautiful day, let's walk." He flashed his Hollywood smile, then pulled on a black leather jacket and held the door for me. I stepped onto the deck and squinted in the sunshine.

Lunch was going to be difficult.

Hyde Park Bar and Grill was busy as usual. The restaurant serves large portions of Southern cooking to the largely white-collar but vaguely bohemian crowd.

When we stepped through the doors, I could see that every bar stool was occupied. Men in business suits and college kids in baggy pants, wool socks, and sandals leaned against walls or stood in groups, drinking glasses of wine and frosty mugs of beer. Many were trying not to block the waiters' stations or loom over tables already full of hungry customers busily stuffing their faces with burgers and fries and buttery Wom Kim's peach pudding.

We made our way up to a smiling, chubby woman carrying a clipboard. She told us the current wait would be forty-five minutes to an hour so we stepped back outside and huddled together on a sunny bench near the porch. I stared out past the giant fork statue and watched the Duval traffic lumbering over the speed bumps in front of us.

Thatcher turned his blue-green eyes my direction. "Tell me something."

I raised an eyebrow.

"How did you get that scar?"

My stomach clenched involuntarily. The gun, the articles, and now Thatcher was asking me about my scar? It was all happening too quickly. I still hadn't been able to make sense of my feelings and the growing suspicion. I shrugged nonchalantly. "Old story. Why do you ask?"

"Just interested," he responded. The hair stood on the back of my neck and I shivered as the wind picked up.

I paused, staring into the distance, and tried to figure out what to say. When I turned back his direction, I caught him staring at me. He smiled self-consciously and dropped his gaze.

"I was shot," I blurted out, and turned back to the traffic. "I don't want to talk about it."

I could feel his eyes on me but he didn't speak. We sat that way together for a few minutes before I said, "It was a long time ago. I prefer to leave it in the past." I hoped this explanation would suffice. Fear that he might have been the shooter churned inside me.

Thatcher let the subject drop. We sat in uncomfortable silence. I watched a city bus amble slowly over a speed bump and stop across the street, its air brakes blasting a puff of air. Finally, he broke the silence. "Look, I know it's none of my business, but I'm interested."

I smiled at him. "Why don't we start with some easier subjects, like, tell me about your family."

He smiled back. "Okay, tell me about your family." He was being coy.

"You first," I shot back.

He shook his head. He looked back at the street and said, "Not much to tell, really. My parents died in a car wreck when I was in college. No brothers or sisters." He looked at me with a wry smile. "I have an aunt in New Mexico. She keeps cats. How about you?"

"I'm a dog person," I deadpanned.

"Hmmm…" He pretended to pull a notepad from his pocket and write on it. "Avoids all kinds of subjects. Perhaps he's in the mafia…or CIA."

I grinned. "FBI, but don't ask."

"Or you'll have to kill me…I know."

A flock of green parrots flew past us and landed on the fork. I took their unexpected appearance as an omen of good fortune.

"Look at the wild parrots." I gestured toward the fork.

We both looked that direction. "Don't they generally roost around Town Lake?" he asked.

"Yeah, it's pretty rare to see them this far north. I think they feed on seedpods from the mesquite trees along the golf course."

He nodded and we watched the bright-green birds groom themselves for a few seconds. A couple of joggers ran by, drawing our attention back to the street. Thatcher asked, "So do you have family?"

"Unfortunately." I shrugged

"Well?" He prodded gently.

I sighed heavily before answering. "My parents live in the mountains of New Mexico. I have one sister and two brothers, and more nieces and nephews than I care to count." I dropped my tone conspiratorially. "My siblings are very prolific."

He smiled again. "New Mexico...I wonder if they know my aunt."

I laughed. "Hope not. You see, they're dog people too." The humor was lame, but he grinned anyway.

I sat back and closed my eyes. The parrots cooed and clucked and rose together from the fork in a bright-green flutter. After a few minutes, Thatcher lifted his arm and laid it along the top of the bench rail. His hand softly grazed my shoulder.

"Matt, I didn't mean to pry...earlier, I mean."

He said it so tenderly my heart warmed. "I know." The two of us fell silent again.

Inside, my mind churned. I wanted to ask him about the gun and the articles. I wanted to get the subject out in the open. But I hesitated.

His voice brought me out of my self-absorbed contemplation. "It's just this thing I've been working on," he said.

I lifted my eyes and watched him in silence. He was clearly struggling to find the right words.

"Just like you, I have an old story."

He paused and seemed to search the sky for assistance. The breeze began to pick up and it gently played with his sandy hair, lifting and dropping it in seemingly random patterns. The sunshine twinkled in his blue-green eyes. Still, the visual effect of his features was so captivating that I found myself lost again gazing at him.

Slowly those blue-green pools turned back in my direction; the twinkling of his eyes was actually the glistening of tears. I dropped my head immediately and began playing with the lining of my coat. I was conscious of a building feeling of intrusion, an awkward awareness of imposition as if I had somehow stumbled upon a quiet, personal moment between old friends.

Thatcher said, "I need to tell you about someone."

His voice caught in his throat as he spoke. I concentrated on my coat lining. The time seemed to tick by. More traffic rumbled past. Thatcher waited for the silence to return before he spoke again.

"I need to tell you about Adam."

This was an important step for us. It meant something in a way that nothing before had—not our first encounter, not our first date, not the first time we made love. I waited for his words, motionless as a moth encased in amber.

But it was not to be. Just then the chubby hostess appeared at the door and called Thatcher's name. He looked at me with a pensive smile and shrugged. We followed her inside and snaked through seated guests to a converted porch area where three small tables were crushed together into a sunny, intimate setting. It would have been an acceptable location to continue our conversation if the other tables were empty, but they weren't. Three familiar heads pivoted our direction from the next table.

Jim smiled, Danny dropped his jaw, and Marco just rolled his eyes.

"I guess they let just about anyone in here," Jim said, standing. He hugged Thatcher, extending a hand in my direction over his back. I nodded at Danny and winked at Marco, who continued to sulk silently in his seat across the table.

The hostess asked Thatcher, "Do you want to sit with your friends?"

I gave Thatcher a reluctant nod, before he said to Danny, "We don't want to interrupt."

"Nonsense," Jim said, "let's just pull these tables together."

The tables were rearranged and greetings were exchanged. I found myself scanning a menu perched between Danny's chicken-fried steak and Marco's chili cheeseburger. Across the table, Thatcher was next to Jim's spinach salad.

The two of us ordered quickly and I said, "Please, go on and eat. Don't wait for us." They were the only words I managed during the entire meal.

The situation left me feeling out of sorts. Jim and Danny worked to fill the conversation with light-hearted banter and humorous tales of their volunteer work at the Salvation Army. The three of them had just returned from serving breakfast at the shelter.

Thatcher smiled distractedly as Jim filled us in on their collective adventure. Marco's participation amounted to the occasional sarcastic remark. For the most part, I tried to listen but my thoughts were elsewhere.

About midway through lunch I noticed that Thatcher had stopped eating. It was obvious that he was very engaged with the conversation. I focused my attention on what was being said. Jim was telling a story about a vagrant pulled from under the bridge just before they arrived at the shelter. Evidently filthy, the guy was so drunk he had to be helped in the shower. Danny was "volunteered" for the duty.

"Talk about disgusting. This guy hadn't bathed in months. He smelled really bad," Danny said.

Marco said, "Like most of your tricks."

Danny ignored him. "He was wearing every article of clothing he owned. Layers of filth. It took twenty minutes to get him undressed."

"Like most of your tricks," Marco repeated.

"What did you say his name was?" Thatcher asked.

Danny looked at Jim. Jim answered, "Philips, I think." He shrugged.

"Willy?" Thatcher asked.

"Yeah, that's right. Willy," Danny said. "He asked me to call him Willy."

"So did you enjoy bathing him?" Marco's sarcasm was getting old.

"Ever seen him before?" Thatcher asked.

"Yeah, he's a regular," Danny said. "He's been there every weekend I've worked since I started in January."

Jim nodded.

Thatcher ignored his half-eaten smoked-turkey sandwich. "Where did you say he came from?"

"Under the bridge." Danny answered the question as if everyone knew what "under the bridge" meant.

Thatcher raised his eyebrows in a quizzical expression.

"It's shelter speak," Jim explained. "It means he sleeps in the open. I think he stays at the Fortress."

"Fortress?"

"I know." Danny nodded at Thatcher. "The lingo's confusing. These guys have their own language. The Fortress is a clearing in the brush down by the river, near where Waller Creek spills into Town Lake. A lot of homeless guys live down there."

"Yeah," Jim added. "It's not far from the interstate."

I watched Thatcher, wondering where this sudden interest in the plight of the homeless was coming from. For my part I was anxious to find a way out of this conversation. I wanted the two of us to get back to our earlier discussion, but Jim wasn't through with his explanation.

"Most of these guys lost their jobs with the economic downturn. Now they have no way to get one. They have no shower, no car, no job skills, and no money. Most of us don't—"

I couldn't hear the rest because Marco leaned over and whispered in my ear, "Spare me the feed-the-needy speech. I swear this guy drives me crazy with this overblown do-gooder shit. It's like he's padding his resume for sainthood."

I fought to keep the grin off my face.

Mercifully, lunch went quickly. After paying the check, the five of us exited into the sparkling sunshine and congregated around the fork.

Jim asked, "So where are you guys off to now?"

I shrugged uncomfortably and Thatcher said, "Tell you what. I've got some work to do. Maybe one of you guys can give Matt a ride?" I looked at him, confused. He just ducked his head and avoided eye contact. I wondered what was going on. I'd assumed Thatcher was as anxious to continue our conversation as I was, but evidently not. I sighed in frustration.

Jim said, "Sure. Tell you what, I'm on my way downtown. You want to come?"

I shook my head. "Not right now, I'm getting a headache. Maybe you can drop me at home."

Marco stepped forward. "No need for that, it's the other direction. You can come with us."

We murmured quick good-byes.

As we pulled out of the parking lot in Marco's Taurus, I caught a glimpse of Thatcher jogging up Park Avenue in the direction of his house.

"Okay, spill," Marco said.

Danny looked at me over his shoulder from the front seat. "What?"

"What is going on with you and Thatcher?"

I should have expected the question. I decided the only appropriate response was to ignore it, so I asked, "Do either of you guys have anything for this headache?" I squinted into the sunshine. Marco's eyes cut across the front seat to Danny and both of them sighed in dissatisfaction.

❖

Carla Sandoval pulled her battered old Toyota Celica to the curb and sat for a few moments getting ready to do battle. She scanned the neighborhood. The rundown house itself sported a wide two-story screened-in porch. The yard, though bare and ugly, showed patches of yellow grass that just might struggle back to life when the rains returned in spring.

She opened the car door and stepped onto the pavement, then grabbed her purse from the backseat, pulling the straps over her shoulder as she kicked the door shut. She climbed the steps to the porch, avoiding a dark-gray cat that darted across her path. The door swung open before she had a chance to knock, and a large, angry-looking man sneered at her through the screen.

"What do you want?"

"I have an appointment with Mr. James." She tried to make her voice sound happy and efficient, but the man just stood there staring.

"He ain't here."

Carla paused for a moment, unsure how to proceed. Finally, she asked, "When do you expect him back?"

The man's face broke into a wide smile. "Fooled ya." His laugh was brittle, but not disdainful. "Fooled ya," he repeated. "He's here but you didn't think he was, did ya?"

Carla noted the innocent, childish delight in the words and realized she was talking to a resident. She smiled and played along with the game. "You got me, all right."

"You didn't know he was here, huh?"

"Nope, that was a good one."

She heard the sound of footsteps thudding down the carpeted stairway behind the man, and a cherubic bald head appeared over his shoulder.

"Harvey, what are you up to?"

"She didn't know you was here, Mr. James. She thought you was gone. I told her you was gone and she thought you was gone."

"But I am here, Harvey. Why would you want to tell her that?"

"Jus' cause, you see."

"It was a game, Mr. James," Carla answered. "Right, Harvey?"

Harvey laughed.

"You must be Ms. Sandoval, come to talk about placing your brother, right?"

Carla nodded, "Yes, Stanley Church."

"Yes, of course, please come in." He opened the door and held it while Carla stepped into the foyer.

CHAPTER FOURTEEN

THATCHER

Thatcher stood in the shade of the aging sweet-gum tree and looked up the pathway that skirted the shoreline and climbed the bridge over Waller Creek. Behind him, the waters of Lake Austin glowed unearthly gray-green with silver streaks highlighting the choppy surface. The sun was about to drop below the horizon and a southerly wind strengthened with the dropping temperature. The freshening gusts lifted six-inch peaks on the water's surface. Beyond the bridge, tall grass, waving in the breeze, encircled an untamed mass of bushes. A footpath cut through the grass and trailed off into the brush.

Thatcher leaned against the trunk of an elm tree and watched the pathway. He had been there for the past twenty minutes. During that time four rough-looking men, each wearing dirty jeans and old work boots, and carrying liquor bottles wrapped in brown paper sacks, had staggered over the bridge and followed the footpath. They had all disappeared behind the limbs of the bramble bushes and scrub-oak trees into the marsh. Thatcher looked up above the tops of the trees. He could just make out a plume of smoke and sparks trailing off into the purple northern sky

Two hours before, Thatcher had paid ten dollars to a grimy panhandler lounging next to a dumpster in the parking lot outside a

South Congress liquor store. In exchange, the toothless old man had delivered nearly incoherent directions to the Fortress. It had taken Thatcher longer than he'd expected to discern the location from the instructions, and he'd backtracked across the bridge several times before spotting the footpath. But he knew, finally, this was what he had been searching for.

Thatcher stuck his hands into the pockets of his leather jacket, pushed away from the tree, and walked toward the entrance to the Fortress. He made his way cautiously over the bridge. The footpath was just muddy enough to make footing uncertain as he cut through the grass. Once inside the bushes, he could hear the soft tinkle of laughter. The path zigzagged through the brambles and Thatcher's senses heightened as fear crackled up his spine.

The sound of laughter grew louder as he neared the campfire. Thatcher was aware of unseen eyes following his progress through the brush. The campfire became a hazy beacon that grew progressively brighter as he maneuvered through the tangle of limbs. Before breaching the final layer of branches, he stopped and peered through the thin veil of vines to the scene in the clearing. Four figures sat on fallen logs surrounding the fire. Off to the side, under a makeshift tent made of old blankets draped over the branches of a magnificent oak tree, a couple of supine figures lay splayed on top of what looked like a tarp. In the darkness, Thatcher could barely make out the glint of a bottle being passed between the two. Other figures, some sprawled in sleeping bags while others were wrapped in blankets, were positioned around the perimeter of the clearing in groups of two and three. He could see two solitary shapes on the edges. Each was wrapped in newspapers and appeared to be sleeping, near the distant creek shore.

"If you move, I'm gonna cut you."

The voice came from behind and Thatcher froze, fear shooting through him like electric current. His heart pumped wildly and adrenaline rushed to his brain, heightening his senses. He could make out the sound of labored breathing close to his exposed back.

"I don't want any trouble," Thatcher said softly without turning.

"What do you want then?" The voice was hard with a phlegmy edge and a soft Southern undertone.

In spite of the cool breeze, sweat trickled between Thatcher's shoulder blades. "I just want to talk with someone. I'm looking for Willy Philips."

The figure shifted behind him and Thatcher caught a peripheral flash of leathery skin and tightly curled gray hair. The old man said, "What do you want to talk with Will for?"

"I need to ask him some questions about something that happened a long time ago."

"Shit, Willy's not going to remember a long time ago." The old man rattled out a raspy laugh and stepped in front of Thatcher. Slowly, Thatcher dropped his hands and scrutinized the old man. Red-rimmed eyes stared out from under a nest of unruly white eyebrows. He wore a ratty, military-green peacoat and a tattered turtleneck sweater. His hands were stuffed into the coat's frayed pockets. There was no blade. "Right now, he's gonna have trouble remembering this morning."

Thatcher smiled and the old man laughed again. It seemed to dislodge something deep down in his chest and he bent over in a nasty fit of coughing. The painful, racking cough ended abruptly and the old man cleared his throat with a hacking discharge. He spit into the bushes before straightening up and looking at Thatcher.

"Scared you, didn't I?"

Thatcher nodded. "A little."

The old man laughed again and nodded toward one of the men down near the river. "That's Willy over there, but he's been drinkin'. And when Willy's been drinkin' he don't stop 'til he passes out."

Thatcher gazed at the lanky creature sprawled in the grass. Even from this distance, he could tell that the man had vomited on himself. It probably explained his banishment from the group.

The old man laughed again and left Thatcher to join the men at the campfire. Thatcher heard his raspy voice murmuring, and the others turned to look at Thatcher with blank faces. But the scrutiny only lasted a moment, and they focused on a bottle the old man pulled from his pocket.

Thatcher dropped his head, pulled his jacket tight, and stepped toward Willy Philip's sleeping form.

❖

"Two days, Sam, we've got just two days until this nut strikes again." Dorothy Bowles hitched one shapely hip onto Lieutenant Griggs's desk and peered down at him.

Sam leaned his chair back against the wall, crossed his feet on top of his desk, and sighed in exasperation. "Don't you think I know it? Look, we're trying everything we can think of. Right now I've got fourteen men on Fourth Street. They've been staking out the alleyways, gay bars, and bookstores for a week." He ran his fingers through his gray hair and stared back at Dorothy with tired eyes. "Hell, I've even got one guy running background on all the released sex offenders living in the Central Texas area and another checking the chat Web sites in the hope this asshole has morphed into some kind of cyberkiller."

Sam looked tired, tiny wrinkles around his red eyes. His crumpled shirt looked slept in. Dorothy was pretty sure he hadn't had a full night's sleep since this case went hot. She cut him some slack. "I know you have, Sam. And all that's good too. I'm just frustrated. All this time, all this information, but still no suspects... and the clock's ticking. I really want to find this psycho."

"Me too." Sam dropped his head and shot a quick glance her direction before turning his eyes toward the window. "If you've got any ideas, I'm all ears."

Dorothy followed his gaze out the window. After a few minutes, she said, "Checking the sex offenders was a good idea. This guy's a sicko, he might have a record, but I doubt it. He's too careful, too controlled."

Sam looked up at Dorothy. From her, any recognition he was doing the right thing was high praise.

"Any luck?" she asked.

"Not yet. We figured it might explain the gap in the murder spree." Sam shifted in his seat and dropped his feet to the floor. "Maybe he was in prison."

Dorothy nodded, still gazing at the moon.

Furtively, Sam scrutinized her body as she leaned against the desk with her arms crossed. Wisps of silver-gray hair trailed down her neck and seemed to fall in place whenever she moved her head. She wore black slacks and a white silk blouse pulled tight across her breasts. Dorothy Bowles is an attractive woman, he thought. She wasn't small, but something about her was delicate, almost fragile. It wasn't her manner. From what Sam had seen of Dorothy in action, he knew she could be brusque—direct to the point of rudeness.

Still, he found himself fighting with an internal desire to protect her.

"Did you crosscheck the medical facilities?" Dorothy asked.

"Not yet. Do you think it's important?"

"Jesus, Sam, everything's important! The research indicates that this guy has some medical knowledge…"

Sam grinned playfully and raised his hands in surrender. "Hold on, hold on. I'm just playing with you. Reed's on it."

Dorothy shook her head in mock disgust.

"I know, I know, the humor was lame. I'm sorry, I'm tired."

Dorothy dropped her head to hide the smile that played across her face.

"He's checking doctors' offices and hospital-staff records, also pathology labs and even the morgue—looking for a correlation with employee records and the attack timeline." Sam shuffled his foot over and nudged Dorothy's shoe. "You need to lighten up a little."

Dorothy looked at Sam. She really didn't know what to make of this guy, and she didn't trust her growing attraction to him. She lowered her voice. "I'll lighten up when this guy's in custody."

"You and me both," Sam said.

She shot him a wicked grin. "Then we celebrate. Until then it's all work." She stood up abruptly, strode out of Sam's office and down the corridor, leaving the door open in her wake.

❖

Bill shivered in the breeze from the open window. The winding road banked and twisted, rising to the stoplight at the top of the hill. Cautiously, he approached the red light, pulling to a stop with the other cars. The jet-black Mustang's engine whirred and he pushed the button, rolling the tinted windows shut before he scanned the faces of the people in the other cars: a balding old man in a beat-up pickup truck, a couple of high-school girls in a red Honda, a mother with a car full of teenage soccer players. *Typical breeders.* He turned his attention to the eastern horizon. The moon hadn't risen, wouldn't show itself until nearly sunrise. Then it would appear in the east, a tiny sliver of moon chasing westward across the sky just ahead of the sun. *But tomorrow night, the sun will rise first—a new moon, the eyehole, covered.* In his mouth he tasted the sweetness, just as the traffic light changed.

He pulled away slowly, following the turning traffic. Down the hill on his right he could just make out the pool, shining like an aquamarine jewel set in the dusty darkness and shrouded by tree branches. He smiled, remembering the others—glistening, smooth, strong. He felt his rising sexual interest, the heat building below, and licked his chapped lips. Soon, he thought, very soon, but first to prepare. He drove by carefully, smiling unconsciously, the words ringing in his mind like the pealing of a bell. *Tomorrow, I will hunt.*

❖

"Hello."

"Hi, it's Matt."

"Oh, hi, what's up?" A note of anxiety sounded in Danny's voice. He probably wasn't expecting personal calls at work. He managed the training department for a chain of pharmaceutical stores but had to help out with retail when the stores underwent staffing problems. He had recently been assigned to the Walgreens on Forty-fifth Street. It was Thursday morning. Even though Danny was a close friend, I didn't call often and never at work. I hurried on to my point to allay his fears. "Are you planning to swim with the team tonight?"

He paused before answering, and I sensed something was wrong. Finally, he said, "Not tonight." He sounded disappointed. I could just hear the catch in his voice.

"Are you okay?"

Again he paused before answering. "Yeah, I'm okay. Just not in the mood for swimming."

"Are you and Marco going out then?"

"No…I'm busy."

"What's up?"

"I'm tired." His sentences were clipped and terse

"What is it, Dan?" I was becoming concerned. This wasn't like Danny at all.

He hesitated again. "Nothing."

"What's Marco up to?"

More silence. "Don't know."

This was bewildering. In all the time I'd known Danny, he and Marco had been pretty much inseparable. I said, "Are you sure you're okay? You sound down."

"Yeah, I'm fine. Look, I got to go."

"Okay, call me when you get a chance," I said lamely.

He said good-bye and hung up. I sat at my desk and stared at the phone. *What was that about?*

❖

"Damn!"

Thatcher sat on the bottom rung of his stepladder and rubbed a small knot rising on his head at the spot where he'd banged it on the cabinet door.

The storeroom of the carriage house was full of cast-off clothing and Adam's boxed possessions. Thatcher had spent twenty minutes assembling a pile of old shirts and pants for Willy. It had been four days since he had tracked down Philips at the Fortress, and he'd spent most of the first two days trying to sober him up.

Since then, Thatcher had been helping Willy deal with his personal needs.

And Willy Philips had a lot of personal needs. To begin with, he had no clothes except those on his back. He had very few possessions and a voracious appetite for alcohol. Thatcher had fought that from the beginning, offering a place to sleep it off and a chance to sober up a little. But after a few hours, Willy got the shakes so bad Thatcher broke down and brought him some malt liquor. That settled his palsy and put him back to sleep, so Thatcher spent twenty-four hours feeding, bathing, and pampering the man before he felt Willy was settled enough to answer a few questions. Fortunately, the information that Willy provided had yielded a few surprises. It might not be enough to stand up in court, but it was enough for Thatcher.

Now Thatcher was putting together a care package for Willy to take with him back to the Fortress.

Thatcher kicked the cardboard box to the side in frustration, reached back into the cabinet, and tugged at a pile of sweaters. A stack of jeans, mixed with slacks and a single pair of red sweatpants, came out together, knocking over a box of medical supplies. White tape and a roll of gauze rolled out, followed by sealed packets of Betadine solution and a plastic syringe.

Thatcher cringed at the sight. After all this time through all these emotions, and now this. He stared at the syringe in disbelief and felt the darkness surround him, and the edge of his world began to pull away. His mind flashed to an image of Adam.

Adam's emaciated, feverish body was coiled into a ball on the bed. Thatcher gently stroked the sparse hair on his lover's head. He whispered a little prayer, "Please forgive me."

Adam shook uncontrollably and Thatcher knew his fever was spiking. Adam's labored breathing rasped into the stillness as Thatcher gently wiped the crusted blood from his cheek with a washcloth, then pulled the thermometer from his rectum. A hundred and four. He cleaned the thermometer with the cloth, knelt beside the bed, and dropped both the washcloth and the thermometer into the plastic biohazard container tucked under the edge. Thatcher rose slowly, without taking his eyes off Adam's face. He walked to the bathroom and his knees almost buckled so he braced himself against the doorjamb to steady himself. He washed his hands at the sink and reached into the supply box on the counter for an unused syringe. He grabbed a small brown-glass bottle from the countertop, then lumbered zombie-like back into the bedroom. He bent and gently kissed Adam's forehead. The tears in his eyes blurred the scene before him and he said, "I don't know if I can do this." He spoke to the darkness because Adam was well past responding.

It had been three days since Adam's last intelligible words.

The absolute stillness in the carriage house, broken only by the sound of Adam's labored breathing, cocooned them in a world of their own. Light from the streetlamp streamed through the bedroom window illuminating the hardwoods with an eerie glow, and Thatcher wiped his nose on the sleeve of his T-shirt. In his head he reviewed Doctor Byrd's assessment.

"Are you sure you want to hear this?"

"Yes, tell me," Adam said impatiently. "Tell me about the end."

"It will be HIV-encephalopathy probably, maybe crypto-sporidiosis."

"Not that, Dr. Byrd. Tell me how it will happen."

"Well, if it's encephalopathy you will go to sleep."

"Don't sugarcoat it, Ron." Adam's eyes darted from Dr. Byrd to Thatcher and back again. "We don't have time."

Dr. Byrd met Adam's stare with a wavering certainty, and the muscles of the doctor's jaw worked as he clenched his teeth before he spoke. "You will have intermittent flashes of recognition but soon that will end." He turned to Thatcher and said, "He will not know you. He will lose his ability to function normally. Speech will go first, probably, the ability to stand, then eating. He will fall asleep and not waken." He turned back to Adam. "You will lose control of your bowel function. You will shake uncontrollably and may vomit, the fevers will spike to one-oh-four, one-oh-five. If the crypto is still working you may bleed out."

"Bleed out?" Adam stared at Dr. Byrd, trying to force an explanation. Dr. Byrd ducked his head but Adam grabbed his arm. "I need the truth, Ron. I need to know how it will end so we can plan."

Dr. Byrd raised his eyes slowly. "You may lose so much blood internally that you die, you will probably vomit blood, you will most certainly shit blood." He closed his eyes and opened them slowly, shooting a look of regret over Adam's shoulder to Thatcher. Then he turned his gaze back to Adam and said, "You will die in pain, Adam, like you are melting."

The room spun and Thatcher leaned his head softly against Adam's back. Adam shook him off.

"Okay, then. What do we do?"

Adam glared at Dr. Byrd in defiance, but Dr. Byrd shook his head slowly. "There is nothing to do, Adam."

*Thatcher viewed the scene spellbound, unable to look away. It was like being captured in the drama of a play or a show on TV. Adam turned to face Thatcher slowly. He lifted his eyes and his soul seemed to pour out at Thatcher. Recognition flashed between them, unspoken communication. A plea from Adam...*Will you be strong enough? *An answer from Thatcher...*For you, I will do anything for you.

Thatcher wiped the tears from his eyes and clicked the needle onto the syringe. He drew three-and-a-half milliliters of morphine from the brown glass bottle and withdrew the needle. He held it point up and pressed the plunger. A small stream of the clear liquid squirted into the air.

Then he dropped to one knee next to Adam. With his free hand he tugged the tape from Adam's chest. The IV tube uncoiled and the free end, capped with a rubber stopper, swung toward the bed. Thatcher grabbed the cap before it touched the sheets. Working with one hand he uncapped the Gershon catheter. He held the tip of the catheter with his left hand and pressed the needle into the rubber stopper. Slowly he pushed the plunger of the syringe and watched the clear liquid flow up the tubing into Adam's chest.

When the syringe was empty, Thatcher flushed the catheter with sterile normal saline, tossed the syringe into the biohazard container, and rushed into the bathroom to vomit.

Then he crawled into bed with Adam and curled himself around Adam's feverish body. Thatcher listened to Adam's heart until it stopped beating, then lay wrapped around Adam's body until the home-health-care nurse arrived, four hours later.

Thatcher sat on the floor next to the cabinet and stared at the syringe. Tears welled in his eyes and he laid his head back against the wall. Thatcher's cold, dark world stopped spinning. The focal point of his life became the question echoing through his mind. *How can I go on living with what I've done?*

CHAPTER FIFTEEN

MATT

The stars shone surreally vivid in the moonless sky and I struggled to catch my breath. Steam rose into the cool night air and hovered over the warm sapphire-blue water. I hung on to the wall, watching the other swimmers finish the set.

I had just finished four two-hundreds fly on the four-minute send-off. It was quite a workout.

Coach Chris's voice floated my direction from his chair on deck. "Swim the cool-down set, Matt…unless you want to do another two hundred fly?"

That sealed the deal. No lollygagging. I shook my head and shot Chris a small smile before pushing off the wall. Cool-down was a two-hundred-yard swim, followed by a two-hundred-yard easy kick. I felt my body elongate as I streamlined through the water watching the thick black line beneath the surface.

I swam easy and let my thoughts float. It had been five days since Thatcher left me standing in the parking lot at Hyde Park Bar and Grill. Since then, I had spent about ninety percent of my waking hours pondering our relationship and the likelihood of his being involved in murder.

I had come to a conclusion: I didn't want it to be true.

Deep inside I knew Thatcher didn't want me to know about something in his life, something dark and solitary, and I feared that...more than I would admit, even to myself.

I finished the easy swim and grabbed my kickboard. Marco pulled up in the lane next to me and grinned nervously. I nodded back acknowledgement and asked, "Where's Danny?"

"Dunno." He shrugged. "Probably still busy working."

Marco skipped the two-hundred swim and grabbed a kickboard too. We pushed off the wall together.

I said, "I called him at the office a couple of days ago. He seemed preoccupied."

"Yeah..." It wasn't a question. Marco was working hard to keep up the pace. "So are you going to dinner after practice?" he asked.

"Nope, I ate early. I'm heading home."

We made the first wall and I turned slowly to give Marco time to catch up. He said, "Thatcher was weird last Saturday."

I remained quiet.

Marco persisted. "What was that about?"

I leaned over and looked at him. He was struggling again with the kicking. I picked up the pace. "No idea," I said.

"And he seemed in a..." he paused for two quick breaths, "hurry to leave."

"I guess," I said noncommittally. We hit the other wall and turned together. I pushed the pace a little more and it had the intended effect—Marco's chatter stopped. As we kicked, I saw Thatcher's car pull into the parking lot up the hill. I watched as he parked and my heart fluttered, but he just sat there in his car, watching from the parking lot.

I wondered what he was doing.

A few seconds later, Danny's car pulled into the lot too.

Marco didn't seem to notice as he concentrated on keeping up. We hit the far wall again and I kicked even harder. This time Marco began to fall off the pace, his labored breathing receding behind me. When I made it to the wall I pushed off and glanced up the hill toward the parking lot again. I could see Danny in his gold Volvo, parked next to Thatcher. Their windows were up and neither of them was paying any attention to the other. They were both watching the pool.

I finished the kick set a full length ahead of Marco and pulled myself out of the water, waving to Chris as I climbed the hill to the dressing room. I showered quickly, dressed, and glanced back at the pool as I climbed the steps toward the lot. Marco was chatting with Chris and Kurt. Others were still finishing the warm-down. At the top of the steps I scanned the parking lot; it was nearly half full of cars, but neither Thatcher's Rav4 nor Danny's Volvo was there.

Feeling let down and confused, I opened my car door and tossed my backpack inside. That's when I noticed a small note tucked under my windshield wiper. My spirits rose on the hope that it was from Thatcher. I couldn't control my elation at the thought he had come all this way to leave a note for me.

I should have known better.

I grabbed the note, which read, *Call me. Danny.*

The pool lights flickered off as Bill watched Chris pull out of the parking lot. That left just one car in the paved area. Good, he thought, and licked his lips.

The night sky was pitch-black. The only illumination came from the stars overhead, the parking-lot lights, and the windows of the men's dressing room. Still, he could easily see the lot and stiffened with excitement. He had parked up the hill on a nearby ridge and now sat watching the dressing room through his rifle scope. The night air smelled of cedar as he reached down and slid his hand along the barrel of the Bushmaster .223. The heat rose from below and he tasted the sweetness. *Not yet. Not until he comes out of the locker room.*

He shuddered with delight and let a small grin play across his face. He gazed up through the open moonroof at the clear night sky. It was cold—the temperature had dropped with the sun—but he felt surprisingly warm. The parking lot had emptied earlier than expected and now he had the perfect view from his position on the ridge. No one would be able to see him in the shadow of the scrub oaks, even as the parking lot glowed like a firefly.

He scanned the horizon through the windshield and listened to the night. The distant hum of traffic on Bee Caves Road seemed to merge with the wind rustling through the trees and the ticking of the cooling engine into a soothing background melody. The closest house, at least five hundred yards down the hill to his left, was the only residence he could see. The dark, un-curtained windows reassured him that it was vacant. He was alone, and the hunt was always best when he was alone. Good hunting, he thought, good hunting in the country. He smiled at his little joke.

He reached into the backseat and pulled out the Styrofoam shield. He slid the barrel into the opening and used duct tape to secure the ends. He wrapped the trigger mechanism in the towel and pulled two cotton swabs from his pocket. He twisted the cotton and carefully stuck it into each ear. He clicked the scope onto the stock and cracked the window. The cool night air rushed into the cabin and the smell of cedar intensified.

It was a full ten minutes before Marco pushed through the dressing-room door, flipping the light off and pausing in the shadows while his eyes adapted to the darkness. Now the only light came from the stars overhead and the lamps around the parking lot.

Bill poked the barrel of the Bushmaster through the window and sighted down the scope. Marco clanged through the gate and climbed the ramp toward his car.

Bill's erection thumped with his excitement. He rested the encased barrel on the edge of the windowsill and aimed. He watched as Marco stepped into the crosshairs of his scope and tasted the sweetness in his mouth. He pulled the trigger.

The shot was on target; Marco slumped to the ground next to his Ford Taurus.

Bill watched through the scope, excited by the shot and the blood. His quarry was down. He could see Marco writhing on the pavement and imagined himself unloading in his shorts.

He inhaled the night air and grinned at his reflection in the mirror. The engine roared to life and he pulled slowly away from the scrub oaks onto the dirt road. He rolled down the hill, stopped at the light, and waited for traffic before turning onto Bee Caves.

The sweetness played across his tongue and he envisioned his quarry, thrashing on the ground. It was a good shot, he thought, he will be mine. He drove carefully, under the speed limit, all the way to Loop 360. He turned onto the highway and headed north.

❖

"God damn it, what's going on out here?" Lieutenant Griggs pulled off the road above the West Austin Athletic Club parking lot.

Dorothy Bowles shrugged and grabbed the dashboard to avoid hitting the windshield as the '80s vintage white Crown Victoria bounced over the uneven pavement at the side of the road. Griggs gave her a weak smile as apology and carefully maneuvered the vehicle down the slope into the lot. They had spent the night waiting for word from a member of the Blue task force. This was the only shooting in the city this evening. Its location, out in the hills west of town, didn't really match the Blue profile, but Griggs had sent John Reed to check it out just in case.

The predawn darkness was broken by the rotating red lights on top of two police units and a harsh white light glaring down from the back of the Austin Police Department Crime Scene van. The units were parked at skewed angles in the lot, blocking Griggs's view of the body, but the van's lights brightly illuminated an area surrounded in yellow tape, next to a silver-colored Ford Taurus. A uniformed officer was busy stringing the final section of tape from the Taurus's bumper to the wheelchair-ramp railing.

Griggs parked as far away from the evidence area as he could. They exited the car together and cautiously approached the activity. They spotted Reed standing off to the side, talking with one of the evidence technicians. Lieutenant Griggs angled that direction, Bowles followed.

Reed looked surprised when he saw Griggs. "Lieutenant?"

Griggs asked, "What you got?"

Reed turned back toward the scene before speaking; the periphery of his curly red hair glowed eerily orange, backlit by the harsh white light. He stepped away from the technician, shaking his head slowly. "The victim's a young male, chief, looks like he was shot in the torso, probably gay."

"Why do you suspect that?" Bowles asked.

Reed stared at her, seeming annoyed. "He swims with a masters' team out here. Owner of this place says the whole team's gay." He turned his back to Dorothy and spoke to Griggs. "We're trying to track down the coach. That's the pool owner over there" He tossed a hand in the direction of a nervous-looking middle-aged man huddled against the side of a cinderblock building talking to a uniformed officer. What was left of the man's hair was matted and flattened on one side, and his eyes were red and puffy from lack of sleep. He looked like he had been pulled out of bed in a hurry.

Griggs asked, "Who found the body?"

"Dunno. An anonymous 911 caller, from a booth about half a mile up the road, convenience store on Bee Caves."

Bowles and Griggs exchanged a glance of confusion. Griggs said, "Okay, tell me about the scene."

"Looks like one shot fired from up on that ridge." He nodded toward the hill across the street. "We've roped off the area, but the ETs say they need to wait for sunrise before searching. The slug's probably imbedded in the pavement. They're about ready to move the body. We'll know for sure when we get him to the coroner's office but it looks like a single shot, upper right abdomen." Reed pointed to his side, indicating the location, and glanced quickly at Dorothy. "Sound familiar?"

Dorothy raised an eyebrow and Griggs tilted his head in an unspoken question. Reed said, "Yeah lieutenant. Sure looks Blue to me."

Griggs nodded. "Good work, Reed. Make sure they don't mess with the scene, and let me know if you find anything else."

Reed shrugged his agreement, nodded toward Dorothy, and walked back to the technicians.

Dorothy took Griggs by the elbow and led him out of earshot. "Something's not right with this."

They both scanned the scene with interest. It was the first time Dorothy had been to one of the Blue crime scenes, and what she saw confused her. She said, "Why way out here?"

Griggs looked at her. "You tell me."

Dorothy shook her head and folded her arms across her chest. She chewed her lower lip as she thought. Sam waited in silence. Finally she said, "It doesn't fit the pattern, Sam."

"It fits."

The look she gave him was cold. "It's not downtown, it's the fucking country."

Sam shook his head. "The victim's a young gay man, shot in the upper right abdomen and left to die on site. No sign of struggle, no witnesses." He paused before asking, "How many of these killers do you think we have in Austin?"

"That's not what I mean." Dorothy touched Sam's shoulder and turned him to face her directly. "It's obviously the same guy. It's just that his pattern is changing." A gust of wind caught the edge of the silk scarf wrapped around her neck. The scarf lifted and tossed in front of her face. Dorothy said, "I think he knew this guy."

"Knew *this* guy?" Griggs pointed toward the crime scene.

"Yeah, I think so."

Griggs didn't wait for an explanation. He turned abruptly and jogged back to where Reed stood. When he stepped around the Taurus, the body came into view.

A pool of blood puddled around the young man and extended underneath the car. He wore blood-soaked jeans and a T-shirt. Griggs stepped closer and strained for a better view. Something about the slope of the young man's jaw looked vaguely familiar. The face was turned awkwardly toward the pavement and only one eye showed. It glinted in the halogen light.

Griggs was sure he had seen the man before but couldn't place him. A small Asian man wearing glasses and rubber gloves was on his knees snapping pictures. He waved to Griggs.

"Have you got an ID on the body yet, Charley?"

The Asian man lifted a hand signaling Griggs to wait. Griggs watched impatiently while the man worked.

After a couple of minutes, Charley lowered the camera and said, "No ID yet, Lieutenant, but we'll pick through his pockets in the lab. My guess is it's his car. See the keys?"

Griggs glanced where Charley pointed, at the dead man's hand. A key ring was looped through an index finger with a Ford ignition key clearly visible.

"Just ran the plates."

Griggs flinched, startled by the unexpected reply coming from behind him. "Sorry about that." Reed stepped backward before saying softly, "The Taurus is registered to a Marco Padilla."

That name, Marco Padilla, sounded familiar too. Sam had a good memory for detail, and the fact he couldn't place it bothered him. He turned his back on Reed. "Charley, let me know as soon as you have a positive ID."

"Sure thing."

Griggs strode purposefully back to his white Crown Victoria where Dorothy waited, leaning against the passenger door. She was looking at the eastern horizon. The darkness was just beginning to lift and they could see an indistinct border of indigo forming above the scrub oaks. The sun would be up soon. Where had Sam heard that name?

Dorothy sat quietly as Sam pulled out of the parking lot. She had a lot to think about. Quietly she scanned the ridge where the shooter had been waiting. She turned back to look down on the parking lot from the road. The pool shone in the early morning gloom like an obsidian disk. She tried to create a mental image of the attack and pictured the shooter, shielded in his vehicle, hidden in the shadows, waiting quietly for his victim.

If she was right, he had to know the victim, and he had to know the victim would be the last one out of the locker room. He wouldn't risk the shooting with a witness around. Or was she wrong? Could this have been another crime of convenience? Way out here? Dorothy pondered the possibilities.

They were halfway back to Sam's office before he remembered where he'd heard Marco Padilla's name. He turned to Dorothy and said, "We're making an unscheduled stop."

Dorothy's eyebrows rose but she didn't speak. Griggs turned north on Loop 1.

❖

The knock on my door was louder than it had a right to be this early on a Monday morning. I pulled my head off the pillow reluctantly and squinted in the dark. The knock sounded again, louder this time. I called, "Hold on a minute," and looked at the clock. It was 5:45.

When I opened the door, a middle-aged man in a rumpled suit showed his badge. I could see a woman standing just behind him on my porch. My eyes refused to focus, but the badge was silver, about the right size, and looked official. "What's the matter, Officer? What's happened?" That's when I recognized him. Lieutenant Griggs had put on a few pounds and his hair had gone gray.

He said, "Mr. Bell, I have some disturbing news. Can we come in?"

I tried to tether the panic building inside me. "What is it? What's wrong?"

"Please," the woman said, scanning the street traffic. "I think this would be easier if we could come inside."

"Yes, come in." I stepped aside and pulled the door closed behind them. I turned around with my arms folded across my chest and waited in silence for them to speak. Though my body language was giving a lecture on the rudeness of their unannounced early arrival, I knew they could read the fear in my eyes. Finally, Lieutenant Griggs found his voice. "I'm afraid someone you may know was shot last night. He was killed."

"Who?" I softened my stance.

My first thought was for Thatcher. Fear rippled up my spine and anxiety tightened my stomach. I focused my attention on Griggs, but the lady spoke next. "We're not sure. That's why we're here. The lieutenant believes you may know him." She shot an unreadable glance at Griggs. "We need you to come with us—"

"Who are you?" I snapped. I stared at her for a second before I noticed her puffy red eyes and rumpled clothing. Griggs's exhaustion was also evident.

Griggs ducked his head in apology, then shrugged and said, "I'm sorry, son. This is FBI Special Agent Bowles, and I'm Lieutenant Griggs from the Austin Police Department. Please forgive me. It's been a long night." He ran his fingers through his hair and sighed. When he spoke again, his voice was milder. "Do you remember me?"

I nodded, and he said, "Please, come with us."

"It's the shooter, isn't it?" I heard the words in my head before I spoke them. They sounded foreign floating through the air.

Griggs answered my query with a cold stare.

"I'll get dressed," I said, and didn't wait for a response. On my way back to my bedroom I tossed another question over my shoulder. "Where are we going?"

"West Austin Athletic Club," Griggs said.

I lost my center of gravity at the mention of the pool. I flashed to an image of swim practice and Thatcher sitting in his truck in the parking lot. The hair rose on the back of my neck. I forced images of Thatcher's Bushmaster .223 out of my head and tugged on a pair of jeans.

Griggs made a call on his cell phone while I dressed. I could hear the deep muffled sounds of a one-sided conversation emanating from the living room. By the time I joined them, the plan had changed. He explained we would be heading downtown instead of out to the pool. I shrugged, and the three of us piled into the white car parked in front of my house.

We made it to the coroner's office before the body. After parking the car, Lieutenant Griggs and Agent Bowles escorted me down the side stairs, through metal doors, and into a long tiled hallway. I felt like a death-row inmate heading to the gas chamber.

In fact, the examining room would do nicely as a gas chamber. The room was an overly bright, sterile, cold, concrete box with no windows. I took a seat on a cheap plastic chair and Griggs asked Bowles if she would stay with me for a minute. She nodded and set her briefcase on a folding card table before sitting in another plastic chair. I watched as Griggs pulled his cell phone out of his pocket and strolled off down the hallway. Bowles pushed back with her heels and leaned the back of the chair against the far wall. She sighed and closed her eyes.

When the two of us were alone I asked, "Who is it?"

The question seemed to startle her. "Hmmm?" she asked, opening her eyes and pretending like she didn't hear me.

"Who is it that died...that I'm supposed to know? You know... the body..."

She shook her head slowly. "Sorry. You need to tell us."

"Oh, I see. So that's how it works? You jerk me out of bed, drag me down here to identify a dead body, and don't even give me any indication who you think it is." My anxiety was building. I wanted a chance to get ready for this. I wanted a heads-up on whom to expect lying on the table—or the stretcher or whatever.

"I'm sorry. That's the way it needs to be."

"Why?" My voice sounded ragged, echoing off the bare walls.

"Look, I know this isn't easy—"

"Do you?"

She ignored the sarcasm and tipped her chair forward. It landed with a sharp click that hung in the still air of the stark room. "Yes. I do," she said. "But if we tell you who we think it is and you make an incorrect ID, based on our suggestion, it gives the appearance that we are trying to..." She gave up on her explanation. "It's just better this way," she said with a sense of resignation.

Hurried footsteps tapped up the hallway and Griggs pushed through the doorway. "They're here. Come this way," he said, holding the door open. We stepped through and Griggs led us into another cinderblock room, this one even more sterile. A lab bench leaned against a steel partition near the back, lined with beakers and metal equipment with serrated edges and sharp points that made me uncomfortable. A row of silver doors was inset into the wall to the right. A wiry Hispanic man scurried around a gurney parked in the center of the room. As we watched he stepped onto a little lever at each wheel, locking the gurney in place. I raised my eyes slowly to the top of the cart. A surgical green sheet was draped over the body.

Griggs said, "Thanks, Chas. Can you give us a minute?"

The Hispanic man shook his head, "No way, Griggs. I have to be here, we still haven't processed the body."

Agent Bowles placed her hand on my shoulder. Griggs stared hard at Chas for a second before Bowles said, "I think we need to get on with this."

Griggs dropped his eyes and turned his back, mumbling, "Okay, it's your show."

Bowles nodded to Chas and he carefully lifted the sheet with gloved hands. I fidgeted uncontrollably as he folded the sheet back. Marco's face stared at me from the gurney. Someone had tried to close his eyes but the lids had slid partway up and his jaw had dropped open, allowing his tongue to loll out of the side of his mouth. Just then I became aware of red stain seeping through the sheet. Blood began to drip onto the cement floor. The sound of each drop echoed in the silence. I turned to Griggs and said, "His name is Marco Padilla." I pulled away from Agent Bowles's grasp and bolted out to the hallway.

I made it halfway back to the staircase before I threw up.

❖

It took a full hour to answer all Lieutenant Griggs's questions. Agent Bowles sat at the far side of the table with her briefcase open, listening silently. Griggs explained that when he found out that the car in the lot at the pool was registered to Marco Padilla, he recognized the name from his notes of the investigation of my shooting years ago. Marco had been the one who found me in the alley that evening and was interviewed by the investigating officer while I was rushed to the hospital. Griggs figured I might be able to confirm that Marco was the victim and save time in their investigation. He was taken by surprise when I told him I had seen Marco not long before the shooting.

"So let me get this straight. You were swimming with the team, at West Austin Athletic Club last night?"

"Right."

He scribbled a note on the pad in his lap. "And Mr. Padilla was swimming with the team at the same time?"

"Right."

"So you and Mr. Padilla...are *friends?*" He emphasized the word and I knew he was asking me if we were lovers.

"We were friends," I said flatly. "We were not intimate."

"But you were...close?"

I wasn't sure what he was getting at. "Yeah. We were good friends. But like I said, we weren't involved, sexually."

Griggs nodded and looked down at his pad. "Can you give us some names of the others who swam with the team last night?"

"Sure, I guess so. You should probably ask Chris though."

"Chris?"

"Yeah, Coach Chris. He takes attendance."

"We will. But why don't you give us the names you remember?"

So I did. I pictured the pool and stepped mentally from lane to lane. I started with Chris, then Mitch and Marco and Kurt and sixteen others. I think I got everyone, though I might have missed one or two in the far lanes. I even mentioned noticing Danny pull into the parking lot.

I didn't mention Thatcher.

When I finished, Griggs took the list and scanned it quickly and handed it to Agent Bowles, who tucked it into her briefcase. Griggs asked a few more questions about my friendship with Marco. Every time I tried to find out about the investigation, he steered the conversation in another direction. I was unsteady and grateful when he said they were just about finished.

That's when Agent Bowles leaned forward. "Do you know if any of these men owns a rifle?" Her question hit me like a sucker punch.

My heart seemed to sink and an image from Thatcher's closet welled up in my mind's eye. Slowly, I shook my head.

Bowles watched me closely, but Griggs stood and stretched. "Okay, I think we have all we need right now."

I concentrated on Griggs, trying not to look at Bowles. He let me go, warning that they might need to speak with me again. He arranged for a handsome Hispanic officer to drive me back to my home. It was eight thirty when he dropped me off. I was so unnerved I was shaking before he pulled away from the curb.

Two questions kept echoing in my mind.

How am I going to tell Danny? Did Thatcher do this?

❖

"I will always be grateful."

Adam stood at the foot of Thatcher's bed. "Look at me, Thatcher."

Thatcher gazed up with bloodshot eyes. Adam's hazy image glowed in the sunshine. Adam said, "I will always be grateful. You know that."

Thatcher turned his head away and tears streamed down his cheeks. Adam stepped around the bed and lifted Thatcher's chin with his hand. When Thatcher opened his eyes, it was like he was staring into the light.

The knock at the door was unexpected. Adam's image dissipated slowly, leaving Thatcher squinting into the sunshine pouring through the blinds. All he could see was a shimmering rainbow halo. He closed his eyes again.

The knock was louder the second time. Thatcher opened his eyes and tried to focus on the murky image visible beyond the door's glass panes. The outline of Matt's form looked like an angel to Thatcher. *I'm dreaming,* he thought, and closed his eyes again.

The next time the knock was so loud it rattled the door. Thatcher raised his head and tried to concentrate on the glowing numbers on the face of his bedside clock: 9:10. He shook his head and looked again at the door. Matt's face was pressed to a glass pane, his cupped hand shading the glare. "Just a minute," Thatcher yelled, grabbing a pair of gym shorts from the floor.

❖

Thatcher's eyes were red and puffy, his face sporting a few days' growth. His hair was flattened on one side and a cowlick stood up on the other like a rooster tail. I could see sleep clinging to the corners of his eyes. His face looked bloated, and the skin around his mouth looked sallow and blotchy.

Still, as he struggled clumsily to unlock the door, I couldn't help thinking he was the most beautiful man I had ever seen. When he finally tugged the door open, I fought to keep from throwing my arms around him. Silently, he stepped back and motioned for me to come inside.

The room looked like the aftermath from a tornado. Clothes were strewn from the bedroom to the bathroom. The floor was scattered with remnants of take-out dining, half-empty Styrofoam cups, wadded waxed paper, a red-and-white box containing the bones of a chicken, and a banana peel. I could see piles of unwashed dishes stacked on the counter and a half-eaten pizza in a grease-stained cardboard box resting on the floor next to his desk. A mostly empty peach Snapple bottle sat next to his computer screen. Neglected houseplants drooped in yellowing dehydration.

Surveying the damage, I said, "What happened here?"

Thatcher blinked, scratched his chin, and shrugged. "I've been busy."

I moved through the room and tried to peer through the passage into his bedroom closet. A stack of cardboard boxes blocked my view.

Before I arrived, I had carefully planned what to say and do. I wanted to confront Thatcher about the gun and tell him I'd seen him at the pool last night. I wanted to drop Marco's name in conversation and gauge his reaction.

But as I stood in the midst of this destruction, I felt a sinking feeling in the pit of my stomach and a growing conviction that Thatcher was troubled, unbalanced…perhaps unhinged.

My soul didn't want to admit it but my mind would not let me ignore what I was seeing.

I looked at Thatcher and tears began to well up in his eyes.

In spite of my growing conviction, I pulled him toward me. He laid his head on my shoulder and sobbed. I held him for a few minutes, steadied my voice, and said, "We need to end this now, Thatcher."

He stiffened and I pushed him away gently, holding him at arm's length by the shoulders. I stared directly into his impossibly blue-green eyes. He looked back at me through his tears.

My voice was calm as I said again, "It's time to end this, right now."

Thatcher's tears stopped almost immediately. He seemed to harden himself, to draw from inner strength. He shook off my grasp and I was struck by the look in his eyes. It reminded me of the first time I'd seen him, before we met. There was pain in those eyes, a pain I didn't understand, couldn't comprehend.

He pulled the door open and in a steady, cold voice said, "If that's the way you feel, then go."

I looked at him. "Thatcher, you need…"

He just held the door and I looked into his eyes. For the first time, I saw a flash of anger. "What are you waiting for," he screamed. "Get the hell out of here!"

I left with my jaw clenched but one thing was for sure. I loved this man. That hadn't changed and it never would. I didn't know why he was driven to kill, but I did know he was out of control.

"You said that before, but I don't see the connection."

After a full night's sleep and a good breakfast, Sam was in the office early, determined to follow up every possible lead in the Blue investigation. A couple of hours of reviewing the case log had convinced him it was time to pull the team together to discuss the latest revelations. The Blue taskforce was assembled inside the conference room.

"You have to think of it from the perspective of opportunity, Sam." Dorothy Bowles scanned the faces in front of her. "We've been going on the assumption the killer has been selecting his targets at random. But that doesn't ring true with this last victim. Think about it. If the killer was looking for a convenient gay man to shoot, what was he doing out in the boonies?"

Sam sighed heavily. "Isn't it obvious? He was stalking the swim team."

"Exactly, Sam. A thrill killer, he kills at random. But a serial killer, he stalks *specific* victims." She made her way to the coffee urn. "This guy's smart. We know that. He's been killing for years without being caught." She added, "In spite of all the good work from you guys. I just don't see him parking in the bushes way out in the country, on the off-chance that a gay man might stroll through that parking lot alone." She shot a challenging glance in Griggs's direction. "That's what I mean, he knew this team. He might have even swum with this team. He had to know their schedule and their habits. And I'd bet money that he knew this victim too."

Sam nodded agreement. What Dorothy was saying made sense. So this guy knew this team…or about this team anyway. At last, he thought, something to go on.

He said, "Okay, I agree. This changes things." He strode to the whiteboard. "Reed, I want you and Connors to canvass the team members. Interview everyone that was at practice and everyone that wasn't. Find out where they were Thursday night. I want to know any connection with the victim as well. Find out if anyone has experience with guns."

He turned to Dorothy and asked, "What do you think we should be looking for, Bowles?"

"Find out who works, or used to work, in the health-care industry or has some knowledge about the human body. Like I said before, this guy knows his anatomy. You might also pay attention to the handedness of the guys, in case we get access to optometric records."

Sam asked Reed, "You heard her?" Reed nodded.

"Good. Johnson, I want you to go over the list of swimmers, cross-reference with changes in employment or residence and check out incarceration records. Look for someone who was out of Austin during the lull in the shooting schedule."

"Benson, you follow up with the victim's close friends. Find out whom he worked with and whom he played with. Then add their names to Johnson's list." Sam put his hands on his hips and glared down at his officers. "We've finally got what we've been looking for, gentlemen, suspects. Follow every lead. Blue has been on the books a long time. It's time to find this asshole."

There was a murmur of assent as officers rose in twos and threes and left the room.

❖

The wound in Bill's heart felt deep and profound. He tossed the paper to the floor and wept. Not again, not another one, he thought. His tears flowed freely.

Six weeks since the Ticket. Six weeks alone. How long must I wait? Why can't my targets make it through? Like the Ticket. Why? Even as he asked the question he answered it. *He isn't the one, there's another.*

Bill picked up his glasses and put them on before peering out at the rising moon, which was just a sliver in the late-evening sky. It would grow slowly into a shining disk and then shrink again. He poured another glass of Silver Oak merlot and toasted the moon.

"Next time," he said to the gathering darkness. "Next time I will not fail." *I want...no, I need my Ticket.*

Then he smiled briefly, realizing there was another...with sandy hair and sleek body. His thoughts trailed off into the nasty and he felt his cheeks flush in embarrassment. *No, not yet. This time I will not fail. This time I will have him.*

He turned slowly to the image on his computer. He wiped his eyes and peered into a grainy photo taken from a distance in fading evening light. It showed Marco at practice, wearing his swimsuit on deck. Just over his shoulder, Thatcher's upper body was barely visible.

He pressed the mouse button and dragged a rectangle over Thatcher's image. When he released the button, Thatcher's blurry image magnified to fill the screen.

There is another, he thought, and once more tasted the sweetness.

CHAPTER SIXTEEN

MATT

I thought about Thatcher for two days before I made my decision, my bewilderment only slightly tempering my anger.

Thatcher killed Marco. That thought just would not register in my brain. I know it's true, I told myself, though I couldn't really believe it. I had seen the gun. I had seen the destruction of his apartment. It had to be true. He was disturbed. He was sick. My logical mind kept repeating the words like a mantra: Thatcher was dangerous. Thatcher was a killer.

Still, a little voice in my subconscious rebelled. It ignored the evidence. It ignored the logic. It pleaded with me to rethink the whole thing. And I wanted to listen, but try as I might, I couldn't come up with another explanation that fit the facts.

Marco was my friend. I had to do something. And not just that, if I was right, Thatcher had shot me too. What was I going to do? Wait until he killed someone else, or shot me again? No. Finally, reason had to prevail. This had to stop.

With conviction, I said to myself, "This ends now."

I dug Lieutenant Griggs's card out of my wallet and sat down on my couch, grabbing my cell phone from the side table. My hands shook as I punched in the numbers.

A female voice answered. "Austin PD, Homicide."

"I need to speak with Lieutenant Griggs."

"Can I tell him who is calling?"

I told her my name. Griggs came on the line almost instantly.

"Hello? Matt?" It sounded like a question.

"Lieutenant, I have something to tell you."

He waited while I gathered my thoughts.

"I have a…friend." I cringed at the word. Thatcher had become so much more to me. "The other day I was at his house and he has a Bushmaster .223."

Silence filled the connection; Griggs waited for me to continue. The pause was very uncomfortable. A knot began building in my throat before I spoke again. When I finally gave him the details my voice sounded higher and less confident.

I told him about discovering Thatcher's gun and mentioned that Thatcher swam with our team and that he knew Marco. I told him about seeing Thatcher in the pool parking lot the night of Marco's murder. I told him about my trip to Thatcher's place two days before and the confused condition that I found there. I told him my fears that Thatcher was mentally unraveling. I paused and told Griggs I was afraid Thatcher might be the shooter.

I waited for his response.

Griggs waited before he said, "So you think this guy, this Thatcher Keeney…you believe he may be the shooter?"

With my voice wavering, I said, "Yes." After another uncomfortable pause I added, "God, I truly want to be wrong, Lieutenant. But it just…it just makes too much sense."

Griggs asked me for more, and I gave it to him in spades. I told him about finding the stack of newspaper articles covering the shootings stuffed in Thatcher's desk drawer. I explained how I became suspicious after seeing Thatcher try to hide them from me when I showed up unannounced that afternoon.

I could tell Griggs was becoming excited about the possibility. By the time I finished, I sensed he couldn't wait to get me off the line.

Before he hung up, he warned me to stay away from Thatcher and asked me to keep him informed of my whereabouts over the next few days.

My head began to pound and my stomach began to churn. Finally, I bolted to the bathroom. For the second time in two days I threw up.

❖

"So tell me again why this guy...what's his name again?"

"Bell, Matt Bell."

"The guy who IDed the body?"

Griggs nodded.

"Why does Mr. Bell think Keeney's the killer?" Dorothy was sitting in her temporary office. The mid-morning sun shined surreally bright through the windowpane.

Griggs squinted into the glare and said, "Several things. The gun, for one, and he also noticed a change, you know, in Keeney's behavior. At least that's what Bell says. And the articles, Bell said he saw Keeney hiding articles about the shootings. What do you make of that?"

Dorothy looked at him. "What do you think?"

"I don't know. It's complicated."

"How is it complicated?" Dorothy moved around to the front of her desk so Griggs wouldn't have to squint into the sunshine.

"Keeney's connected to the investigation."

Dorothy raised her eyebrows, surprised, and waited.

"He's a friend of one of the early victims." Griggs quickly scanned his notes. "A...Adam Malloy, the second—no, wait—the first survivor. They lived—"

Dorothy held up her hand. "Wait a minute. Are you saying Keeney lived with one of the survivors? Do you mean they were lovers?"

"I don't know for sure but...yeah, I guess so. Looks that way anyway."

Dorothy pulled a notebook from the top drawer in her desk and snatched a yellow pencil from the tray on her desk. She began frantically scribbling on a page. "Go on."

"So like I said, they lived together, Keeney and Malloy. When I tried to reach Malloy…"

Dorothy stopped writing. "You tried to reach Malloy?"

"Yeah, I promised all the survivors when the trail went cold, I would let them know if the investigation ever heated up again."

Dorothy sat motionless, examining Sam's face. He looked tired mostly, but beneath that she saw concern for the victims. The more she knew about this guy, the more she liked him. She looked down at her notes and said, "Go on."

"Like I said, when I tried to contact Adam Malloy, this Keeney guy answered the phone. He told me that Malloy had died."

"How?"

"AIDS. He said it was AIDS."

Dorothy made a notation and idly twisted her hair. An idea started to form on the periphery of her consciousness. Quickly she flipped back in the notepad scanning the pages. When she located what she was looking for, she carefully read the entire page before asking, "Did you ask when Malloy died?"

"No, is it important?"

"Everything's important, Sam."

"I know," he said. "There's something else."

"What, Sam, what aren't you telling me?"

"This Bell guy?"

"Yeah."

"So, he's the one who called."

"That's what you said, so?"

"So he's one of the survivors too."

Dorothy sat back and exhaled loudly, tossing her pencil onto the table.

"This is Danny. After the beep, tell me who you are."

I hung up without leaving a message and stared at my phone. Four days had passed since Marco's death, two days since I'd called Griggs about Thatcher and *still* I hadn't heard from Danny. Marco's funeral service was set for tomorrow, and I'd left countless messages at Danny's home number and cell phone.

Reluctantly, I grabbed my keys and trudged out to my car; the time had come to track him down. The afternoon had been sunny and mild, and the shadows were starting to lengthen as I drove up Duval to Forty-fifth. The traffic was light and five minutes later I pulled into the drugstore parking lot.

A skulking cashier frowned when asked if I could speak with Danny. He directed me to the back of the building where I found a young woman standing behind the pharmacy counter. She stood in front of a computer wearing a white smock, a nametag pinned above her right breast that read, HI, I'M SANDY. I leaned on the counter until she raised her eyes from the computer screen. She said, "Sorry, Can I help you?"

"I'm trying to reach Danny Mills."

"I'm sorry. He's not in this afternoon. Is there something I can do for you?"

"No…Well, yes, actually, there is. You see, I'm a friend of Danny's and I've been trying to locate him for the past few days without any luck. I'm…well, I'm just worried, I guess. Can you tell me if he's been into work this week?"

She didn't answer.

I found it pretty easy to sound pathetic. "Normally I wouldn't ask but we've just lost a mutual friend. He died a couple of days ago and I need to let Danny know."

"I'm really not supposed to…" she said.

"I know it would be so hard on Danny if he missed the funeral. It's tomorrow."

That did it. She reached into a file stored under the counter, turning her back on me, and shuffled through the papers in the file for a few seconds When she turned back around she said, "Look, if anyone asks, you…you didn't hear this from me. The time sheet says Danny called in sick last week, but he should have been here this morning and never showed. Maybe you should check his house."

I thanked her and dashed out of the store.

❖

In the foggy grayness, Adam wavered into view. Thatcher wasn't sure if he was really there or if he was having another hallucination. He hadn't eaten in three days. He felt dizzy and weak, so he eased slowly to the floor.

Adam said, *"Are you going to let it end like this?"*

"End what? Like what?" Thatcher answered.

"Your life," Adam said. "Like this." He tilted his chin toward the destruction in the room.

Thatcher lay back against the wall and sighed. "What good is it, Adam? What else can I do?"

"You can go after him. You can get yourself together and go after him."

"But he doesn't want me."

"He doesn't know what he wants."

"He told me it had to end, Adam. He doesn't want me."

"No, Thatcher, he wants you." Adam crouched down next to him and ran his fingers gently through Thatcher's hair. "That I know. He wants you. Probably more than he knows."

Thatcher raised his eyes to Adam. With tears rolling down his face he asked, "Then why? Why did he..."

Thatcher dropped his head, softly sobbing.

Adam nudged him over and sat down next to him on the floor. Thatcher laid his head on Adam's shoulder and closed his eyes.

Adam said, "I want you to do something for me, Thatch, just one more thing for me. I want you to fight for this guy. I want you to get up, clean up, and pull yourself together." Adam held Thatcher's chin in his hand and gently turned his face so he could look into his eyes. Adam said, "I want you to go after this guy. Make him tell you why he said what he did to you. Make him tell you, Thatcher."

Thatcher's tears washed down his face and he dropped his head slowly. Adam pulled Thatcher close and gently snuggled his face into Thatcher's hair.

When Thatcher woke, he was alone. He sat in the gathering darkness of the room for a long time listening to the echo of Adam's words in his head. Through the window, he watched as the light seeped from the sky. He kicked off the covers and eased out of the bed. He tried to stretch as he stood, but he had to reach out to steady himself against the wall as the ceiling began to spin. His knees gave out and he sat down hard on the side of the bed. Slowly his surroundings shifted back into view. He waited until he felt steady again and stood, more slowly this time, testing his strength. His head remained clear.

He shuffled toward the bathroom.

"He works in a pharmacy—that's sort of medical. Lots of people named him as a close friend of the victim, so he definitely knew Padilla. We've been trying to get in touch but so far no luck. Turns out he's sort of disappeared since last Thursday. And he swims with the team, but according to the coach's records he wasn't in the water that night. And here's the main thing, Lieutenant, he's the guy Bell says he saw sitting in the parking lot in his truck." Benson's bald head pivoted from Lieutenant Griggs to Dorothy Bowles. "Two other team members mentioned they noticed him in the lot too."

"So he was at the scene," Griggs said, "which makes me wonder what he was doing at practice if he wasn't going swimming."

"That's one of the things we need to ask him, but like I said, so far we haven't been able to track him down."

Griggs nodded, and Agent Bowles asked, "Is he left-handed?"

"Don't know yet."

"What about a record? Has he been in trouble before?"

"Clean as a whistle. Parking tickets, that's all I found."

"Go talk to the guy, Benson. Track him down and bring him in for questioning if you have to. I don't think we have enough for a warrant, so go easy. But ask him if he has a gun, see what he says. Let me know if he's not being cooperative." Griggs nodded. "If he says yes, I'll take that to the judge and argue that he has something to hide."

Griggs turned his back to the table and scribbled on the whiteboard. The members of the Blue task force sat in high-backed leather chairs sprawled around one end of the conference room. A few had pulled their chairs up to the table, taking notes. Others had shoved their chairs back, but everyone was concentrating on Griggs at the head of the table. A quarter moon in the west was visible through the window.

Griggs sat down and flipped through the casebook. "What did you find out about this Keeney guy, Reed?"

"Connors is on his way to talk to him. It took a while to get the warrant, but we finally got it a few minutes ago. He's going in after the gun. We got Bradley watching the place, but the guy hasn't moved in a couple of days."

"You sure he's inside?"

"Neighbor lady says it's his car in the garage, and we're seeing lights coming on in the back of the house. Someone's there."

"Good, what else you got?"

"Finished the preliminary background checks on the rest of the list. Three guys have a medical background and fit Bowles's profile. But one of them has an alibi. Turns out most of the swimmers met at a Jason's Deli after practice. This guy was with them, name's Johnny Billings. He's a physical therapist, spent some time in the system too." Reed shook his head. "Times don't check out though."

Griggs nodded. "What about the other two?"

Reed ran his finger down the page of an open spiral notebook. "Martin Hansen, a home-health-care nurse, worked in a hospital for a while. No adult record, had some trouble as a juvenile, and…" he flipped the notebook pages…"a Jim Avery—doesn't swim. He's a friend of Padilla's, worked as an X-ray technician for a while just out of college. This guy was in the military, a member of the US Army Marksmanship Unit, selected marksman of the year in '92."

Griggs glanced at Bowles. "Good. Follow up on them and let me know. Let's see," he looked up to the lunar calendar tacked to the bulletin board, "we've got twenty-two days until the next new moon."

"Lieutenant." Bowles pushed back from the table and stood. "If I can just…"

Griggs yielded the floor and Bowles said, "I just want to caution that this guy could be deconstructing."

Blank stares around the table.

"What does that mean, Agent Bowles?" Reed asked.

"It means the pattern has been broken. And this guy's becoming more dangerous, less predictable."

Griggs sighed.

Connors spoke next, his voice sounded contemptuous. "This guy's a cold-blooded killer. We've chased him for years. We know he's dangerous."

Griggs glared at Connors. *What was his problem?*

Dorothy shook her head. "That's not what I'm saying. Things have changed, he may be coming…"

Every eye watched Dorothy as she searched for the right words. "Look, when this type of compulsive killer changes his pattern it means something. Usually it signals a *deconstruction*. That means the inner system that he has built his murderous paradigm on— the story he's built around the murders—it no longer applies. He becomes less stable and the patterns can shift. I'm just cautioning. The rules of the game have changed. That's all, Sergeant."

Reed asked, "What pattern, exactly? Are you talking about the victim profile, the pacing of the attacks…the weapon?"

"Exactly, Detective, the entire MO. He could search out different targets, possibly use a different weapon, and we can't count on the carefully timed attacks based on the phases of the moon anymore. He's already changed his MO by hunting in a rural area and stalking a specific target. Just keep that in mind."

Griggs stood. "Okay, you've got your assignments." He tossed his notebook into his briefcase and clicked it shut. The task-force members stood and gradually filed out the door. When Griggs returned to his desk he found a stack of messages in the center. He scanned the pink slips quickly, pulling up abruptly when he reached one in particular He looked toward the office bull pen and called, "Reed, Benson…"

The heads of both detectives poked over the tops of the gray paneled partitions like prairie dogs popping out of their holes. Benson had a phone to his ear. Griggs said, "Can I see you in my office?"

Benson pointed at the phone and Griggs shook his head. "Now!"

Benson hung up quickly and fell in behind Reed, who was already heading toward Griggs's office. Griggs closed the door.

"I just got a call from Danny Mill's place," Griggs said, then nodded to Benson. "I want you guys to get over there pronto and check this out."

❖

Light shining through the garage apartment's windows cast yellow rectangles onto the paved alleyway. Glass shards sparkled in the pale light as I clanged through the wrought-iron gateway and climbed the stairs. A breeze ricocheted up through the metal stairway, sucking the warmth from my legs, and I shivered. Pressing the doorbell with my head leaning against the screen door and my arms wrapped tightly around my chest, I listened to the electronic ding-dong dissipate into the atmosphere.

I waited. The wind died, but the cold worked its way into my body. Already my toes and ears were numb and a slight tingling was starting in my calves. I looked down the steps and scanned across to the yard that separated the garage apartment from the main house. The main house looked deserted. I could see through French doors to a softly lit area where warm light reflected off brightly colored ceramic Talavera tiles. I pressed the doorbell again and the chimes sounded.

I waited, straining to hear movement inside. I leaned against the porch railing and peered through the window. Small slits of

Danny's front room came into view between the slats of his mini-blinds. I could just make out a shredded jumble of paper piled on top of the coffee table. Otherwise, the room was immaculate. Every light in the apartment blazed. No sign of Danny, no sleeping form on the couch, no headset-wearing figure boogying across the carpet, no rigid body lying in a pool of blood.

I waited some more. Finally I gave up. Disappointed, I crept back down the stairs, wondering where he could be. At the base of the stairs I looked around the building's corner and peered into the garage. Danny's car was parked in the first stall. Uneasiness mushroomed in the pit of my stomach.

What was going on?

I stepped into the driveway and gazed up at the bedroom window. The blinds were open and the lights were on. My heart began to flutter.

I searched the garage for a way to climb up and see into his bedroom window. There was no ladder, no tree growing next to the building, no fence or railing. I climbed the steps again, resolving to get inside one way or the other.

At the landing, once again I leaned over the railing and studied the scene through the window. The window was far from the railing and seemed latched. I knocked on the door as loud as I could. No answer. I tugged the screen door open and examined the door lock. It was a double-cylinder dead bolt.

Great, now what?

I kicked the door. I laid my head against the silver knocker, sighing in frustration and, with waning hope, gently twisted the doorknob. It turned. The door edged open. I stared through the crack, not believing my luck.

Danny would not leave his door open!

My heartbeat racing, I hurried through the door and scanned the living room. "Danny?" I called.

The sound of a car engine in the alleyway startled me. I turned in that direction and almost screamed when I saw a figure staring at me through the window. It was my own reflection. My palms sweaty and my heart pounding so fast it sounded like a drum roll, I lurched to the back wall and twisted the rods on three sets of mini-blinds. They closed with a snap.

I stood for a minute, trying to still my nerves. When my head finally cleared, I moved around the couch and examined the pile of paper I'd noticed on the coffee table. It was a jumble of fettuccini-shaped strips, obviously machine-shredded. On one side the surface was colored and glossy—a photo. It was several photos, actually. I tried to put together the pieces and quickly assembled a Picassoesque image of Marco.

Dropping the shredded photos, I bolted toward the bedroom door.

Danny's body reclined on the bed. I went through the motions of checking for a pulse, but it was obvious that he had been dead for quite some time. I reached for the telephone and dialed 911.

Walking unsteadily out onto the landing, I pulled the door closed and lumbered down the stairs in a state of shock. In the alleyway I leaned against the limestone wall and threw up.

I wiped my chin on my sleeve and sat down on the bottom step of the stairway. As I waited for the police, I bent forward, wrapped my arms tightly around my knees, and gently rocked myself. Frosty stillness settled over the area and I began to shake.

This time, it wasn't from the cold.

Chapter Seventeen

Matt

The next morning broke cold and clear. I pulled up to the curb in front of my house exhausted, after spending much of the night answering questions.

Two detectives grilled me for what seemed like an eternity before Lieutenant Griggs showed up with Agent Bowles. Griggs nodded and led the way up the stairs. I watched the two of them speak briefly to a group of crime-scene investigators on Danny's porch.

After dismissing the other officers, Griggs looked at me shivering and asked me to follow him. I nodded and the three of us trudged over to Griggs's car. The lieutenant held the passenger door open, while Bowles slipped into the backseat. Griggs kicked on the engine as soon as he closed the door. The three of us sat together in the car for about an hour.

Bowles and Griggs's questions were mostly about Danny and his relationship to Marco. I answered them as best I could. After a few minutes, I tried to get them to reciprocate, to no avail. They were not interested in sharing information with me.

Neither one would tell me anything about Danny's death or its connection to the serial murders. Griggs refused to enlighten me as to whether he thought this death was connected to the serial murders, and Bowles simply would not talk about the investigation at all.

I really wanted to know whether Griggs had followed up on my tip about Thatcher. But I never asked because I wasn't ready to hear the answer. When he finally let me go, it was four in the morning. I was sent home with instructions to get some rest and to expect a call from him soon.

I left Danny's neighborhood and drove through the dark, still night, trying to lose myself in aimless wandering. I navigated the streets for a little over two hours, waiting for the sun to rise and my head to clear. I didn't relish the idea of entering an empty house alone.

I opened the door to my green Miata, slogged up the sidewalk, and froze when I spotted him through the cedar slats in the fence. He wore an oversized, dark-green goose-down coat pulled tight around him. He leaned back against the bottom panes in my French door, his chin tucked neatly into the crook of an elbow, his eyes closed. As I peered at him through the fence, a brisk morning breeze freshened and lifted the hair from his forehead.

He was beautiful, and I wanted him more right then than I had ever wanted anyone.

I pushed through the gate. The sound of the latch jangling woke him and he scrambled unsteadily to his feet. I moved toward him, pulling him close in my arms and smelling the scent of shampoo in his hair. I said, "Please, don't leave me." Tears began to well up in my eyes.

He squeezed me tight, murmuring, "It's okay, Matt, I'm here now."

I was surprised by my own reaction. If it had been a normal day, I might have turned away. But not after what I had just lived through. Right then, my heart trumped everything. I let go emotionally, weeping.

Thatcher shushed me softly and rocked me in his arms, patiently waiting while I pulled myself together. I had just lost my two best friends, and the spate of recent killings had stirred painful, deeply buried memories. So, I cried on his shoulder until my legs became weak and the two of us finally had to sit down on my porch. As we settled I noticed how pale and thin he looked. His features were sharper than I remembered—the line of his jaw, his drawn lips, and his sunken cheeks. And his eyes, those beautiful haunting eyes, had a hollow, lonely look. I wiped the tears from my face and asked, "Are you okay?"

"Yeah, I'm okay," he said.

Just then a yellow cab turned the corner and parked behind my car. I cringed when I saw my mother's petite frame step out of the back door. She tugged an oversized carry-on bag behind her and set it on the sidewalk. Searching through her purse, she found her pocketbook.

Thatcher and I sat spellbound, huddled together leaning against my door.

The overblown emotion I had felt just minutes before soured in a sea of churning anger, and I felt an unwelcome wave of nausea as I watched her spin in our direction, towing her luggage up the walkway with the determination of a steam engine.

She reached the gate and pushed through it without looking up. When she did, Thatcher and I, still holding each other, stared up at her from our seats on the porch.

She pulled back and clutched at her chest like she feared her heart would leap through her sternum. She glared at the two of us. Her eyes darted back and forth between Thatcher and me for what seemed like hours before finally settling on my face.

"What are you doing? People can see you out here." She glanced up the street nervously.

As I sat holding Thatcher on my porch gazing up at the wispy streams of breath trailing out of my mother's nose, I wondered what fantasies she had concocted about my life and what fallacies she had selected to support them.

After an uncomfortable moment of silence, I said, "Thatcher, this is my mother."

The two of us scrambled to our feet, and he held his hand out to shake, saying, "Thatcher Keeney."

To my total surprise, she shook it and asked, "So, why are you wrestling with my son on his porch?"

I asked, "Mom, what are you doing here?"

Just then Thatcher's knees buckled and he crumpled slowly toward the ground. I caught him by the shoulders and the two of us sat down hard. I let his body lean my direction and carefully cradled his head in my lap. Mom let go of her bag and bounded toward Thatcher with an agility belying her age. She straightened his legs and touched his forehead with a practiced hand.

"He's burning up. This man is burning up." She grabbed the handle on the door.

"Unlock your door," she commanded, lifting his head gently from my lap. I stared at her but she nodded, nudging me out of the way. "We need to get him inside and call a doctor." Her voice had softened.

I stood and fumbled through my pockets for the key, unlocked the door, and we carried Thatcher inside together. He came to as we laid him on the couch. He struggled to sit up but gave up after a few seconds, finally deciding to lean on one elbow. He looked at me with a dazed expression. Mom knelt in front of him and softly guided his head down onto a cushion. "I'm okay," he said without conviction.

"You're not okay," Mom said. "You have a fever, you're light as a feather, and you just passed out on the porch. You need to see a doctor."

"It's just…I haven't been eating well…" Thatcher looked up at me with sad eyes. He raised his head and shook it gently. "It's been a tough time, stress…"

Mom's focus shifted my direction. She said, "Are you okay? You've lost weight too." She stood and placed her hand on my forehead.

"I'm all right." I shook off her touch.

"You look sick. Both of you." Her eyes scanned my face.

Tears welled in my eyes. She wrapped her arms around me and held me for a few minutes, shushing me and rocking me like I was still her baby. Finally, she led me to the couch. Thatcher swung his legs around and I sat next to him. Mom tugged her carry-on bag from the porch, laid it flat on my living-room rug, and sat on it in front of us.

She propped her elbows on her knees and looked up at me with imploring eyes. Her voice was without malice and didn't waver in the least as she said, "Now, you're going to tell me what is going on here."

I didn't know what to say, so I started with Lieutenant Griggs's phone call and the first murder. She grimaced when I mentioned the shooter.

I knew she'd remember Griggs. She and my father had raced to Austin right after I was shot. Marco had called them from the hospital. They were waiting in the hallway when Griggs first tried to question me in the recovery room.

I told her about the bartender who had been murdered in the alleyway behind the Can. I told her about swimming with the team on Thursday and tried to tell her about Marco, but I broke down again.

She was waiting patiently for me to continue when the three of us heard the gate jingle open. We watched through the windowpanes as a gangly, uniformed police officer trailed his fingers across his holstered pistol before wiping his feet on my mat. He unclipped the safety strap on his holster with his right hand and knocked with his left.

I lurched toward the door and opened it abruptly. The young police officer stepped back, obviously surprised. I said, "Do you need something else?"

His expression went blank and I could tell that he was trying to figure out what I meant. I attempted to smile reassuringly. "Did Lieutenant Griggs send you? Does he need to ask me something else?"

"No, sir," he said formally. "I need to speak with Thatcher Keeney." He lowered his voice when he said, "It's police business."

Thatcher's expression was a mixture of astonishment and curiosity as he stood shakily and moved to the door. I stepped aside, a sensation of dread building in my stomach. Mom now leaned against the bar with an astonished expression.

Thatcher said, "I'm Thatcher Keeney. What seems to be the problem, Officer?"

The policeman said, "It would be better if you could come with me to the station. We have some questions for you."

Thatcher glanced back at me. "Sure."

They walked together to the police car. I watched Thatcher grab the doorframe to steady himself as he slid into the backseat. The officer closed the door and paced quickly around the car to the driver's side. I felt Mom standing beside me, and the two of us peered through the slats in the gate as the police car pulled away from the curb.

"Well, I never." Mom sighed.

I just shook my head.

Thatcher had no idea what was going on, but he did realize this was no ordinary police inquiry. On his way out of his carriage house that morning, he'd noticed the police car parked down the hill near the golf course. The cruiser had a clear view of the carriage house. It crossed Thatcher's mind that the officer might just be watching him. He dropped the thought, convinced his paranoia was unwarranted. But as soon as he saw the uniform on Matt's porch, he knew the officer had come for him. On the drive down to Seventh Street, his mind roiled with uncomfortable possibilities.

Thatcher sat on the ratty couch in Lieutenant Griggs's office, watching a different policeman fidget nervously as he leaned against the doorjamb. Thatcher considered asking what was going on but the young man was studiously avoiding eye contact.

A large oak desk facing the door dominated the tiny office. A matching chair on rollers had been shoved back against the wall behind the desk. A row of small, streaked windows built into the wall above the desk looked northward. The couch Thatcher sat on had clearly seen better days. One frayed armrest pressed against a bare stucco wall while the other nudged the door frame. A computer terminal sat at an angle on a corner of the desk. Thatcher watched a dizzying, kaleidoscopic pattern of colored lines flow across its face. A collection of silver-framed photos clustered along the edge of a desk pad. Two ceramic coffee cups holding a mismatched assortment of pens and pencils sat sentinel, guarding a desk lamp sporting a glass shade tinted green.

Griggs finally came in, carrying a folder. "Thanks, Bradley," he said. "Could you ask Detective Reed to step in, please?" Officer Bradley nodded and eased into the hallway. Thatcher listened to the dull slap of his footsteps on the concrete floor before focusing on Griggs. He watched as the lieutenant stepped gracefully around the desk and sat in the oak chair, rolling it smoothly forward. Griggs flicked his gray eyes quickly up at Thatcher before dropping them to the folder in his hands.

Finally, Griggs said, "Mr. Keeney, I'm Lieutenant Griggs. We spoke on the phone a few days ago."

The door opened and a pudgy man with a shock of curly red hair stepped inside.

Griggs introduced the man as Detective Reed, and Reed shook Thatcher's hand before sitting on the side of the lieutenant's desk. Griggs said, "Mr. Keeney, I had you brought down here this morning to ask you a few questions. Would you like some coffee?"

Thatcher shook his head.

Griggs opened the bottom drawer of his desk and pulled out a tattered old notebook. He set it on the desk pad and flipped through the first few pages before finding what he was looking for. He read the passage several times before fixing Thatcher with a determined stare.

"Where were you on the evening of December 12th…last Sunday?"

Thatcher stared at him for a moment. "I don't know. I guess I was home alone most of the night."

"Are you sure?"

Thatcher closed his eyes as he tried to remember. It wasn't easy; the week had been fractured and difficult. Finally, he looked up and said, "I think so. I remember dropping by the pool, but didn't stay long. I just drove back home and went to bed early."

Griggs changed tack abruptly and asked, "Do you have a gun, Mr. Keeney?"

Thatcher stared at him, unsure what he meant. Finally, he said, "A gun? What is this about, Lieutenant?"

"Please just answer the question."

Thatcher's anger flared and he responded, without thinking, "No, I don't."

Griggs waited. After a few seconds he said, "Are you saying that you don't own a gun?"

Thatcher then remembered the Bushmaster and blanched. He tried to shake the fogginess from his head and said, "I mean, yes. Well...sort of...I mean, I guess, yeah—I own one. But I've never even fired it. I was just...I was..." He sighed heavily and sat back dejected. This was not going well. He wiped his tired eyes.

Mother seemed to sense my anger and frustration. She retreated to my guest bedroom with her luggage in tow, after announcing she would be staying overnight.

I was exhausted. My whole being seemed to droop with the weight of the loss of my two best friends and the guilt of turning Thatcher in. I slumped onto my couch and let the world spin around me. In my head, recrimination ebbed and flowed.

After a few minutes, Mom padded across the hardwood floors, wrapped in a terry-cloth robe. She carried her makeup kit under her arm.

"I'm going to take a shower," she said, as if the only thing that mattered was cleanliness. "You should decide what you're going to wear to the funeral."

A blank expression covered my face. I asked, "You know about Marco?"

"I know," she said, and spun on her heel, her slippers slapping the hardwoods as she marched toward the restroom. "Muggy called."

When she reached the bathroom, she leaned against the door frame and said, "You think I'd come all this way without an invitation if it weren't an emergency?" She stepped into the bathroom and closed the door firmly.

Muggy (Margaret) Padilla had been Mom's best friend since grade school. The two of them were raised on adjacent farms in the east New Mexico desert. Together, they comprised the entire 1953 graduating class of Shady, New Mexico. After graduation, Mom headed to Las Cruces and New Mexico State University, where she met my dad. Muggy followed her brother Buddy to Southwest Texas State in San Marcos, where she met Marco's dad, Paulo.

Through the years the two women had monitored each other's lives with an intensity bordering on insanity. They were each other's maid of honor and were in the delivery room together for my birth, then Marco's fourteen days later.

In the years since, their friendship had survived the rigors of living miles apart, the death of Paulo, and the varied frustrations of two lives diverging in separate directions—Mom's more and more conservative, Muggy's steadfastly, stridently liberal. After Paulo's death in the late eighties, Marco was sent to stay with my family while Mom traveled to Texas to stay with Muggy while she "pulled herself together."

Marco and I became fast friends after discovering our mutual sexual orientation and shared reluctance to explain things to our families.

After graduation, Marco and I decided to attend the University of Texas together. Muggy and Mom were ecstatic. Personally, I have always suspected their excitement resulted more from the realization the situation would lead to more chances for interaction than from happiness their children would not be alone in college.

Regardless, Marco and I remained close. A few years later, we would run into Danny and the troupe would be complete. My stomach lurched at the thought of my two dead friends, and an edgy emptiness began to gnaw at the pit of my stomach.

Of course Mom would be the first person Muggy called after Marco's death. I should have expected it.

The shower kicked on and I lifted my tired body from the couch. Wearily, I shuffled to the bedroom and threw open my closet. I flipped through slacks and shirts and hanging bags until I located my black Bill Blass suit. I tugged it out of the suit bag, laid it on the bed, and turned to stare at my reflection in the wall mirror. Dark circles surrounded my eyes, and my face looked drawn and tired. I sat on the bed and ran my fingers through my hair. *What was I going to do now?*

❖

When we pulled into the parking lot at the Weed-Corley-Fish Funeral Home, Mom took Muggy's hand and led her gently inside. I waited in the car, letting them go in together—alone. Muggy had been distraught. I was hurting too. And I didn't feel like I could share my feelings. I didn't want to bottle them up inside, but I didn't know any way to express what I was feeling around Muggy.

True to form, Mom was preoccupied with Muggy. I could read it on her face: *There is nothing as bad as the suffering of a mother who has lost a child.*

Maybe not, I thought bitterly, but try losing your two best friends in two days and watching the police carry off the love of your life.

Add in the guilt of being the one to turn him in, along with the possibility that he may be a cold-blooded mass murderer.

I nearly bolted from the car when Jim Avery pulled up in his red Toyota Highlander.

"Matt," he said, opening his car door. "I'm so sorry about Marco. Are you okay?"

"No," I said, fighting to control my emotions.

Jim stepped close and, as we hugged, he murmured soft words of encouragement. I tried to explain the entire situation. "It's not just Marco. It's Danny too—and Thatcher."

He looked at me with a puzzled expression. "What's wrong with Danny and Thatcher?"

"Danny's dead, Thatcher was arrested." I tried to make my voice flat and emotionless.

"What?"

I nodded slowly.

"Wait," he stammered. "I don't get it. Danny's dead?"

I nodded again.

"How—did he die, I mean? Are you saying Thatcher murdered Marco—and Danny too? I don't believe it."

I shook my head. "I don't either…I mean, I don't think so, I mean…I hope not." My voice began to crack and I worked to choke back a sob. A single tear rolled down my cheek.

The parking lot was beginning to fill. Carloads of mourners clad in dark colors shuffled in twos and threes toward the funeral parlor. Through the sunny glare I recognized Coach Chris's shiny red Tundra pickup truck parked in the shade, and in the distance the odd-shaped, bulky Stephanie, Sean's nurse, walked across the parking lot. Sean had been Marco's lover before the injury left him a quadriplegic.

Jim grabbed my arm and led me toward the building. We stepped through the entrance and he guided me down a hallway to a seating area. The spot was sheltered from the entrance hall by a flimsy felt-covered divider. We sat down on a small floral sofa so close together our knees touched. He leaned forward and said, "Now, tell me what's happening."

So I filled him in. He sat speechless through my entire presentation, waiting patiently for me to finish.

"God, Matt, what's going on here?"

I was so exhausted I couldn't answer. I just stared back at him, shaking my head. Thirty hours without sleep was affecting me. I felt light-headed and disconnected from reality.

"Are you okay?" he asked.

"No. I just want to get through this, then go home and sleep for a month."

"Then that's what we're going to do…get you through this." He nodded with conviction and took my arm again, leading me toward the shuffling crowd filing through the double doors on their way to the service.

There was a small delay before the service started to allow mourners time to view the body. We sat on the hard benches near the back of the chapel and watched a small contingent shuffle past the open casket near the altar. I scanned the room looking for Mom and Muggy. They were huddled together in the first pew. Mom looked fashionably severe in a sleek black dress that emphasized her slim figure, and Muggy was swathed in billowing folds of black taffeta. Muggy was fragile despite her bulk. She leaned on Mom and dutifully acknowledged the condolences proffered from those that approached. The crowd surrounded the two women, and occasionally people would step forward individually and in small groups with their heads bowed. With hugs and handshakes Muggy sent them on their way, all the while studiously avoiding looking in the direction of the casket.

The atmosphere in the chapel was artificial. What was meant to pass for soothing organ music hissed softly from a set of audio speakers hidden in the foliage. Baskets of Boston ferns bracketed the altar and enormous floral arrangements, piled deep on either side, spilled down the nave and bathed the chapel in gaudy color. The whole effect made me wince. If Marco were here he wouldn't have liked what he saw. It was too traditional, even slightly cheesy. It was like a funeral satire instead of a solemn ritual.

The service was mercifully quick. The Episcopalian minister Muggy had selected filled the service with references to love and lost opportunities. I was enormously relieved and hoped my mother was listening to the part of the homily that talked about the Christian history of loving our individual differences and withholding judgment for individual choices.

"Remember, it's God's province to judge. We're but followers. He is the shepherd, the light we follow."

I was fading fast, resting my head on Jim's shoulder, waiting for the crowd to dissipate.

"So Thatcher's in jail?" Jim asked.

I shrugged. "I guess so. He went with the officer this morning. That's really all I know."

"I should tell you something about Thatcher."

I sat forward and tried to focus. In my exhaustion I couldn't even muster a look of confusion.

"Two years ago, he was institutionalized."

Jim dropped his head and continued in a low tone. "Thatcher believes he's responsible for Adam's death."

"You mean his lover, the one who died of AIDS?" I asked.

Jim nodded and leaned closer. His voice dropped to a whisper and I had to strain to hear what he was saying.

"Two-and-a-half years ago Thatcher tried to commit suicide. He was in treatment for six months. In fact, I just happened to be the one who stumbled in on him at his house one afternoon. He had a loaded handgun in his mouth."

I looked at him, stunned. "I don't understand. Adam died of AIDS, right?"

He nodded.

"How can that be Thatcher's fault?"

He looked at me without speaking.

I said, "I know he's negative. I mean, Thatcher's HIV negative, he told me himself…so he didn't give AIDS to Adam."

His eyes clouded before he dropped his gaze to his lap. "It's complicated."

I wasn't sure what this meant but it fit the picture. After what I'd seen of Thatcher over the last few days, news about his emotional instability didn't surprise me.

Jim continued. "I managed to talk him out of it—the attempt, I mean. He agreed to get help. Like I said, he was institutionalized for six months."

The notion that Thatcher felt responsible for Adam's death touched me deep inside in a way hard to explain.

❖

Kay Bell shivered in the cold and pulled her lined trench coat around her, tight, like a sausage casing. She stood next to Muggy Padilla in the receiving line outside the funeral parlor. She kept one eye on her bulky friend as she greeted the crowd that slowly filed past. During the service a mass of clouds had slithered in from the north. Now, the gray sky hung thick and heavy with the threat of icy precipitation, but even that didn't spur the guests to their cars. They seemed reluctant to leave, like they needed to be together, needed this time to grieve en masse, sharing their sadness.

The turnout had surprised Matt's mother. The throng was much larger than she expected, maybe two hundred well-dressed young men and a handful of women. The absence of children was what really surprised her.

There weren't any teenagers either.

For years Kay had defined her place in the world through her interaction with children. That was part of her problems with Matt. She was a mother, a grandmother, and a schoolteacher. Children—her own and those she taught—were the focus of her life. Her children were grown now, married and living their lives with their own children.

All her children, that is, except Matt.

Once he had left New Mexico for college, Matt seemed to cut his ties to the family. He simply did not feel comfortable in her world anymore, the world of children and toys and chattering happy little ones. His life was full of adults. His friends were grownups, other gay men mostly. His job did not involve children; he rarely visited his siblings' families and avoided his nephews and nieces like they were contagious. Kay realized that children made him uncomfortable. She could understand the feeling, but it was alien.

In fact, the complete dearth of little ones that she'd experienced since she arrived in Austin had left her uncertain and out of place. But Kay realized she would have to overcome the feeling if her trip was going to be successful because she had a goal, an ulterior motive for traveling to Austin. When Muggy called and tearfully informed her about Marco's death, Kay felt an uneasy discomfort. It hadn't been that many years since Matt had been shot himself. *Attacked by that madman, a random act by an insane person.* Matt had survived, of course, but the episode had acutely affected Kay, and now Muggy's disconsolate voice over the phone brought it all back.

After promising Muggy that she would make it to Austin, Kay hung up and said a little prayer, guilty words of thanks to God. Thanks that it wasn't her son lying in a casket at the funeral home. And she knew right away that Marco's death was God's way of making her rethink her relationship with Matt. Kay had taken Muggy's pain to heart and it changed her. Right then and there she decided to make amends and so, as she made her plans to come to Austin, she plotted a different course with her son. A new plan emerged from her subconscious and she embraced it with the zeal of a born-again convert. She had come to Austin to help Muggy, but she had also come to seek forgiveness from Matt. She wanted desperately to turn over a new leaf and find a way to become part of his life, to work her way back inside his world again; to hold him and love him and be there for him in the way she hadn't been for such a long time.

Muggy wobbled on her feet and Kay leaned over to steady her. She watched as Muggy fought to keep her knees from buckling and thought, God, it could have been Matt, this could be me. Marco's death had done to Kay what Kay could not have done for herself; it changed her. She could still hear the echo of Muggy's words. *I have lost my son, Kay.* She thought about what it had been like for Muggy to lose her husband; to lose a son would be more than Kay could bear. The image of a giggling six-year-old Matt floated back to her from her subconscious and she realized that if she lost Matt she would be broken-hearted forever. The time had come for reconnecting.

Kay was determined that before she left this earth she would find a way back into his life because she loved Matt, but more than that. If she didn't he would continue to feel guilty. His guilt was unfounded and unfair and, to a large part, her fault. It shook her to the core when she finally realized that she was the source of Matt's pain. Her heart ached when she thought about him and how lonely he had become. But more than being lonely, he was alone. Matt had always had friends. People liked him. But Matt was unable to connect on a deeper level, to find a partner to share his life, and she felt responsible. In light of this new revelation, it became obvious that her conservative Christian upbringing had led her to heap guilt on his shoulders for the way he was. And it had gone on for years. Without meaning to, she had fallen into a pattern of recrimination and blame. For all the "right" reasons Kay had made Matt miserable, had made him feel wrong, and had driven him to be this lonely creature.

Well, no more. Kay's trip to Austin hadn't started off well. She winced as she recalled her harsh words on his porch earlier that morning. She had been startled seeing him in the arms of a man and had reacted without thinking. That was one more thing she would have to change. She vowed not to let Matt's lifestyle startle her again. She was going to find a way to assure him that she loved him, just the way he was. She planned to let him know that she was proud of the man he had become; she would overcome her prejudice and ask him to forgive her. Kay hoped with all her heart it was not too late to help him be happy.

❖

Bill parked on the side street and watched the lot slowly empty. He thought about the look of sadness in Matt's eyes and a sour smile played across his face. Only the weak show their feelings, he thought, and the smile faded.

He turned his focus back to the hunt. He tried to think what he should do. His mind flashed to the crystal-blue eyes and the sparkle of wet skin, and he shivered involuntarily. He let his hand drop from the steering wheel and trailed his fingers across the floor mat below his knees. He felt the gun where it lay tucked under the seat, fingered the cold, hard steel carelessly, and his heart began to pump harder. A thought skittered through his mind like a kite in the breeze. The smile flickered on his face again and sweetness filled his mouth.

If he isn't here, I will hunt him somewhere else.

But first he would change clothes. He never hunted in clothes like this.

CHAPTER EIGHTEEN

MATT

The sound of soft breathing right next to me made my blood run cold. Muddled, I couldn't fathom where I was. The world was total darkness and I lay still for a few seconds, trying to get my bearings. Finally, the shadowy surfaces shifted into view and I rolled slowly onto my back. I waited motionless, straining to hear. The figure inhaled again and my heart began to pound. My senses, sharpened by the adrenaline rush, brought my bedroom into view and I could just make out an indistinct form in my peripheral vision. Someone was definitely lying in bed beside me.

As stealthily as I could manage, I slid my feet to the floor and tiptoed across the hardwoods. The door whispered on its hinges as I opened it and crept into the dark hallway. I pulled it closed again and stood with my arms folded, staring at the wall and trying to remember going to bed—nothing. Then I noticed light pouring under the door to the front room. Someone was up.

I was compelled forward, like a moth attracted to the light, and my body seemed to float that direction without conscious effort. The door to the front room swung open easily, to reveal my mother sitting on the worn leather chair with her hair in curlers and her head buried in a book. She was wearing a pair of my father's oversized pajamas and a cotton robe. She looked up with a surprised expression as I entered the room.

"You're up," she said in a low voice, pushing her reading glasses to the top of her head.

"Yeah, I'm up." I closed the door and squinted as my dark-adapted eyes adjusted to the relative glare. "Who is that?" I asked, pointing in the general direction of my room.

She looked at me with a puzzled expression.

I said, "In my room?"

"Why, Mr. Keeney, of course."

"What?" I shook the sleep from my head. "Say that again?" This wasn't making sense at all. She stared at me and the heater kicked on in the attic.

"Mr. Keeney," she repeated.

"Thatcher?"

She laid the book on the side table and settled back into her chair so she wouldn't have to crane her neck to look at me. "Yes, Thatcher, Thatcher Keeney's in your bedroom." She quirked a wry smile and grabbed my hand. "You were already asleep when the police dropped him off outside."

"Why did they drop him here?"

"For his car, they brought him back for his car. I saw him from the front window. Naturally I thought he'd want to join us. He looked so tired...and hungry...and...well, we have so much food." She waved her hand in the general direction of the kitchen.

I looked at the counter, littered with items. A platter of cookies covered in cellophane sat next to two half loaves of fresh-baked bread wrapped in plastic bags. The outline of a cake was visible through a white Tupperware container. Clean dishes were stacked on the counter. Mom said, "You were exhausted by the time we got back so I took charge. I didn't think you'd mind." She shrugged. "Besides, I didn't want Muggy to be alone. We had a few friends over here, kind of a little wake." She smiled and said, "You should see the refrigerator."

Though the invitation to Thatcher was unexpected the rest of the story was in character. If Mother was anything she was in charge. That's when I noticed the sheet and blanket on the couch. I looked from the couch to her and raised an eyebrow.

She answered my unspoken question. "Muggy's in the guest bedroom." And then as an afterthought she smiled and said, "I guess we have a full house." She shifted uncomfortably in the chair. "Why don't you sit down? We need to talk."

The invitation, like the rest of the conversation, was eerily out of place, as was my mother inviting me to sit down in my own home. A sudden flush of unease washed over me. This scene reminded me of so many times before when Mom would calmly, almost coldly, lay down the law. I steeled myself for the inevitable onslaught, but then a voice in my head spoke. *Not this time, not in my own house.* I clenched my teeth and felt the fire build inside.

Okay, if this is how she wanted it, this was how she was going to get it. No holds barred, Muggy in the bedroom or not, Thatcher in the bedroom or not, I was going to have my say and let the pieces land where they may. I was almost glad its time had finally come. I let go of her hand, pushed the covers aside, and sat on the couch.

"Good," I said. "Because there are a few things you need to hear from me."

Her brows rose in surprise. "You're not angry about the party?" she asked. "Muggy just lost her son, for Christ's sake. She needs—"

"No, Mom. I'm not angry about the party."

"Is it Mr. Keeney? Was I wrong to invite him?"

"This isn't about Thatcher either, and I think you know that."

"I don't know what you're talking about." Her voice was steady; she stared at me, calmly waiting for me to continue.

One of the most amazing things about her was her peculiar ability to remain calm in the face of confrontation. I wanted her to feel the seriousness of the situation, to shake her from her complacency, from her control. I wanted her to show a little frustration or discomfort or concern for what was about to be said; but she sat there tranquil, like this conversation was just like any other, like I was going to tell her about my day and ask about hers.

"This is about the two of us." I struggled to remain composed. "First, I'm a gay man. I don't care what you think, I will always be a gay man and I am glad that I'm a gay man. No amount of pressure from you will change that and…"

She leaned forward and started to speak but I waved her off. "No," I said emphatically. "You are going to hear this all the way through without interruption. If you don't like it you know where the door is." I nodded at the door without lowering my gaze. She bit her lower lip and slid back in her seat. I almost felt sorry for her. I swallowed my discomfort and barged on. "No amount of pressure, from you or anyone else, will change that. I will be gay until the day I die. If you don't like it, tough. If you don't respect me, like I said, there's the door."

She shifted uncomfortably in her chair.

"Second," I said, my voice beginning to steady. I felt like I had practiced this speech for years. "You will stop trying to change me. I will not put up with it. That means no more 'Christian Cure' tapes, no more behavior-modification therapy, and no more pressure to meet 'nice' unmarried women.

"Third, if you are ever rude to any of my friends, like you were this morning to Thatcher, I will tell you to leave. If you refuse or make a fuss I will drag you to the airport and put you on the next plane back to New Mexico myself."

She tucked her tiny frame back into the corner of the chair, her arms folded over her chest. I could see the glint of tears in her eyes but I kept on. "Finally, I recognize your right to believe what you will, but I do not recognize your right to foist your beliefs on me. I'm as serious as a heart attack here, Mom."

I fixed her glassy eyes with a frozen stare, and with a tone as cold as the Arctic Ocean I said, "I will not put up with this anymore. Those are my terms. You can take them or you can leave now and never come back."

Finally, in a hoarse whisper she said, "You're right." And with that she slumped back into her chair. The effort it took to speak seemed to have sapped her strength.

I was unsure what I should do next. My gut told me to rescue her from her misery, to tell her that everything was okay, but I couldn't. Somehow the point had to be made very clear. So I sat and watched and waited.

The silence in the room settled softly around us and she raised her eyes to mine before she started to speak. Her voice was tiny and distant.

"Please forgive me. I've been wrong in the things that I expected of you and I've been wrong in the way I tried to manipulate you. I'm not ignorant of the influence a mother can have over her children, and I used that influence to try to mold you into the image that I truly believed was best."

She wiped a tear from her cheek. "I was wrong to try to change you, Matt. I know that now. But I want you to know that I did it because I truly believed it was in your best interest." My eyes followed her gaze as it dropped to her lap. We both stared at her delicate, porcelain-like hands folded together as if in prayer.

"I did it because I love you." Her words seemed to catch in her throat again and the first warm tear trailed down my own cheek.

"I did it because…" Her voice caught again. "Well, the truth is I believed it would protect you—from the world…from the haters in the world. Do you see?"

Her voice became tinny as she fought back sobs. "I thought it was my fault, that I had made you this way, that my smothering love…I did this to you. A mother should be able to protect her children."

I could hear the ticking of my mantel clock in the near-silence as she searched for her words. When she continued her voice was shaky.

"But I couldn't even protect you from myself."

I hadn't considered that her behavior was a product of misplaced guilt.

I felt uncomfortable and slightly sick. The emotions were overwhelming my ability to reason. It was hard to follow the thread of her logic.

"And when you…well, when I found out you were…not… normal."

The words stumbled out of her like stones thrown from a rooftop; they cut me like the lash of a whip.

"You were gay…well, I thought God would punish you if you lived like…like…a gay man, I guess. I know now that I was wrong." She seemed to gather strength and gain momentum as she talked. "My efforts have hurt you and I will always be sorry for that. I hope you can forgive me. I was wrong."

She swallowed hard and sat back. I watched as she collected her thoughts before starting again. Her voice sounded much stronger now. "I want you to know that I have changed, Matt. I want you to be happy and I want you to be who and what you are." She grabbed my hand and stared straight into my eyes. "All I want is for you to be happy."

I pulled my hand away. I wanted to believe her. The mother that I had always known, this woman that was the dominant force in my youth, this dynamic, relentless, and manipulative person was now telling me that she wanted me to be happy. She was not beyond using emotion to get her way; that I knew. And she was ruthless in the pressure that she applied on her children. *But would she do this? Would she really push this hard?* It just didn't make sense. None of it made sense. *How could she change her ways so abruptly? Why?*

Even as my mind asked the question the answer floated into view. *Because of Marco.*

Marco's death had shaken Muggy to the core. And Muggy's reaction would have forced my mother to look at our relationship in a new light. She would empathize with Muggy and ask herself what she would do in the same situation. And she would worry about me.

She loved me. That was not in question. But was it enough to force her to change? *Maybe.* The word hung in my mind like a streetlamp in the fog, uncertain, yet somehow illuminating.

Even though I was exhausted, I slept fitfully when I returned to bed. Mother's words bounced around inside my head and would not let me be. They shaped my dreams when I slept and filled me with uncomfortable awareness when I lay awake thinking. In my restlessness I pondered the fact that events were overwhelming my ability to process them, coming together and conspiring to distort my view of the world. Long-held beliefs, like the conviction that Danny and Marco would always be around and the unshakeable determination of Mom to oppose my "lifestyle," now lay in ruins at my feet.

I fought the urge to toss and turn, trying not to wake Thatcher. In the still before dawn, I slipped out of bed and sat in the club chair by the window. I watched Thatcher sleep and tried to make sense of recent events. Listening to his slow and gentle breathing, I wondered about the gun and the police. My thoughts wandered back to Marco and Danny. But no matter how hard I thought about the situation, things just didn't add up.

Soft light from a streetlight filtered through the mini-blinds and quietly caressed Thatcher's shoulders. He slept like a child. He lay on one side, turned in my direction, but the room was so dark I couldn't see his face. So I watched the gentle rise and fall of his form and concentrated on the slope of his shoulder. His breathing was deep and slow and hypnotic.

I was about to crawl back into bed when a glint of light shot through the blinds and split the darkness. It drew an arch across the room and then pivoted the other direction. It seemed to slow down as it traced over Thatcher's sleeping figure, illuminating his face.

Then it scanned my direction. I held my breath, stood, and stepped to the side of the window. The light skimmed across the club chair and moved slowly back to the bed. Again, it paused when it reached Thatcher. Quietly, I hooked my finger around the edge of the blinds and opened a small gap.

A dark figure stood in the flowerbed outside the window. The movement of the blinds drew his attention and the light beam shot through the gap. The brightness blinded me and I dropped the blind just as I heard a thump against the outside wall. I bounded through the house in my boxer shorts, my momentum carrying me into the hallway wall.

"Shit," I cursed, and rounded the corner in the living room. Mom looked up from the bed she'd made on the couch. I sprinted across the floor and slammed through the front door just in time to hear the squeal of tires on pavement echo down the darkened street.

Standing in the front yard in my boxer shorts, I could just make out the silhouette of a pickup truck rounding the corner onto Thirty-eighth Street. I stood shivering in the cold, straining to see the truck, listening as it drove up the slope and turned south on Red River, but it was too far and too dark to see the license plate.

❖

Bill's heart pounded as the black Toyota Tundra fishtailed onto Thirty-eighth Street; he punched the accelerator again and lurched down the hill toward the bridge. He looked nervously toward the rearview mirror, but the darkened street remained empty. The truck rattled over the bridge and slowed to the speed limit. He relaxed his hands on the steering wheel and lowered the driver-side window. He inhaled the cold, predawn air as the truck continued to climb toward Red River Street.

He turned south at the stop sign and breathed deep, sucking in the fresh morning air, and held his breath, letting out air very slowly—a little trick he had found to force his body to relax. The corners of his mouth curled into a dark smile as the truck neared St. David's Hospital.

He was there. I will have him soon.

He glanced across the seat at the Bushmaster tucked in the gap between the passenger door and seat.

And once more he tasted the sweetness in his mouth.

❖

"What?" Griggs spit the word out in a hoarse whisper. He swung his legs over the side of the bed and pressed the cell phone to his ear, squeezing his eyes shut and trying to concentrate.

"We just got a call from a Matt Bell." The voice on the other end sounded high and reedy. "He says he chased an intruder away from his house. Evidently the guy was looking in his bedroom window. He called in asking for you, says it has something to do with the Blue investigation."

Griggs shook the grogginess from his head and slid out of bed quietly. He carried the phone to the living room.

The movement woke Dorothy and she reached out, searching instinctively for the gun she kept in her bedside table. Then she remembered where she was. She sat up feeling oddly disconnected and concentrated on the shadowy shapes in front of her until the room came into focus. Sam's muffled voice, coming from the other room, was barely audible. She strained to hear the conversation but it was too distant, so she grabbed her blouse from the pile of her clothes left neatly folded on the dresser top. She dressed quickly without turning on the light, looped the strap of her purse over a shoulder, and carried her shoes into the living room.

Sam sat on the couch in his boxer shorts with his cell phone cradled between a shoulder and ear, scribbling quickly on a notepad in his lap. He looked up and gave Dorothy a sweet smile, then patted the couch.

Dorothy sat down beside him and peered over his shoulder, trying to read from the notepad. After a moment Sam cupped his hand over the phone and whispered, "Our guy's been spotted."

Her face flushed with excitement but Sam could see her struggle to keep it hidden. She nodded nonchalantly and bent down to straighten her stocking.

Sam watched her as she moved. He smiled to himself, realizing that she didn't want him to know that she was just as engaged as he was. Sam was not like that—no pretense, no games. He wore his emotions on his face for all to see. This was his case and this was a break—a big break. Quickly jotting down Matt's address, he slapped his cell phone shut. He tossed her the notepad and tramped back to the bedroom.

Sam stepped out of the closet carrying the same suit he had worn the day before. He tugged his pants on quickly and sat on the side of the bed to tie his shoelaces. His mind raced through the implications of the phone call as he pulled on a freshly laundered shirt and selected a matching tie from the rack screwed to the inside of the closet door.

"If the Blue shooter was stalking Bell maybe we can set up surveillance, perhaps set a trap," he mumbled to himself.

"Sam?"

The sound of Dorothy's voice brought him back to the present. They locked eyes briefly. She held the notepad up and looked at him questioningly. She tossed it onto the bed and reached over to help him straighten his tie.

"We got a peeper at Bell's house," he said. "Bell just called in, says he saw the guy standing in his flower bed. I think it's our shooter."

"Did he see him? Did you get a description?"

"Not much of one, or at least not that he gave the night sergeant, but you never know. That's where I'm headed. The call just came in to the station."

Dorothy smoothed Sam's collar and said, "I'm going with you." Her voice was emphatic.

"I don't know if that's a good idea."

She shook her head. "This time I need to be there, Sam."

He looked at her without speaking, worried about the team finding out about their relationship. Still he knew she wouldn't let office politics keep her from doing her job. It was one thing they had in common.

"Look," she pleaded, "if our guy is circling around Bell, I don't know why, but I need to be there. I need to be there when you talk to him, Sam."

Sam stood motionless for a moment, thinking. Dorothy watched in silence. Finally, he shrugged and said, "Okay, but you better take your own car. I'll drop you at your hotel."

She nodded and stood up quickly. Sam pulled her into his arms. She pressed herself against him and he murmured softly, "Thank you for last night." He grinned mischievously.

Dorothy smiled back and laid her head on his shoulder. He felt her warmth and the smoothness of her face as it brushed his cheek. They kissed passionately.

They would have to be careful to not let their budding relationship cloud their judgment or interfere with the investigation. But now as Sam held her, he knew that things would be all right. They were in it now, for better or worse, in all the way. Both of them would need to do all they could to keep their eye on the target and the investigation focused, but then that's the way they were.

The job comes first.

❖

I paced the room like a caged animal; Thatcher sat in the leather chair and sipped tea. Mom was in the guest room checking on Muggy. "It was the shooter, I know it was him." I mumbled the words to myself, but Thatcher heard me.

"You really think so?"

"Yeah, I really think so."

I felt exhilarated. It had to be the shooter at the window. No other scenario made sense. And that meant it wasn't Thatcher. Sheer relief washed over me like a spring storm. But I saw restlessness in Thatcher's eyes as he set his cup on the side table and stood up. "Show me," he said.

We grabbed our coats and stepped out onto the porch. The eastern sky was brightening but the sun had not yet cleared the horizon. We made our way around the side of the house.

"He must have stood right there." I pointed to the flower bed where someone had stomped a mass of brittle Asian jasmine flat just below the bedroom window. "He had some kind of a light, like a penlight, and he was looking through the window."

The ground was frozen solid so there were no footprints in the bed. A line of scuffmarks cut through the early morning frost on the grass, toward Montrose Street. Thatcher saw them too.

"He must have parked over there," I said, pointing to where the steps ended near the curb. "By the time I got out here, he was already down the street."

"Which way did the car turn?" he asked.

"It was a truck, black, I think. He turned right toward Red River."

We looked at each other with our arms wrapped across our chests and our coats pulled tight against the early morning cold. Even as my mind drew chilling images of dark figures in black trucks aiming assault rifles at my house, I was mesmerized by his image. Thatcher's words broke the spell. "I need to tell you something."

His voice sounded thin and unsteady. He fidgeted nervously for a few seconds. "I don't know where to start."

I attempted to smile as I shivered in the cold.

"Look, I know how you were shot."

I hung there, holding my breath waiting for the rest of the story.

"But you don't know about Adam."

I looked into his eyes and remained frozen in anticipation. Obviously this was difficult for him.

"You see, Adam was shot too, just like you, during the first shooter spree. He was my lover and the same guy that shot you shot him."

He tugged the coat's zipper up and down, and his whole body seemed to shake in a flurry of nervous energy. "In fact, he was shot a few months before you were. He survived the attack. Well, he survived until the virus took over…He died five years later." He stepped closer. "AIDS that was the result of…well, I mean, was caused by…I mean he was infected in the hospital. The treatment he received after being shot, you see?" His blue eyes pleaded for understanding.

I nodded even though I didn't see.

"He was shot here." He lifted his coat and pointed to just below his rib cage. "Just like you were, and his scar was shaped like an eight, just like yours."

I stared back at Thatcher, searching for answers as a heavy, sickening feeling dropped into the pit of my stomach. These murders were swirling around the two of us, enveloping us in a mesh of distortion. I was too close to see the pattern.

Perhaps we both were.

Thatcher, still twitching and shaking, seemed to read my mind. "Every single day since I lost Adam, I've tried to make sense of this. I've been obsessed with understanding what happened, because understanding *what* is easier than understanding *why*. I've dreamed about stopping this monster, catching him and putting an end to it. Maybe it would, I don't know…maybe it would make it better."

"Make what better?" I asked.

Thatcher looked down and paused before speaking again. His voice was softer now. "It really doesn't make sense, I guess" He shook his head as if to clear it. "The truth is I want to—need to..." His eyes filled with tears, and he dropped his head. "Do you understand? I need to set this straight...for Adam." His voice trailed off and his body shook again. I could barely hear him say, "for me."

"Is that why you bought the gun?"

Thatcher looked up at me. "You know about it?"

I nodded sheepishly. "I saw it in your closet, when I was at your house."

He shrugged. "Yeah, I guess." He looked down again. "I bought it, trying to understand. Trying to figure out how someone...how he could..."

I knew what he meant. Thatcher wanted to understand the attack on Adam, the same way I had once wanted to understand why it had happened to me. Like a key in the lock, I could feel the pieces fall into place. I said, "I guess I owe you an apology."

He gave me a look of incomprehension.

"I'm the one that told the police about you...about the gun and the articles."

The corners of his mouth twitched for a moment and he said, "You reported me to the police?"

I fought the temptation to look away. "It was the gun and the articles, I saw the photocopies of the shooter stories in your desk drawer. I didn't understand—"

"You thought I was the shooter?"

"I thought you *could* be the shooter. I didn't really believe it but it was the gun...a Bushmaster...the same gun that shot me, and I didn't know your connection to the murders. I didn't know about Adam and I—"

"And that's why you called the police."

I looked down at my feet and kicked a small stone into the garden. "I didn't know, Thatcher. I didn't understand. I..." My stomach tightened and a wave of nausea rolled over me. When I found my voice again I said, "I was wrong and I'm very sorry."

He looked away for a moment and I watched him as the morning sun crested the horizon. After a minute of silence he grabbed my hand and said, "I understand."

Lieutenant Griggs's car turned the corner from Thirty-eighth Street. We both glanced at it and I asked, "Did you tell the police everything?"

"You mean about the gun? Yeah, I told them yesterday."

I shook my head. "No, about Adam being shot."

He paused, squinting at me, trying to follow my line of thinking. "Not really, but they know…I mean they called me asking for Adam, after that bartender was shot."

We heard the thump of a car door at the curb and a rumpled Lieutenant Griggs waved when he saw us and stepped gingerly across the frosty surface of the yard. In the distance, a police car turned onto Montrose with its lights rotating. It pulled to a stop behind the Ford.

Griggs stared back at the cruiser and made a slicing motion with his thumb across his neck. The rotating lights went off. Griggs plodded toward the two of us with a somewhat surprised expression. "Good morning, Mr. Bell, Mr. Keeney."

We murmured greetings.

"What have we got here?"

I told him about the guy in the flower bed, pointing out the window and the trail of steps across the yard. He nodded and listened patiently. When I finished, he asked the two of us to wait inside for a moment. Griggs stopped me as I was about to follow Thatcher through the door and said, "One quick question, Matt."

I stepped back down to the yard from the porch.

Griggs said, "When did Mr. Keeney get here?"

"He spent the night."

He stared at me for a minute. "The two of you were alone when the guy showed up?"

I shook my head. "No, my mother and a family friend are inside. She came in for Marco's funeral."

"Marco Padilla?"

"Yes, Mom is a friend of Marco's mother. In fact it's Marco's mother that stayed in my spare bedroom last night."

Griggs nodded, pulling a notepad from his coat pocket and writing on it.

"And I see you ignored my advice about Mr. Keeney." He said this without looking up from his notepad.

"Well, it's complicated, Lieutenant."

"I'm sure it is." A small smile played across his face. "You'll be happy to hear that Keeney checks out. His gun is not the weapon our shooter used. In fact it's never been fired."

I smiled as Griggs said, "Okay, thank you, Matt."

Dorothy Bowles pulled the rented red Metro to the curb and opened her briefcase, extracting a folder. In the distance, she could see Griggs chatting with a young female officer. When Sam noticed the Metro, he motioned for Dorothy to join them. She tossed the folder into her bag, opened the door, and stepped into the cold morning air.

Sam introduced Dorothy as she approached. "Agent Bowles, this is Officer Lee." He turned to Lee, "I want this entire area searched carefully. Look for anything out of place, anything that could have been dropped or left behind. Bag everything. I doubt this guy's gonna leave much but you never know."

Officer Lee nodded and strode off toward the curb. Dorothy watched as she opened the cruiser door and searched the backseat, pulling a pair of gloves from the side pocket.

"What do we have here, Lieutenant?" Dorothy asked.

"The peeper was standing in the flower bed, looking through the blinds. That's the bedroom." Sam pointed to the window. "He used a small flashlight. Bell says he took off before he could get outside."

Bowles nodded, pulling Sam to a stop just in front of the porch. "Did Bell get a description?"

"Not much of one. The guy wore dark clothes and a stocking cap, average height, average build…nothing more. But Bell saw him drive off in a dark pickup, probably black. It's almost certainly too late to search the area. I've got a couple of uniforms driving the neighborhood just in case."

"Why does Bell think it's him?" Dorothy asked.

"Timing probably," Sam said. "You have to admit it's a good guess."

Dorothy nodded. "Yeah, but does he have any other reason?"

Sam shrugged. "Not that he mentioned. I haven't had time to question him thoroughly. That's what we do next. There is one other thing."

"Yeah?"

"Keeney's inside." Griggs tilted his head toward the porch. "He spent the night."

Bowles stared at him.

After a moment of awkward silence Griggs asked, "What do you make of it?"

"I don't know. Right now it's an interesting coincidence— maybe more."

Griggs nodded. "Yeah, maybe. So now we talk with them."

Bowles bobbed her head and they climbed the steps toward the house.

CHAPTER NINETEEN

MATT

Lieutenant Griggs and Agent Bowles questioned everyone in my house. Predictably, the police presence upset Muggy. She slumped on the couch wrapped in a quilt and gently rocked side to side with fat tears rolling down her chubby face. Occasionally she nodded or whispered a response, but only when asked a direct question. Griggs and Bowles warned us to report anything suspicious and left just before noon. Mom took Muggy to her hotel a few minutes later.

Thatcher and I sat together, in the relative calm of the front porch, until exhaustion overwhelmed me. I left him on the swing and climbed back in bed. Sleep came quickly.

I woke with the late-afternoon sunshine streaming onto my face. The mini-blinds on the bedroom window were pulled up slightly, and the falling sun had dropped low enough to shine through the gap. I stood and stretched and was surprised to see that I was alone, so I tugged on my jeans and ambled through the house.

Thatcher had left a note on the dining-room table explaining that he'd snuck home to shower and clean up, and asked if I wanted to get together for dinner. The request made me smile on my way to the kitchen where I poured myself a glass of iced tea and padded softly in my cotton socks through the screen door to retrieve the mail.

It was mostly bills and advertisements but one letter caused me to pull up short.

I dropped the rest of the mail in a pile on the counter and sank into the couch holding the envelope gently. I stared at the address written in Danny's distinctive cursive, full of large looping letters. I traced the writing gently with a finger. The postmark was Monday.

I opened it and started to read.

Dearest Matt,

I guess it's only fair for you to know the truth. And now that it's over, that my life is over, and Marco is gone, you should know. It's all such a travesty.

For years I've watched Marco wander from man to man, and all the while I knew that he would never be happy. Never truly happy, because what he was looking for was not out there for him; Marco wanted you.

But you were so oblivious, you surrounded yourself in a cocoon of ignorance. You were unreachable.

All those years I waited, hoping Marco would one day see the light, that he would finally realize that you would never love him that way. That he would give up on you because…you see…I loved Marco like he loved you.

When you began to date Thatcher I thought that maybe he would finally let go of his dream, that maybe I would have a chance. I was so hopeful, so happy.

But it was not to be. I woke this morning to find that Marco is gone, butchered like an animal, and there is simply nothing left for me. Life is a farce, a cruel game, and now it is over.

Danny

What a strange triangle the three of us had become.

I couldn't believe Marco and Danny were dead. That reality was just beginning to hit me and I felt disconnected and numb. The tears, when they came, took me totally by surprise.

❖

"So, what do we have?" Griggs asked.

Reed answered. "Total confusion, disconnected nothing, absolute bewilderment. It's an enigma wrapped in a mystery, stuffed in a burrito, and smothered in taco sauce." He smiled. "Sorry, Lieutenant, I'm a little hungry."

"Anyone else?" Griggs asked. When nobody responded, he snapped, "Connors, detail the suspect list."

Connors carried his laptop to the whiteboard and set it on the table. He opened it and maneuvered the touchpad pointer and clicked a few keys, opening a document. Then he turned to the board and grabbed a marker. "Okay, Lieutenant, from our last meeting we had three suspects, but now we're down to two—looks like Mills committed suicide." He drew a line on the board and wrote the names Martin Hansen and Jim Avery on either side, then copied the relevant details of each suspect-action item and follow-up questions from the last meeting.

Both Hansen and Avery had been under surveillance since mid-morning. It was good to have real suspects. They were closing in on the killer, Griggs could feel it. He heaved a sigh of anticipation, realizing they were closer now than they had ever been. Still one thought played through his mind.

When are we going to catch this guy?

❖

Jerry Philips shoved his eyeglasses to the top of his head and stared blankly at the screen. The notes from the series of sniper stories that had earned his paper a Pulitzer Prize lay open on his lap, and the screen in front of him glowed in the eerie filtered light of his office. It was Saturday and the neon overheads were off. Jerry blinked in disbelief and reached for the telephone. First he had to check the facts, that's what he had to do.

And then what? What if it was all true? What if it checked out, he asked himself. *Then what should I do?* He shook his head again. *No, better not to get too far ahead.* He would check this out first, find a confirming source, and then decide.

He punched the numbers from the screen into his phone.

❖

Bill directed his hazy focus across Eastwoods Park. He was in his truck parked on Harris Park Avenue. In the bright sunshine, the UT Law School loomed above the bare branches of the trees lining Waller Creek. Bill's thoughts were scrambled. He was dressed for work and had been sitting in the shiny black Tundra for twenty minutes, his mind a muddle. He shouldn't be in the Tundra, he knew that, not dressed like this. But his own car had failed to start and it was his only alternative. He couldn't be late for work. But when he arrived, Tanya was already on duty and he remembered he had been rescheduled for the late shift. He had never forgotten his work schedule before. He drove to the park in search of a quiet place to sit and clear his mind, but the swirl of anger and confusion would not go away.

A sharp sound drew his attention and he turned to see a scruffy man in tattered, mud-soaked, camouflage cargo pants amble unsteadily out of the bushes. The unwashed man lugged a plastic trash bag partly full of aluminum cans over one shoulder and clung to a liquor bottle in the opposite hand. He moved from garbage can to garbage can, across the park, dropping the bag at his feet and taking a slug from the bottle before setting it aside and sorting through the garbage.

Bill watched in silence, until another sound drew his attention back to the bushes. Stanley Church rose like an alien creature from the murky shade along Waller Creek and shuffled along the wooded path. He ambled past the man at the trashcan.

The garbage-can man ignored Stanley and continued to pull aluminum cans from the refuse. He crushed each one with his heel and shoved it methodically into the bag. When it was more than halfway full the man began dragging it behind him. The way the hair curled at the base of the man's neck and the shadowy shape of the bag stirred a memory from Bill's past, a bad memory.

Bill couldn't quite pull the image into focus and that made him angrier. And the anger muddled his thinking even more, making it harder to focus.

His frustration grew.

Frantically he struggled, searching for an image to make the connection.

Then rage overcame him. He raised the Bushmaster from his lap, sighted down the barrel, and pulled the trigger. It seemed to Bill there was a measurable pause after the garbage-can man's head exploded and before the morning erupted with the sound of the blast.

The body crumpled to the ground like a marionette with its strings cut.

Bill's temples began to pound with the rhythm of his heartbeat.

The Tundra's tires chirped and the truck pulled away from the curb quickly. He turned onto Twenty-sixth Street and was climbing the hill back toward the freeway when he glanced in his rearview mirror. Stanley Church's reflected image scurried up Harris Park in a hobbling trot, and Bill slammed his palm on the dashboard.

"Goddamn motherfucker…"

He turned the Tundra around at the intersection.

Carla Sandoval was surprised to see her brother at her door. Stanley had never before come to her house on his own. She opened the door and Stanley stepped inside, his eyes darting from corner to corner. He wrung his hands incessantly, the slow scrubbing motions a pantomime of washing them under a faucet. Something had upset him badly. This was Stanley's way. His psychosis made it difficult for him to communicate with others, the incessant nervous tic a sign he was really distressed. Carla wanted to hold him but she knew better. Touching him would set off a whole other set of issues.

Instead she led Stanley to the kitchen and sat him on a barstool at the counter. She pulled a haphazard armful of newspapers from the recycle bin and piled them next to him on the countertop. Without speaking, he began sorting through the pile, separating the papers into two stacks, one containing shiny advertisements and the other regular newsprint. He meticulously aligned the edges of the stacks as he worked his way through the heap. Carla watched the routine in silence.

❖

It took ten minutes to confirm with Nell the information Jerry had mined online from the Department of Social Security's Web site. Two minutes after that, Jerry dialed Brackenridge Hospital and spoke with someone in Human Resources, who refused to confirm or deny the information.

Fair enough, he would have to visit the hospital in person, but he was pretty sure he already had what he was looking for.

Looking at the employment history sketched on the yellow pad in front of him tickled a thought in the back of his mind. He pulled the shooter folder from his cabinet and shuffled through the documents until he found the timeline his source at the police station had given him. He laid the timeline next to the pad and compared the dates.

Bingo! Excitement quickened Jerry's heartbeat. It was too bizarre to think that this could be a coincidence. The schedule matched up with the shooter's timeline perfectly.

He grabbed the phone and punched in the numbers for his contact at the police station without hesitation. When the far end answered he didn't wait for a response.

"Detective Reed, this is Jerry Philips. I've got to talk with you right away."

Reed read the note of excitement in Jerry's voice and let him tell his story the first time through without prompting. He scribbled notes on a yellow notepad, and when Jerry was finally finished his voice betrayed no emotion as he walked Jerry back through the explanation of his findings one more time, filling in pertinent details. When he was finally satisfied, Reed offered to have a police car sent around to pick Jerry up and bring him down to the station.

"That won't be necessary. It would be faster if I just drove over."

"How long will it take you to get here?"

"I'm at my office at the *Statesman*—ten minutes or so."

Reed hurried down the hall toward Lieutenant Griggs's office clenching the yellow notepad in his fist. Griggs's door was shut but he heard the sound of soft voices on the other side so he knocked once and opened the door without an invitation. The lieutenant was talking to Dorothy Bowles—their conversation died as soon as the door opened. They both turned to look at Reed.

Reed said, "Lieutenant, I got something here you need to hear."

The urgency in his voice made both Griggs and Bowles sit up.

"I just got off the phone with a Jerry Philips. He's a reporter with the *Statesman*—"

Just then Griggs's cell phone chirped and he held up a hand, signaling Reed to wait. He glanced at the screen of the phone and said, "I've got to take this, hold on."

❖

The sound of the gunshot brought me to my feet. I could tell that it echoed in the distance and immediately I thought of Thatcher. I grabbed the phone from the counter and called him. The phone rang three times before his answering machine picked up. I hung up and dressed quickly. I snatched Lieutenant Griggs's card from the top of my dresser and called him on my cell phone as I raced to the garage. I was backing into the alleyway before Griggs picked up.

"This is Griggs."

"Lieutenant, there was a gunshot, just now a gunshot."

"Matt?"

"Yes, sorry, it's me. I just heard a gunshot."

"Okay, was anyone hurt, are you home?"

"No, I don't know...I mean yes, but I'm heading over to Thatcher's house."

"Okay, slow down. Who was hurt and where are you?"

I forced myself to inhale. "No one was hurt, not that I know of, but I was at home, a minute ago, I mean when I heard the shot. It's him, Lieutenant, I know it's him, and Thatcher's not here, he went home and I'm going to find him. I'm driving to his house—"

"Matt, I want you to turn around right now, turn around and go back home. Do you hear me, go home right now. I'm on my way. We will find Mr. Keeney but you need to be home."

"But Lieutenant…I mean, he's out there…I need to find him."

"Matt, listen to me. You do not need to find him, we will find him, and you need to go home."

I disconnected, closed my cell phone, and drove on.

Thatcher wasn't at his house and his car was gone. I had driven the most direct route but didn't see him. And then my cell phone rang.

"Hello."

"So what happened to you, sleeping beauty? I'm at your house."

I said, "Uh, well, I'm at your house."

"Couldn't wait for me to come back?" he teased.

I said, "Listen, Thatcher, there was a shot, just a few minutes ago."

"What?"

"A gunshot, not far from my house. I heard it from the porch."

"It's him," Thatcher said, excitement in his voice.

"Stay there, okay? I'm heading that way."

But I was talking to dead air. Thatcher had already hung up. I backed out of his driveway, spinning my wheels as they caught the pavement.

❖

Bill caught up with Stanley Church just as he entered the little house on Carolyn Street. He parked the Tundra on a side street and thought about what he was going to do. *It's all falling apart. This isn't the way it was supposed to go.*

Bill shook his head and stared at the house. The drapes in the front windows were drawn but he could see the shadow of two figures in the front room. He tried to think of a way out of this mess but nothing came to mind. He kept returning to the fact that now, for the first time, he had a witness to deal with. As he watched the house, the people inside made their way to the kitchen. From where he sat he could see them clearly now through the kitchen window. There was the guy, the witness from the park, standing at the counter, next to a woman.

As he watched them, he considered his options. The only solution was to kill them both, but here he was, dressed for work, in the middle of the day. This wasn't the way it was supposed to be. He tried to concentrate, to make a plan, but his mind was jumbled, his thoughts scattered.

And then he tasted the sweetness.

He cradled the stock of the Bushmaster in his lap, the Styrofoam sleeve abandoned in the backseat.

Bill balanced the gun's stock against the doorjamb and sighted down the barrel.

❖

Lieutenant Griggs parked his blue Subaru wagon in front of Matt's house, and Thatcher Keeney waved a timid greeting from the porch swing. Griggs jogged to the porch. "Where's Matt?"

Thatcher nodded toward the street and Griggs looked in that direction. They both watched Matt's little green Miata climb the Montrose Street hill and pull to a stop next to the curb. Another shot echoed up the street. Matt ducked instinctively and Griggs signaled for him to get inside the house. Thatcher tore off in the direction of Matt's car and Griggs yelled at him to go inside, too, as he drew his service revolver and jogged up the street in the direction of the shot.

Judging the echo on the run, Griggs determined the shot came from Carolyn Street, the next block over. He took the north alley, crouching low, darting behind bushes and edging around garages, scanning the buildings on the Carolyn Street side as he ran. He spotted two figures, a woman and a man, huddling on the rear porch of a limestone house in the middle of the block. The terrified eyes of the woman glared at him as he jumped a small fence from the alley. He pulled the badge from his inner jacket pocket and flashed it their direction as he bounded across the backyard. Holding a finger to his lips, he signaled silence and hugged the edge of building with his revolver drawn. All three shrugged down farther as a second shot rang out, followed by the tinkle of glass.

❖

Carla wrapped her arms around her terrified brother's head and shoulders, trying to use her body to physically shield him from the attack. Stanley would normally fight the physical contact, but when the first shot missed, she grabbed him and pulled him out the back door.

Now, he was nearly comatose in his bewilderment.

They were squatting together on the back porch, leaning against the house, when she caught sight of a man jumping the alley fence and sprinting through the backyard in her direction. Her terror at being trapped turned to relief as the man bounded through the backyard, then held up his badge. A second shot rang out and adrenaline pulsed through her again, like a bolt of electricity. She pulled Stanley closer and together they slid down below the edge of the window on the porch.

❖

The first shot had shattered the glass in the kitchen window and ricocheted off the counter. Bill lost sight of the figures at the counter, but when the last of the glass dropped he glimpsed faces moving just above the windowsill at the back of the house. He was on autopilot now, barely noticing the activity in the neighboring houses. He was focused on the target; from his seat he could just make out their heads. He sighted down the barrel and pulled the trigger again just as both ducked lower.

Griggs hunkered down and slowly peered around the corner of the house. Across the street he could see a black pickup truck, its occupant obscured in the shadows of the cab. Then he saw the shiny blue-black glint of the gun barrel in the sun and raised his revolver. He hesitated, trying to steady his aim, when movement behind him drew his attention.

Back in the yard, Thatcher stepped around the edge of the building with his rifle aimed toward the street.

Griggs lowered his handgun and hissed, "Don't do it, Thatcher." The words came out in a harsh whisper.

But Thatcher steadied himself and sighted down the barrel.

Bill's head rang with the sound of the explosion and his ears hummed in the roaring after-blast that echoed through the truck's cab. The first sound he picked up when his hearing came back was the distant whine of a police siren, and then he saw the two figures aiming at him from the edge of the building. Blackness edged into the corners of his world and he smiled to himself, almost in relief.

"It would be over soon," he told himself, and he tasted the sweetness again.

"Don't do it, Thatch." Adam's words resounded in Thatcher's ear and he felt the gentle touch of Adam's hand on his shoulder.

"You don't have to do this, Thatcher," Adam said.

Thatcher swallowed hard and sighted down the barrel at the shooter, the sting of hatred flaring in his mind. "When are you going to let it go?" Adam asked. Thatcher's throat constricted and hot tears smoldered in his eyes. He blinked hard.

"It's not your fault, Thatch," Adam whispered from over his shoulder, so close he could feel the warm breath on his neck. "It was never your fault."

Thatcher tried to shake off his confusion and ignore the illusion, but Adam's steady voice sounded again. "It's time to let it go."

And the weight of the gun seemed to press down on him with an overwhelming force. Thatcher fought, but to no avail. The gun barrel dipped and then tilted slowly downward, drifting to the ground like a leaky helium-filled balloon. It slapped to the ground with a hollow, clanking sound.

When Thatcher turned to look at Adam, Matt stood in his place with his hand on his shoulder.

❖

Thatcher and I had seen Griggs sprint up the alley together. But instead of following me into the house, Thatcher bolted from the porch toward his car, grabbed the Bushmaster from the backseat, and tore off after Lieutenant Griggs. In the time it took my mind to engage, Thatcher had disappeared up the alley. I heard the second shot as I followed.

The scene played out in front of me like a play in the park. Griggs slouched against the limestone wall, his revolver drawn, Thatcher standing behind him, with the Bushmaster at his shoulder, the wild, far-away look on his face—so much like the first time I'd seen him. I fought to keep my voice steady and told Thatcher not to do it, and he must have heard me because he dropped the gun. The third shot brought all of us to a halt. Time seemed to compress.

We watched as the head of the shooter in the cab jerked violently backward and whipped forward. A spray of blood erupted inside the cab.

❖

Griggs moved quickly, picking up Thatcher's gun and pulling his cell phone from the caddy attached to his belt. He hit speed-dial, staring at Thatcher, waiting for someone to pick up on the other end. When they did, he shouted coded phrases into the phone and dashed across the street toward the truck. Then he grabbed the shooter's blood-drenched gun and glanced warily through the window. He set all three guns on the ground at his feet and opened the door.

She was dressed in pastel-blue nursing scrubs and white shoes with comfortable crepe soles. Blood streamed from the hole in her forehead down her chin and through the gap in her cleavage. It pooled in her lap and was already beginning to congeal.

She was dead.

I don't know why I followed Griggs across the street. I should have stayed with Thatcher, but something propelled me forward. Griggs's movements were careful, practiced, and automatic.

The thing I remember most was the blood.

It sprang as if from a fountain, gurgling and splashing over everything. It stuck to Griggs's hands as he checked her pulse and dripped from the truck door, forming puddles on the pavement.

Blood also covered Stephanie.

Chapter Twenty

Ruth

I t's not all that surprising, really. Shocking but not surprising."

"You mean the fact that he was living as a woman?"

Lieutenant Griggs and Dorothy Bowles sat on the sofa in Griggs's office.

"Yeah, we knew his fixation was sexual, that he had sexual problems. But we didn't expect the extreme nature of his sexual obsession."

"We know that Bill Hansen, as Stephanie Sheldon, had access to all the victims in the hospital. In fact he carefully staged the shootings in the hopes of getting to the victims in the emergency room. As a trauma nurse working in the Brackenridge emergency room Sheldon had access to gunshot victims, and the attacks all occurred just before she went on duty, all in the general vicinity of the hospital where Sheldon worked. It was part of the plan."

"So you're saying she wanted to treat them in the hospital?"

"Exactly. In fact, that was the main focus of the attacks."

"But that doesn't make sense. Why would she do that?"

"Well, that's the point, I guess. It wasn't sane. It doesn't have to make sense to us. All that matters is it made sense to him." Dorothy shook her head slowly. "Very seldom do we really understand *why*. Usually we can only hope to understand *what*."

Griggs nodded. "But it never seems to be enough."

Dorothy smiled. "There are four levels of understanding. First it's the *what*, the simple one—the facts of the situation. Then it's the *what from*—the middle level of understanding, which means understanding the underlying mental illness. In Bill Hansen/ Stephanie Sheldon's case it was a psychosis, that's a given—a definite loss of contact with reality. Mentally he was both a man and a woman, mentally his world made sense...to him. The psychosis drove him to do the things he did."

Griggs nodded.

"Then there's the *how*," she said. "We usually have to understand the *how* to catch these monsters. It's their pattern, the connected series of events, their MO. Understanding their pattern is the key. The *how* is the most important thing for us because it helps us catch up with them."

"Yeah, I guess I follow you."

"That one we have down pretty good in this case. His pattern was easily definable. But the fourth level is what we all really want to know. Unfortunately it's also the thing we almost never understand. It's the big one, the *why*, the root cause of the sickness or obsession. We all want the story tied up in a neat little bundle from beginning to end."

"So how did this begin?" Griggs looked at her with expectation but she shook her head.

"Your guess is as good as mine."

❖

A gentle misting rain puddled the pavement and dappled the car's windows as Jerry Philips drove slowly through the stone archway. The rain darkened surfaces and shrouded the tree-lined sidewalks in a hazy blanket. Impossibly green lawns, spiked with stone angels and monuments, rolled gently across the hills in the distance, and traffic from the freeway hummed in a muffled buzz. Ruth Brookes sat silently in the passenger seat, clutching a bundle of blue irises with her twisted, arthritic hands. Her eyes brimmed with tears.

Jerry stopped the car alongside the pathway and carefully unfolded the wheelchair from the trunk, holding an umbrella awkwardly to keep the rain off both of them. The fragile old lady clutched his neck tight as he lifted her and maneuvered her into the chair. Then he repositioned the umbrella, squeezing its handle between his cheek and shoulder, careful that the rim covered her, and rolled the chair awkwardly across the soggy grass. They stopped next to the grave.

Jerry knelt down to wipe the moisture from the surface of the headstone with his handkerchief. When he stood, Ruth tossed the bundle of irises down atop the grave and peered over her knees at the flat slab of blue-gray granite. The family's brand, a simple lazy figure eight, was carved on the surface, and under it the phrase "Darkness begets darkness, the only true light is forgiveness."

She wiped a single tear from her cheek with a claw-like hand and said, "You may find it hard to believe, Mr. Philips, but he was such a gentle boy."

Jerry nodded acknowledgement. She reached into the pocket of her overcoat and pulled out a small dark book in a plastic bag tied with a purple ribbon. She leaned over the side of her wheelchair and gently tossed the book onto the grave next to the irises.

"It's Silas's cookbook, the only thing I have left from him. I think it belongs here, don't you?

Jerry just nodded. They were silent for a while, each lost in their own thoughts, until Mrs. Brookes said, "Please take me home now, my time is almost up."

Her words stuck with him as he drove them both back up the hill, the car shrouded in the falling mist. Somehow he knew she did not mean making it back to the nursing home before curfew.

❖

Later that evening in his motel room in Clovis, New Mexico, Jerry shoved the tape into the video player and turned on the television set. Snow covered the screen until he pushed Play; then the image of an old, wrinkled woman sitting in a wheelchair flickered into view. She was sitting in the sun next to a window in a hallway with a linoleum-tiled floor. Rustling sounds and the squeaking of rubber-soled shoes were just audible in the background. Then Jerry Philips voice spoke from off-camera.

"Interview with Ruth Brookes November 19, 2004. Mrs. Brookes, feel free to speak whenever you are ready."

The camera focused on an arthritic hand waving with palsy, then pulled back and framed Mrs. Brooke's face. She glanced out the window. Sunshine reflecting off the dewy surface of her eyes glistened like chipped flint. Her lips smacked together before she spoke.

"The first thing I want to tell you is that my brother Silas was a hero, a decorated World War I hero. But the war changed him."

She paused, searching for the right words, then turned her gaze toward the camera and slowly focused her stare. The effect was unsettling, like the ancient eyes were pouring through the screen and into the viewer's mind. "No, that's not what I mean. I guess I mean that we—well, Momma, Poppa and I—we all didn't really know him until he came back. So for us it seemed to change him, do you understand?"

Jerry Philips was heard off-screen. "Yes, I think so."

"It was a hard-fought war, a man's war, an ugly war. We didn't know that then, mind you. It wasn't talked about—just wasn't done. But the effect it had on those young men, boys really, most of them, well, they were never the same. So when Silas came back from the war, he was different. Poppa accepted it, but he was different. Momma and I blamed it on the war, the changes. What I mean is, the first thing he wanted to do when he came back was leave again. And that wasn't like the Silas I knew before, to come and go right away again. Anyway Poppa said he was a man now and could make up his own mind…and he did. He moved off to New York right away, and we didn't hear much from him until the trouble.

"I think he didn't want Momma and Daddy to know that he was queer—but no one knew. He was…what do they call it nowadays?"

Jerry said, "In the closet."

"Yes." Mrs. Brookes's head nodded slowly. "Because it was different back then, do you see? It was bad, really bad. And it would have been especially bad for us…'cause we're Baptist, staunch Baptists, and we lived in a small place, a country place.

"The first I knew about the trouble was when we heard he was in Sing Sing. You have to remember that things were very different back then, but I'm getting way ahead of myself."

She blinked her glassy eyes and stared directly at the camera.

"Silas fell in love with another young man and they began to see each other. I won't tell you his name, because I don't know it. Silas never told me. We were close but some things he kept to himself.

"Whoever he was, this young man, his daddy was rich and powerful. And that was the problem, you see. Because his daddy didn't like what was going on. I don't know the particulars really. All I know is that this man, the daddy, used some of his connections to have Silas charged for attacking his son.

"I think the charge was rape or sodomy or some evil thing. When my daddy found out, it pretty much killed him. He just lay down and never really got up again."

She turned her glassy eyes toward the window again and looked into the streaming sunshine.

"Well, that's pretty much all I know of Silas's first big secret. He went to prison and stayed there for a lot of years. Of course Momma and Daddy both died with him still in there.

"When he came out he just stayed away from the family. I think he was still hurting or, more likely, embarrassed." There was a catch in her voice and tears pooled in her eyes.

She swallowed hard and started again. "I heard from him once in a while. From time to time, he'd send a letter. He moved around a lot, never seemed to settle down. Never told me much about who he was with or what he was doing."

"Until he got sick."

"That must have been in the summer of 1962, because my Floyd was still with us and Lula's family had just moved back to the farm. We raised cattle and Clarence needed the work, of course. Clarence was Lula's husband."

"Lula's your daughter?" Jerry Philips asked.

"Yes, that's right. Anyway, that summer Silas called on me, for the first time needing something. He was sick with the cancer then and wanted to come home. I remember Lula was mad as a wet hen about that. She didn't know him, had never met him, so all she knew was about him going to prison. I'm pretty sure she was afraid he would try something with her little boys; she had two little boys and one girl, precious children. Anyway, we argued over that. She didn't want him around, but he was my big brother, a war hero, and he was sick. What was I to do? The way things turned out, I know she was really glad he came home."

Her chin quivered momentarily and her eyes closed.

"You see, I sent a letter and a plane ticket. Lula and I met him at the airport in Albuquerque. I remember seeing him stumble down the stairway of that airplane. The sight of him was shocking; he was so weak and thin, and the cancer…it had really changed him. I think seeing him like that melted Lula's heart a little. He was as frail and thin as a sapling.

"The problem happened a few weeks after we got him home. What I remember was that Clarence was beating Billy up real bad. You see, Billy was Lula's eldest boy, but Billy was not Clarence's child, though no one knew that at the time, of course, except Lula and Clarence…and me. The plain fact is Clarence used to beat up Billy a lot, poor child. Lord, how I prayed that man would stop. Clarence was really awful, but Floyd said to leave it alone, said they would work it out on their own. Floyd didn't want to get involved. I think he just figured Clarence was a strict father. But I knew something was wrong. Lula was terrified of him too. And Clarence was a big, strong man. It was complicated by the fact that the other children were Clarence's and Lula kept thinking she could get him to stop hurting Billy without leaving him. But I'm getting off my story."

The wrinkled, weathered face broke into a self-conscious smile. "I'm an old woman, Mr. Philips. We tend to talk in circles."

The sound of a gentle chuckle was just audible off-camera.

"Let's see, where was I? Oh, yes, that day must have been a good day for Silas; at least he wasn't bedridden yet, because we were sitting together over coffee in the kitchen. Floyd was out gathering the cattle for Clarence to brand them, and Lula was off somewhere with the little ones—probably gone to town.

"We heard Billy's screams just as we sat down together. The two of us stepped out on the back porch to see what was going on. I remember watching Billy running up the hill and Clarence chasing him with the branding iron. There was blood everywhere and the end of the iron was red hot. Billy got all the way up the hill before Clarence caught him. And that man branded my grandson, right there on the peak of the hill in the backyard. Can you believe that? Lord, it was evil, pure evil. We found out later that Clarence spotted Billy with the Sharkey boy. The Sharkeys were our neighbors. I don't think Billy was queer, really. They were just boys being boys, but any excuse was enough for Clarence to beat up Billy.

"It set Silas off. He looked back at me with murder in his eyes. I know I should have stopped him, I mean tried to stop him anyway, but I didn't. Truth is, I didn't want to."

The old woman's hand shook a bit more and she gazed out the window.

"Silas slapped back through the screen door and grabbed Poppa's rifle from the rack that hung over the door. I remember watching his hands shake with fury as he loaded it, bullets scattering about on the floor. I stood there on the porch and watched as he headed off up the hill."

Ruth looked down at the misshapen hands in her lap.

"The sound of that shot still echoes through the house like it was yesterday."

She paused again and the sound of birds chirping came through the window. Her glassy eyes lifted slowly toward the camera.

"We didn't find out that Clarence had cut Billy down there until later. He butchered Billy that day—neutered him like a steer."

She wiped a tear away with a claw-like hand, sighed, and said, "Well, that's the story, I guess. The sheriff came out and took Silas away. He died in jail. I don't really blame Lula, but after that she turned cold to the boy. In her mind she couldn't accept what Clarence had done to him. You see, that would have been her fault then. I mean she couldn't accept that she had married a man that would do that, so she turned against the boy.

"It doesn't make sense. But that's what guilt will do to you. And poor Billy was never the same, of course. I kept hoping things would work out. But it's all in God's hands now."

She turned to look out the window and the tape ended.

AFTERWORD—APRIL 2005

MATT

I drove through the swirling winds of a dust devil listening to NPR's assessment of the recently departed pope's favorite music. It appeared the pope preferred music with an underlying message and was stirred by powerful redemptive pieces, full of choral passages that required a full orchestra. The dirge-like quality of the music matched my mood. The unsettling appearance of my indigo ghost still unnerved me. My mind raced quickly through the facts of the past six months, searching for resolution.

Stephanie had died there on the street, leaving us without an explanation for the shootings. Despite the incomprehensible nature of the murders, I'm strangely at peace with the whole thing. The FBI agent believed she was searching for companionship and had ritualistically mutilated her victims to fulfill some inner meaning they may never understand. Shockingly she was born a man or still was a man; I never fully understood the details. The insane nature of what she did and who she was somehow renders the entire episode bizarre enough that I feel no need to look further. For me, knowing that the shootings were the irrational acts of a sick mind gives me peace.

Senseless things happen, life goes on.

Danny was buried next to Marco on a hill overlooking the Austin skyline, and it seems in death the pair had assumed the same constant companionship that they exhibited in life. I miss them both more than I would have thought possible.

I have to admit that the relationship I have with my mother is better than it's been in years. She spends most of her time with Muggy, trying to help her through the loss of Marco, but somehow this too has brought perspective. She is no longer trying to cure my sexual preference, and I am no longer trying to avoid her completely.

The afternoon sun blazed through the passenger window as I crested the ridge and angled southward. In front of me I caught my first glimpse of the snow-capped Sandia Mountains floating unreal in the blue haze of the valley. In an hour I would be at the Albuquerque airport and, three hours after that, back home in Austin with Thatcher.

About the Author

Russ Gregory was born and, mostly, raised in New Mexico. He received a couple of technical degrees from the University of Texas and now he lives and writes in Austin, Texas. He also has a job programming computers for a high tech company, though he is adamant about pointing out that he is not a geek.

Russ's stories come from his own unique, slightly quirky perspective, and that perspective is largely a reflection of his upbringing. He is the only gay child of a conservative family with country roots and Republican political leanings. His writing is sprinkled with a wide variety of characters and intersecting plot lines that stem from his experience bridging the gap between relatives and friends with widely divergent viewpoints.

Blue is his first published novel.

Website: www.russgregory.net

Books Available from Bold Strokes Books

Three Days by L.T. Marie. In a town like Vegas where anything can happen, Shawn and Dakota find that the stakes are love at all costs, and it's a gamble neither can afford to lose. (978-1-60282-569-7)

Swimming to Chicago by David-Matthew Barnes. As the lives of the adults around them unravel, high school students Alex and Robby form an unbreakable bond, vowing to do anything to stay together—even if it means leaving everything behind. (978-1-60282-572-7)

Hostage Moon by AJ Quinn. Hunter Roswell thought she had left her past behind, until a serial killer begins stalking her. Can FBI profiler Sara Wilder help her find her connection to the killer before he strikes on blood moon? (978-1-60282-568-0)

Erotica Exotica: Tales of Magic, Sex, and the Supernatural, edited by Richard Labonté. Today's top gay erotica authors offer sexual thrills and perverse arousal, spooky chills, and magical orgasms in these stories exploring arcane mystery, supernatural seduction, and sex that haunts in a manner both weird and wondrous. (978-1-60282-570-3)

Blue by Russ Gregory. Matt and Thatcher find themselves in the crosshairs of a psychotic killer stalking gay men in the streets of Austin, and only a 103-year-old nursing home resident holds the key to solving the murders—but can she give up her secrets in time to save them? (978-1-60282-571-0)

Balance of Forces: Toujours Ici by Ali Vali. Immortal Kendal Richoux's life began during the reign of Egypt's only female pharaoh, and history has taught her the dangers of getting too close to anyone who hasn't harnessed the power of time, but as she prepares for the most important battle of her long life, can she resist her attraction to Piper Marmande? (978-1-60282-567-3)

Contemporary Gay Romances by Felice Picano. This collection of short fiction from legendary novelist and memoirist Felice Picano are as different from any standard "romances" as you can get, but they will linger in the mind and memory. (978-1-60282-639-7)

Pirate's Fortune: Supreme Constellations Book Four by Gun Brooke. Set against the backdrop of war, captured mercenary Weiss Kyakh is persuaded to work undercover with bio-android Madisyn Pimm, which foils her plans to escape, but kindles unexpected love. (978-1-60282-563-5)

Sex and Skateboards by Ashley Bartlett. Sex and skateboards and surfing on the California coast. What more could anyone want? Alden McKenna thinks that's all she needs, until she meets Weston Duvall. (978-1-60282-562-8)

Waiting in the Wings by Melissa Brayden. Jenna has spent her whole life training for the stage, but the one thing she didn't prepare for was Adrienne. Is she ready to sacrifice what she's worked so hard for in exchange for a shot at something much deeper? (978-1-60282-561-1)

Wings: Subversive Gay Angel Erotica, edited by Todd Gregory. A collection of powerfully written tales of passion and desire centered on the aching beauty of angels. (978-1-60282-565-9)

Suite Nineteen by Mel Bossa. Psychic Ben Lebeau moves into Shilts Manor, where he meets seductive Lennox Van Kemp and his clan of Métis—guardians of a spiritual conspiracy dating back to Christ. But are Ben's psychic abilities strong enough to save him? (978-1-60282-564-2)

Speaking Out: LGBTQ Youth Stand Up, edited by Steve Berman. Inspiring stories written for and about LGBTQ teens of overcoming adversity (against intolerance and homophobia) and experiencing life after "coming out." (978-1-60282-566-6)

Forbidden Passions by MJ Williamz. Passion burns hotter when it's forbidden, and the fire between Katie Prentiss and Corrine Staples in antebellum Louisiana is raging out of control. (978-1-60282-641-0)

Harmony by Karis Walsh. When Brook Stanton meets a beautiful musician who threatens the security of her conventional, predetermined future, will she take a chance on finding the harmony only love creates? (978-1-60282-237-5)

Nightrise by Nell Stark and Trinity Tam. In the third book in the everafter series, when Valentine Darrow loses her soul, Alexa must cross continents to find a way to save her. (978-1-60282-238-2)

Men of the Mean Streets, edited by Greg Herren and J.M. Redmann. Dark tales of amorality and criminality by some of the top authors of gay mysteries. (978-1-60282-240-5)

Firestorm by Radclyffe. Firefighter paramedic Mallory "Ice" James isn't happy when the undisciplined Jac Russo joins her command, but lust isn't something either can control—and they soon discover ice burns as fiercely as flame. (978-1-60282-232-0)

The Best Defense by Carsen Taite. When socialite Aimee Howard hires former homicide detective Skye Keaton to find her missing niece, she vows not to mix business with pleasure, but she soon finds Skye hard to resist. (978-1-60282-233-7)

After the Fall by Robin Summers. When the plague destroys most of humanity, Taylor Stone thinks there's nothing left to live for, until she meets Kate, a woman who makes her realize love is still alive and makes her dream of a future she thought was no longer possible. (978-1-60282-234-4)

Accidents Never Happen by David-Matthew Barnes. From the moment Albert and Joey meet by chance beneath a train track on a street in Chicago, a domino effect is triggered, setting off a chain reaction of murder and tragedy. (978-1-60282-235-1)

In Plain View, edited by Shane Allison. Best-selling gay erotica authors create the stories of sex and desire modern readers crave. (978-1-60282-236-8)